Good Medicine
Bobby Hutchinson

D0207777

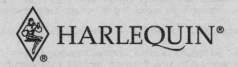

HARLEQUIN®

TORONTO • NEW YORK • LONDON
AMSTERDAM • PARIS • SYDNEY • HAMBURG
STOCKHOLM • ATHENS • TOKYO • MILAN • MADRID
PRAGUE • WARSAW • BUDAPEST • AUCKLAND

ISBN 0-373-71265-0

GOOD MEDICINE

Copyright © 2005 by Bobby Hutchinson.

Printed in U.S.A.

To Marie Donahue and the other Nuu-chah-nulth women
who greeted me in the Ahousaht Health Centre one
rainy morning. Truly, the Ancestors were there.

Books by Bobby Hutchinson

HARLEQUIN SUPERROMANCE

CHAPTER ONE

DOCTOR JORDAN BURKE walked over to the automatic sliding glass doors and peered out at the wet April night, not really seeing the eerie fluorescent glare or the deserted cement apron that led to St. Joseph's Emergency entrance.

It was her birthday. A glance at her watch told her it was 12:40 a.m. She had no idea the exact hour she'd been born, so she might as well make it midnight on the nose. Which meant she was now thirty-two.

Spending the first six hours of her birthday working the graveyard shift in Emerg suited her fine. John Frankel, one of the other doctors, had the flu, and since Jordan was on her long break from day shift, she'd eagerly volunteered to fill in.

It wasn't as if she'd be sleeping much, anyway. She might as well be working tonight as lying in bed tossing and turning, wide-awake and worrying.

She shivered, even though it wasn't cold, and crossed her arms, hugging the front of her white lab coat.

Where the hell are all the patients? On most

nights, the E.R. was so busy there wasn't time to do anything except concentrate on the stream of desperate, frightened people needing medical assistance. But it had been nearly an hour since Jordan's last patient was treated and released, and she was restless. *Anxious.*

She ought to be used to the anxiety. It never really went away these days.

"Quiet tonight, eh? Downtown Vancouver must be closed for spring break or something." The tiny Asian nurse was new, and she laughed at her own joke.

"It is quiet." Jordan nodded and attempted a smile. When did smiling become such an effort? "Calm before the hurricane," she commented, aware of how callous it was to long for patients. It was just that she needed action, needed the degree of intensity that drove everything else out of her head.

"At least it gives us time to think," the young woman replied.

"Yeah." Jordan forced herself to nod, even though time to think was the very last thing she wanted. She glanced at the ident tag pinned to the nurse's shirt. Jordan had been introduced when they came on shift, but now she couldn't remember the woman's name.

Lola. Her name's Lola, numskull.

Forgetting things had become the norm. She'd lost her keys today, she'd misplaced her cell phone yesterday, she hadn't remembered what she needed when she got to the grocery the day before last. Thirty-two was nowhere near menopause, but she knew that constant low-level anxiety could cause memory lapses. Eight months of anxiety. Ever since her husband's accident.

She thought of Garry now, and her gut heaved as an all too familiar mixture of emotions coursed through her: anger, sadness, guilt, longing and an overwhelming sense of frustration and futility.

Two years, is that all it had been? She felt as if she'd been Garry's wife for at least two long, painful lifetimes. She wanted desperately to help him, she longed for an end to the problems they were having, she—

Stop. Stop.

She would *not* obsess over her personal problems here, not while she was on shift. She turned away from the doors and walked over to the admitting desk. So there were no patients, okay, she could catch up on patient files. That tedious task was every doctor's least favorite activity.

"No point getting your blood pressure up doing paperwork, Jordan." Eddie, the desk clerk, grinned at her, revealing crooked teeth. "There's an 18-year-old female on her way, severe headache, vomiting, recent history of stomach pain. Her dad called, he's bringing her."

A few moments later the patient arrived, a college student named Ardyth Malone, slender and very fit looking, but obviously in severe distress. Jordan escorted the girl to a cubicle and began taking a history.

Ardyth responded with negative answers to questions about drugs, alcohol, allergies, blows to the head. A careful physical examination ruled out appendicitis, inflamed ovaries, gallbladder problems. Each successive test was normal, until Jordan examined Ardyth's eyes with the ophthalmoscope. There was a slight papillidema, a swelling of the optic nerve.

By now Jordan was beginning to feel really concerned, wondering if this was a brain tumor, but there were a few questions she still needed to ask.

"Ardyth, has there been any change in your diet recently?"

The girl shook her head. "I'm a vegetarian. I'm very health-conscious and careful about what I put in my body." Her expression was virtuous. "I take tons of vitamins and I don't eat sugar or saturated fat. *Oww! Oh my God, do something! It hurts.*" Bent double, she cradled her stomach, moaning.

A warning bell went off in Jordan's brain. Taking iron tablets on an empty stomach could lead to excruciating cramps.

"Exactly what vitamins do you take, and how many?"

As the pain eased, the girl rattled off a dozen or more names, adding that she swallowed massive quantities.

"Have you taken any new ones recently?"

"Only more vitamin A."

"How much more?"

"Seven extra pills. My skin's been breaking out—vitamin A cures acne."

"How long have you been taking that dose?"

Ardyth shrugged. "A couple of months now, I guess."

"How many international units per pill?"

"Five thousand."

"And when did you take your last mega dose?"

"A few hours ago."

Thirty-five thousand units of A, ten to twenty times a normal dose, taken daily for sixty days. Jordan was pretty sure she had the answer to Ardyth's symptoms, and it gave her a feeling of satisfaction. At least her personal problems weren't interfering with her diagnostic ability. *Yet.*

"My guess is you have acute vitamin A intoxication, Ardyth," she said gently. "I think if you stop taking it, your symptoms will disappear. We'll run some tests, though, just to be absolutely certain we're not missing anything here."

Jordan was jotting down orders for a CAT scan and an upper GI series when Lola stuck her head into the cubicle.

"Jordan, a guy's just been dumped outside Emerg. He's unconscious—whoever brought him sped off in a car. They're bringing him in now. Billy says he's got track marks, so it's probably an overdose. Can you come?"

"Be right there." Jordan handed orders to an aide and then sprinted after Lola. There'd been a series of drug overdoses in the past two weeks, a result of exceptionally strong heroin having hit the downtown Vancouver streets. Usually the Emergency Response Team brought the victims in, but sometimes bodies were dumped at the door by people who didn't want to get involved.

Orderlies and nurses were lifting the limp male figure onto a stretcher when Jordan arrived. The patient's face was obscured by a nurse's arm, but Jordan saw at a glance that this wasn't the usual skid-row addict.

Caucasian, well-dressed, charcoal sports jacket, black trousers, blue silk shirt—

She struggled to get her breath as a wave of dizziness swept over her. *She recognized that shirt.* Reaching past the nurse, Jordan took hold of the man's jaw and turned his slack face toward her, and her worst fears were confirmed.

Garry. It was her husband. She'd bought him the shirt for Christmas.

Someone on the medical team was calling out his vitals, but Jordan barely heard it. One of the nurses was holding Garry's wallet, going through it to determine his identity.

"Hughes, Garry M., DOB 1968, March 13." As the woman read out the information on his driver's license, for one shameful instant Jordan was relieved she'd retained her maiden name.

"I'll see if he's listed in the book," the nurse said. "We may need next of kin."

The number was listed, but Jordan knew there was no one home in their Kitsilano apartment. The nurse would get the message Garry had recorded for the answering service.

"Jordan? Hey, Jordan, what's up? You okay?"

She suddenly realized everyone was waiting for her, looking at her—puzzled, impatient.

She should tell them about Garry and have someone else take over. It was against policy to treat a relative. Instead, like an automaton, she began the necessary assessment, even though she knew beyond a doubt what was wrong. Of course he'd taken an overdose. Her husband was a junkie.

"Pulse forty, respiration down to eight," Lola reported. "We're not getting a BP, Jordan. This guy's on his way out…. He's flat! Now we're not getting much of a pulse at all."

"Establish a line. Let's give him Narcan." She felt cold and detached and far away as she picked up the syringe with numb fingers and inserted naloxone hydrochloride into the IV valve.

In cases of overdose, the drug's effect was miraculous. It instantly reversed the action of narcotics, and a patient who'd been on the verge of death only seconds before suddenly became awake and alert, just as if nothing had happened. In the E.R., they called it the Lazarus Effect. Except Lazarus had probably been grateful.

Everybody watched and waited. It only took a few seconds.

"Brace yourself, boys and girls," someone murmured.

The instant the powerful drug reached Garry's bloodstream, his sky-blue eyes flew open. A frown flickered across his smooth forehead as he stared up at the faces of the medical team grouped around the stretcher.

Inevitably his gaze came to rest on Jordan. As recognition dawned, his features contorted with rage. He grasped the sides of the gurney and pulled himself up as staff members struggled to control him. He was a big man, and it looked as if they were going to lose the battle.

"Call a code white," someone yelled. "He's freaking on us."

Code white was an emergency call to security.

"Jordan?" Garry spat her name out. "What the hell have you done to me?"

Her mouth felt numb, her throat dry. She cleared it, amazed that her voice still worked. "You overdosed. I used Narcan to bring you out of it."

It took a moment for Garry to react to that, and when he did Jordan wanted to turn her back and run from the room.

"You *bitch!*" he screamed at her. "You filthy *bitch,* you ruined my high, what the hell's wrong with you? Do you have any idea what you've done, you stupid fool?" He tried to shake off the hands restraining him so he could climb off the table.

Jordan couldn't move. She saw shock on the faces of her co-workers. They were staring at her, some of them open mouthed.

She was surprised when her voice burst out loud and strong. "Call a code white and get him out of here," she ordered.

"You *know* this guy, Jordan?"

"Yes." Her voice was unnaturally calm now. It seemed to come from a long distance away and belong to someone else. "I know him. Of course I know him. He's my—he's my *husband*. Get the equipment off him, I'm discharging him."

She saw the glances that passed among the staff. They knew she could have committed him to the psych ward for treatment. They probably figured that's what she ought to do, and maybe it was, but she just wanted him gone.

She had no energy left to deal with Garry and his problems. Over the past weeks she'd made appointments with the best drug treatment clinics in the city, appointments that she pulled strings to arrange and Garry hadn't bothered to keep. She'd spent hours talking to him, trying to understand, to reason with him. She'd tried every way she knew to help him make the decision to stop. Nothing had worked.

Now, she was worn out. She'd done her best to keep her work and her personal problems separate, and look where that got her. She hadn't wanted her co-workers to know how desperate and degrading her personal life had become. Garry had managed to take away even that last tiny shred of dignity.

Two security guards hurried in, and between them they restrained Garry as the staff quickly removed the IV apparatus from his body.

"Escort him to the exit and see that he gets a cab," Jordan instructed the men.

The guards flanked him, and Garry's broad shoulders sagged as they started to hustle him out of the treatment room. Over his shoulder he gave her the look she'd come to despise in the past months, the contrite, little-boy-lost look from under long, curling blond lashes. Those baby blues had charmed her when she first fell in love with him. At this moment they made her stomach churn with nausea.

Yesterday morning he'd begged her to write him yet another prescription for morphine. She'd refused, and he'd sworn at her, just as he had a moment ago. For a man with an expensive education, he had a limited vocabulary.

"Hey. Hey, Jordie," he called over his shoulder as the guards hustled him out. "I'm sorry, babe, I'm really sorry. I didn't mean it, it was just, you know, the shock of coming to in this place." He dragged his feet, going limp.

"Jordie, tell these goons to back off me, okay? Please, honey?"

She didn't reply. The security guards had stopped, holding him upright. They turned and looked at her, questioning. Her co-workers were all pretending hard to be busy with other things. By morning the whole episode would be all over the hospital, probably posted on some Web site.

"Jordie, talk to me here, okay?" Garry's voice dropped, and he assumed the wheedling tone she'd come to despise. "See, the thing is, I've got no money for a cab. I shot the whole wad on that fix. Could you maybe—? Please, honey?"

Amazed that her legs worked, she hurried to the staff locker room and got twenty dollars from her handbag.

She had to keep swallowing, and her hands were shaking so much she could hardly get her handbag opened or the door to her locker closed.

Security had escorted Garry to the exit by the time she got back, and Jordan marched into the rain and wordlessly held the money out to him.

He glanced at it and his mouth turned down petulantly before he snatched it, jamming the single bill into his pocket. "Twenty isn't enough, not when I'm really in pain like this. I told you how bad it hurt this morning, Jordie, you could have given me something then and this wouldn't have happened." In one lithe motion, he twisted out of the guard's grip.

"C'mon, babe, don't be chippy with me, surely you can spare another couple twenties?"

She jerked her head from side to side and then turned her back on him, fleeing through the doors that led into Emerg. Inside, not one person looked at her, but their curiosity was like a scent in the air.

She couldn't remember anything about the rest of that shift except that the trembling and nausea grew more and more difficult to control. She felt disoriented, far away, watching herself go through the motions of treating one patient after the other, amazed that she looked and sounded so normal.

When morning finally came, she had trouble driving home to the apartment. Fortunately the morning rush hour hadn't really started yet, because she drove through a red light and sat through a green one. She scraped the side of her red Toyota against a cement beam when she tried to park it in the underground lot, and when she got out she didn't even bother to check the extent of the damage.

She took the elevator to the second floor and after three tries, unlocked the door. The apartment was empty; Garry wasn't there. She hadn't expected him home. She'd hoped he wouldn't be.

She knew he wasn't at work, he hadn't been all week. It was Thursday, and his secretary had left increasingly desperate messages for him every day. Up until this week, he'd managed to keep up a relatively professional facade at his law office. The partners had been lenient with him, blaming his erratic behavior on the accident. They'd covered for him the same way Jordan had, she mused as she walked through the rooms she'd painted and decorated with such care.

It felt as if she were seeing her home clearly for the first time in weeks. A great many things had disappeared lately, and she'd tried to believe it had nothing to do with Garry, but now she forced herself to face the truth.

In the living room, an empty CD holder stood beside the equally empty space where the expensive audio system had been. They'd bought it on their first anniversary. Several weeks ago, the apartment had been broken into while they were both supposedly at work. Her few good pieces of jewelry had been taken as well as all the electronic equipment—even the damned microwave.

Garry had taken them. She'd known it even then, but

hadn't been able to face the fact that her husband was an addict who'd steal and lie and cheat to get drugs.

Slowly and painfully as though she were old and brittle-boned, Jordan lowered herself to the dove-gray sofa and forced herself to look at what her life had become.

It had started with that damned car accident. Garry had been driving home late, undoubtedly going too fast. The expensive little sports car he'd insisted on owning had been struck by a pickup truck at an intersection. Garry had come away with a compound fracture of the left arm and a concussion. He'd also complained of excruciating pain from torn muscles in his back, pain that nothing seemed to alleviate.

Garry's physician, Albert Mayborn, had finally prescribed morphine.

Jordan blamed herself for not recognizing that Garry was becoming addicted. She ought to have known, the signs were all there. Garry complained of pain long past the time when any muscle strain should have healed. She'd finally seen the physical signs of drug abuse in her husband's bloodshot eyes, his jumpiness, his inability to sleep, his hair-trigger temper.

At last she'd confronted him about it, and of course he'd denied it. Until tonight, she'd managed to deny the extent of the problem herself.

The awful scene in the E.R. kept replaying in her head, and Jordan's humiliation and shame grew. She drew her knees up to her chest, trying by sheer force of will to impose control over her shaking arms and legs.

She couldn't get a deep breath. Her heart hammered against her ribs. She began to cry, deep, tearing sobs that scared her. Try as she might, she couldn't stop them. Soon her stomach and chest hurt, her lungs felt as if they were on fire, and still the wrenching sobs went on and on. She was completely alone.

Hours passed. The phone rang, and she couldn't answer it. She couldn't move. She was thirty-two today, and she didn't want to live. She began to think of the many ways there were to die.

And then the physician in her recognized that she needed help.

She forced herself up off the sofa, dialed the telephone and ordered a cab.

Sweating and shaking, still gulping back sobs, she found her handbag and made her way outside.

The Native driver gave her a concerned and wary look. "You okay, lady? Where you want to go?"

"St. Joseph's Medical Center," she gasped.

St. Joseph's was an old building, and she knew every inch of it, having interned there. She dragged herself up a set of stairs at the back of the building to the third floor. It was the only place she could think of to get help.

The psych ward.

CHAPTER TWO

THE INTAKE NURSE WAS both intuitive and gentle. Jordan managed to choke out her name, adding that she was an Emerg physician, and without even asking her to fill in any forms, the nurse guided Jordan to a tiny private room with a cot and a chair. She helped her lie down, covering her with a blanket.

Jordan curled into a ball, too exhausted and spent to resist the emotions coursing through her. After a time, the door opened and Helen Moore, the resident psychiatrist, came in. Jordan knew her slightly, and had always liked her kind smile and forthright manner.

"Hi, Jordan." Helen sat down beside the cot and reached for one of Jordan's hands. She took it gently, cradling it between both of hers. "Can you tell me what's made you so upset?"

Jordan tried, but it was impossible to talk through the tears. Helen reached for a box of tissues and handed over a fistful. "Try to take deep breaths."

After a few moments, Jordan was able to put words together. "My hus-husband is —is a drug addict," she began. Once she'd said the words aloud, it became easier to tell the rest of the story. She began with the car accident, the morphine, the prescriptions she'd written him and, when she'd refused to supply him, how the apartment was ransacked. Amid fresh bouts of weeping, she managed to recount what had occurred the previous night in the E.R.

"What—what about—about—Garry? What am I going to *do* about him? How—how can I—help him?"

"This is not about him," Helen said firmly. "This is about *you*, Jordan. What are you going to do about *you?*"

Helen's words shocked Jordan out of her tears. For so long, she'd exhausted herself worrying about Garry and his problems, believing that if only she could help him stop taking drugs, their life together might work.

"Garry is an adult, making choices about the way he lives his life," Helen continued. "Do you want to go on allowing him to make those same choices for *your* life? You're an exceptional physician with a great reputation at this hospital, Jordan, and I know you to be a good and caring person." Her kind face broke into a mischievous smile. "Lord knows you're good to look at. I've seen men fall over their feet like schoolboys when you're around."

Jordan started to cry again. It had been so long since anyone had complimented her. When she'd first met Garry, she'd felt confident and even pretty. Now she felt gray and old. And ashamed, so ashamed of not being able to control herself.

Helen gave her hand a comforting squeeze. "I think

you need to value your own worth, Jordan, and go from there. The scene last night in the E.R. was hard, but sometimes it takes a hard lesson for us to see we're on a path that isn't the most beneficial for us." Helen smiled again and released Jordan's hand. "I've had my share of those tough lessons, I know how much they hurt. But they also help us heal. Right now I'm going to give you a sedative because you need to rest. We'll talk again."

"I feel so—so stupid," Jordan admitted, her voice trembling. "You'd think I could cope with this on my own. It's humiliating to admit that I can't."

"We—all of us—are only human, Jordan. Being doctors means we start out with a higher level of daily stress, and then we have our own personal stuff on top of it. As a profession, medicine carries the highest rate of alcohol dependency, drug addiction, divorce and suicide. Coming here shows good judgment and common sense. And no one needs to know you're here."

Jordan blew her nose. "Thank you. That would make things easier."

"I'll have a word with the staff. Now, I think rest is the best restorative at the moment." She gave Jordan a sedative and gently tucked the blanket around her. "I'll be in this evening to see how you're doing. Relax now."

As the medication gradually took the edge off her panic and her muscles loosened, Jordan was able to think more clearly than she had for weeks.

Garry was a junkie.

As an E.R. doctor, she'd seen enough junkies to

know that no one could help them unless they chose to help themselves.

He wasn't making the slightest effort.

Her eyelids were heavy, and she knew that within a few moments, she'd be asleep.

What are you going to do about you, *Jordan?*

The answer floated to the surface. It made her terribly sad, and it frightened her as well, but it was the right thing for her. The only thing.

As soon as she felt able, she was going to see a lawyer about a divorce.

"THE VERY LEAST you could have done was tell me you wanted a divorce before you saw this—this scumbag of a lawyer." Garry's face was scarlet with rage and disbelief. "How could you do this to me, Jordan?" He threw the copy of the proposed separation agreement she'd just handed him to the floor and stood glaring at her, hands knotted into fists. The pages scattered, landing at her feet.

His voice rose. "You know I'm not well. I'm not over the accident yet! You could help but you won't. What about the marriage vows you made?" Sarcasm dripped from every word. "I could swear there was something in there about in sickness and in health, till death do us part. Have you thought about my parents? They've treated you like one of the family, and now you're doing this to me—to *them.*"

Jordan's heart was hammering. It was true, Meg and Edward had been good to her. She hated the thought of hurting them. She kept her expression impassive and did her best to convince herself that the problems Garry was throwing at her weren't hers to solve.

This was all *his* stuff, as Helen would phrase it. And Meg and Edward had witnessed Garry's recent tantrums. Surely they would understand her decision when they accepted the reality of their son's addiction....

It was helpful to remember Helen's advice. Jordan now viewed the two days she'd spent in psych as an intensive training seminar.

Right now she noticed that everything Garry said related only to himself. Lordy, how could she have missed how self-centered he was? She'd known him two and a half years, and yet she felt that during the past week, since she'd come home from the psych ward, she was seeing him as if he were a stranger.

And it surprised her to realize she didn't even like him anymore. His addiction had turned him into a bully and a whiner, not exactly a sexy combination. There hadn't been any sex for months now, anyway.

He was hollering at her again. "What kind of bullshit is that dyke of a doctor pumping you full of, Jordie? You never acted like this before. What's between us should stay between us. I don't like you dumping your guts to some stranger." His voice grew softer, and he tried to reach out and take her into his arms. "You're my wife, babe. Shouldn't you be talking to me about stuff that bothers you?"

Jordan held up both hands, palms out, and moved away.

He swore a long stream of curses, and then she could

see him consciously turning on the charm again. "C'mon, Jordie. Honey, baby, don't be this way," he wheedled. "I said I was sorry for what happened in the E.R. I just couldn't take the pain in my back anymore, and you wouldn't give me anything for it, remember? I'm not good with pain, honey, you know that."

She moved farther back, out of his reach. She remembered everything. He sickened her.

The second day of her stay in psych, Jordan had called home and left a message for Garry, telling him where she was. Hours later, he'd come to the ward, and on Jordan's instructions, Helen and the staff had conveyed the message that she didn't want to see him. High, he'd become verbally abusive. Helen had threatened to call security, and finally he left.

Now Jordan looked at him, and she couldn't even summon pity.

"I won't prescribe drugs for you ever again, Garry. So don't bother asking."

He tightened his mouth and narrowed his eyes. Taking a step closer, he shook his trembling finger under her nose. His breath was foul.

"You go ahead with this divorce shit and I promise you I'll ruin you financially. I *am* a lawyer, in case it's slipped your mind. Any judge would award me ongoing support when they hear about the accident. And I've got the firm behind me—it isn't going to cost me anything."

He'd already tested his firm to the limit, but she resisted the urge to tell him that. She was grateful that Helen had given her the name of an attorney she liked and trusted, Marcy Davis. Marcy had handled Helen's own complex divorce several years ago. It made it easier to withstand Garry's bullying, knowing Marcy would deal with all the legal issues.

"And I'm not moving out of this apartment, either," he said. "You want a separation, you move out, lady."

"I already have." He hadn't even noticed that her clothes, some of the furniture and the few personal things she cherished were gone. She'd packed up that morning, called a moving company to put the furniture in storage, and rented a housekeeping room at a motel across the street from St. Joe's.

"You're welcome to everything that's left here. But I'd like to put the apartment on the market as soon as possible, Garry." Her lawyer was well aware that Jordan had been making the mortgage payments since Garry's accident.

She could tell by his expression that he hadn't expected any of this.

"My lawyer will handle the details," she said in a quiet voice. "Call her if you have any questions." Exactly what Marcy had told her to say. She'd practiced so that now it came out smoothly, without revealing the effort it took her to speak.

"Where the hell are you going? You come back here!" She heard the panic in his voice as she headed for the door. "We haven't finished talking yet. What if I need you for something? You could at least give me your new address, Jordan."

It was tragic to recognize that the only thing he'd

need her for was money. Prescriptions and money were all he'd needed from her for months.

"You have my cell number." And Marcy had already suggested she get that changed if his calls became too frequent or abusive. "And I'd rather you didn't come to St. Joe's again, Garry."

"Last I heard it was a free country," he snarled. "I can go wherever the hell I choose."

"Okay, then I'll alert security." She prayed she wouldn't have to carry out the threat. She opened the apartment door. "Goodbye, Garry."

"You're making a big mistake, you dumb bitch!"

She closed the door and hurried to the elevator. Her legs were shaking as she made her way down and out of the building. She was crying when she climbed in her car. Some of the tears were for the dreams she'd forfeited, but mostly they were tears of relief.

She'd taken a first and much-needed step toward finding out who Jordan Burke really was, and she was learning fast what she didn't want in her life anymore. If that was a negative positive, so what? She'd take what she could get.

She blew her nose hard and for the first time in days, she smiled wryly. But the smile went just as quickly as it came.

Now she had to figure out what it was she did want.

CHAPTER THREE

IT WAS THE FOLLOWING WEEK when the notice on St. Joe's computer bulletin board caught Jordan's eye.

Resident GP wanted for isolated First Nations village, Vancouver Island's west coast. Ahousaht, Clayoquot Sound, Flores Island. Applicants must be willing to work with Tribal Community Services. Access by boat or floatplane only.

There was a Web address and a phone number, and Jordan scribbled them down. She wasn't sure why. She knew nothing about native villages, and not much about First Nations people. The ones she was most familiar with were the ones who ended up in the E.R., most of them unfortunate residents of Vancouver's troubled Lower East Side.

She was on the early shift, and when she was finished work she had an appointment with Helen, who once again asked the question that was becoming a mantra between them.

"What is it you really want, Jordan?"

"I want to move away." The words came of their own volition, surprising her. "I've always lived in Vancouver. I grew up here, went to university here, trained at St. Joe's. This is the only hospital I've ever worked at. I think I'd like to leave the city, go somewhere where no one knows me, maybe give general practice a shot. Make a fresh start."

Somewhere Garry isn't. She didn't say the words aloud. She didn't have to. Helen understood.

"Maybe that's what you need to do, then. Just keep in mind that you take all your emotional baggage with you, along with your underwear, no matter where you travel," Helen reminded her. *"Wherever you go, there you are,"* she quoted with her teasing smile. "Any idea where you want to go?"

Jordan shook her head. "I'll have to find a job before I make any changes. There's the legal bills to think about." It was too soon to speculate.

But later that afternoon, she explored the Web for Ahousaht. Photos showed a wild and windswept village surrounded by the Pacific Ocean. She learned that until now medical care had been provided by the nurse at the local clinic and a doctor who flew in twice a week. Emergency cases were transported by medevac to the hospital in Tofino on nearby Vancouver Island. But the community's requirements had changed, and now the Tribal Council needed a full-time doctor. The salary wasn't what Jordan earned in the E.R., but neither would there be shift work. And housing was included.

Impulsively, Jordan took out her cell phone and dialed the number she'd copied down.

The number rang and rang, and she was about to hang up when a man answered.

"Hello?" There was a note of impatience in the man's deep and resonant tone.

"Oh, um, yes, hello." Damn, now she was losing her confidence. Her hands were sweating and she could hear the strain in her voice. "My, um, my name is Jordan Burke, *Doctor* Burke, and I'm calling about the medical position. Is it still available, or have you found someone?"

There was a moment's silence. "I don't know for sure. Call back another time. The office is closed for the day." His tone was brusque, bordering on rude.

"Well, can you just tell me—"

"Nope, I can't. You need to speak to Bennie, he's the rep from Tribal Council."

"Bennie? Bennie who? Does he have a last name?" Jordan was over feeling nervous and well on the way to being annoyed. Surely he could be more helpful?

"Just Bennie will do fine. He'll be here in the morning."

"And you are—?" This person should never be answering a business phone. She'd say so, in the nicest possible way, when she talked to this Bennie, Jordan decided.

"Silas Keefer. And I'm hanging up now, Jordan Burke. There's a celebration I need to attend."

"Oh. Sure. But first can you just tell me—"

The line clicked and a dial tone sounded. The bloody man had hung up on her.

Jordan pushed End and shoved the phone into her bag with more force than was necessary. Whoever, whatever Silas Keefer was, he'd succeeded in discouraging her from applying for the position.

SILAS HAD FORGOTTEN about the call by the time he took his place in the welcoming circle. When his turn came to hold the fragile baby, he cradled him against his heart. The tiny boy seemed too small to bear the weight of his sturdy name.

Hello, Cameron Michael John. Welcome, Nuu-chah-nulth warrior.

Cameron was barely a week old. Silas gazed down into the little face. The baby's skin was golden and downy, and he looked up at Silas through big dark eyes. One minute fist, curled into itself like a seashell, flailed and then came to rest on the front of Silas's flannel shirt, and his man's heart swelled in his chest. He never got used to the miracle of new life. He hoped he never would.

You, young Cameron, have plenty of time to grow into your name—and you'll be growing up right alongside your parents.

Alice Pettigrew, Cameron's mother, was barely sixteen, hardly more than a child herself. And his father, Hogan John, had two full years to go before his twentieth birthday.

Children, raising children. At least here in Ahousaht, Cameron and his parents were surrounded by family, mothers and aunts and fathers and grandfathers. Most

of them were here today and Silas knew all of them
were willing to help in any way they could.

The shy young parents sat side by side holding hands
as the members of the welcoming circle cradled the
newborn to their hearts and hummed the traditional
ahhhh nook, ahhhhh nook deep in their chests. Con-
veying love and welcome and support. Then they sang
the welcoming songs, the dancers up and moving to the
beat of the drums. Silas said a prayer, and as soon as
the blessing was complete, got to his feet and headed
toward the door.

His half sister, Christina Crow, caught him just before he escaped.

She gave him her wicked wide grin. "Hey, Silas,
you're coming to Mom's birthday party tomorrow
night, right?"

"Yeah, I'll be there." They both knew he wouldn't
stay, but he'd put in an appearance. He was, after all,
Rose Marie's firstborn. After her divorce from Silas's
father, Angus Keefer, Rose Marie had married Peter
Crow and five years later she'd had Christina. Twelve
years after that, Patwin, her third child, was born, but
Christina was the half sibling Silas really knew well.
Patwin hadn't been home much since Silas had moved
back to Ahousaht. And Silas was profoundly solitary.

But who could help loving Christina? She'd been
born smiling. Tiny and slender, his half sister had thick
black hair permed into a curly, electric frizz. Her dramatic, high cheekbones, deep-set eyes and glorious
copper skin drew the hungry glances of men. But it was

her sunny nature that captivated people as much as her beauty. She had a streak of mischief that made her fun to be around, and her smart mouth brought shocked smiles to even the most dour of the elders.

Over the six years he'd lived in Ahousaht, Christina had somehow wormed her way through all the protective barriers Silas had erected.

And just like all the women in the family, she was nosy as hell.

"So what'd you get Mom for her birthday?"

"That marble pastry board and lazy Susan she's been eyeing in the new kitchenware store in Tofino."

"Super." Christina beamed up at him, dark eyes sparkling. "That's gonna get you brownie points, big brother. Dad and I each got her another one of those copper-bottomed pots she's nuts about." She shook her head and her curls lifted and settled. "Mom's the only woman I know who actually wants kitchen stuff for her birthday. I'd flatten anyone who gave me pots instead of perfume."

"How's it going with Andy?" She'd been dating Andy Makinna for a couple of months now.

"It's over." Christina shrugged and wrinkled her nose. "Him and Eli didn't get along."

"That kid's got a good shit detector." Silas hadn't been particularly fond of her latest admirer, either. Good for his nephew for putting the run on the guy.

"Yeah, well, Eli's gonna end up supporting me in my old age unless he takes a shine to one of these guys pretty soon."

"He's only eight. He's got lots of time to dig up a stepfather before that."

Christina rolled her eyes. "I'd just as soon have a man who's breathing."

"I'll pass that on to Eli, but a woman with a personality problem like you have can't be too fussy."

She grinned and thumped him on the shoulder. "Take your own advice, older brother."

"I'll give it my best shot." Silas gave her a quick hug and eased past her, toward freedom.

Christina grabbed a handful of his shirt and held on. "Why not stay for coffee?"

"Can't. I've got a deadline on an article, and I'm trying to improve the Ahousaht Web site."

She knew it was an excuse, but she didn't challenge him. "Okay. See you tomorrow morning at the meeting, then. No applicants yet for the medical posting, I'm beginning to wonder if we'll ever find a doctor who wants to come and live here." Christina was nursing supervisor for the medical center. She was the one who'd convinced the Council about the advantages of having a resident M.D.

"You know, somebody did call about that posting." He'd forgotten all about it till now. Silas was one of the band's healers, but he was the first to admit the need for both healing modalities. "Just before the ceremony, I dropped by the band office to get some stuff Bennie left for me, and the phone rang. It was a woman. She asked if the position was still open. I told her I didn't know."

"Did you get her name and number?"

"Her name was Jordan, Jordan Brick or Bruk or something." Silas shook his head. "I was late for the welcoming ceremony. But I did tell her to call back and talk to Bennie before I hung up on her."

Christina gave him a look. "Probably the only person who'll ever even think of applying, and you pissed her off right up front, eh?"

Silas shrugged. "You know me, I'm not exactly Mr. Congeniality."

"Mr. Porcupine is more like it." Christina shook her head and rolled her eyes. "You need a crash course in human relations, big brother."

He smiled down at her, not in the least offended. "I'm way too old to change my wicked ways."

"Thirty-six going on ninety-seven?"

"If that woman really wants the job, she'll call back. And she'll have to really want it or she'll never stick it out through the first few weeks of culture shock. She'll find out—" he ticked them off on his fingers "—there's no sushi bar, no movie theater, no health club and it's a forty-five minute trip by water taxi to the nearest pizza joint, which for some strange reason won't deliver. And then there's the rain. Mustn't forget we have an annual rainfall of a hundred and ninety-six inches. So if I was a little abrupt on the phone, it's a good thing—a test. We'll see how determined she is to live on an island populated by wild Indians."

Christina blew a raspberry. "The elders hear you call us that and they'll revive scalping. You make it sound so bad anybody would turn tail and run. If by some fluke she phones back and even comes for a look-see, maybe you oughta lay low while I convince her there actually are advantages to living in Ahousaht."

"If she comes, I'll stay out of the way. Promise."

Christina shot him a mischievous look. "Come to think about it, that's not the best idea, either, big brother. If she's single, the sight of you might entice her to remain in spite of the rain and the lack of a mall. You're not half-bad to look at, although your manners leave a lot to be desired."

Laughing, Silas made his escape when someone else came by to talk to Christina. He took the path that would lead him out of the village, along the forested path to where he'd built his compact cabin.

The rain that had been falling all day had stopped. The rising wind, chill and brisk, blew the clouds away, and overhead the late-afternoon sunset streaked the sky crimson and gold. Boats rocked at anchor in the bay, and kids in T-shirts raced up and down the gravel road on their bikes, impervious to the chill air. He was thinking about what he'd said, about there being no pizza joint in Ahousaht.

Personally, he'd settle for a faster and more reliable connection to the Internet.

CHAPTER FOUR

A CAB DROPPED Jordan and her two gigantic suitcases on the end of the pier just after ten on Monday morning, June 26. As well as her sizeable medical bag, she also had two shopping bags stuffed with groceries. The small convenience store in Ahousaht reputedly carried only the most basic essentials, so she'd just visited a large grocery in Tofino.

"She leaves at ten-thirty or thereabouts," the cab-driver said, waving a hand at a decent-size boat bobbing in the water at the bottom of a walkway. "You got lotsa time." He eyed the suitcases with a distinct lack of enthusiasm. "I'll get these on board for ya."

He was a small, older man, and he walked with a limp. He'd struggled with the bags at the small airstrip the evening before, when Jordan arrived from Vancouver. He'd carried them into the inn where she'd spent the night and then lifted them back into his cab this morning. Envisioning herniated disks and heart attacks, Jordan tipped him lavishly and shook her head.

"Nope, not again. You've been great, and I thank you

for the offer. But I'll get someone on the boat to help me. You've wrestled with these long enough."

He looked relieved. Thanking her profusely, he hurried away through the rain before she could change her mind.

Unsure what to do next, Jordan hefted her medical bag, abandoning the suitcases and groceries on the dock. By now quite wet, she clung to the railing, gingerly making her way down the slippery wooden ramp to the tiny floating pier. Moored to the dock, the aluminum boat the cabdriver had pointed out rocked as she scrambled aboard.

There was no one on the small deck. Feeling awkward, hoping she wouldn't slip and catapult straight down into the cabin, Jordan gingerly climbed down the narrow ladder, surprised by how large the interior was.

There was space for about twenty-four passengers, and so far, she was the only one. Two tall, heavy native men were seated in the cockpit, talking as they drank from gigantic mugs of coffee. They turned and looked at her, dark, weather-beaten faces devoid of expression.

"I want to go to Ahousaht," she began. "I've left a couple of heavy suitcases and a bunch of groceries up on the pier. Could someone help me carry them on board?"

Without a word, the younger man got up. When Jordan turned to follow him, the older man shook his head and motioned at a seat.

"Billy'll get them."

Jordan set her medical bag down and slid into a seat. "Thanks, that's very kind." She reached into her hand-bag for her wallet. "How much is the fare?"

"You're the new doctor." It wasn't a question.

"Yes, I'm Jordan Burke. Hi." She got up and they shook hands, hers swallowed by his rough paw. His scarred face softened into a smile.

"Charlie Tidian. No charge this time, Doctor Jordan Burke."

"Thank you, skipper." Jordan smiled at him. "You make the trip back and forth from Ahousaht every day?"

"Twice a day. The boat's also used as an ambulance, if anybody needs to get to the hospital and it's not urgent enough for the medevac."

"How long does the trip take?"

"Forty-five minutes in good seas."

Billy heaved her suitcases to the deck and then stowed them and the groceries at the back of the cabin, and soon people began trickling aboard, most of them First Nations. A young, pretty girl with a toddler and a huge backpack, an older woman, four young men. A middle-aged couple, obviously tourists, outfitted head to toe in Tilley gear, took the seat across from Jordan. The man whipped out a digital camera and began filming the boat and its occupants, concentrating on the mother and toddler and the older woman. Jordan figured he was being rude as hell, but the three ignored him.

At ten-thirty, the captain started the engines and the boat slipped away from the dock, heading at ever-in-creasing speed out over the gray-green expanse of water.

As the mainland disappeared, Jordan thought back to her first and only visit to Ahousaht three weeks earlier. She'd taken her car that time, driving from Vancouver to Horseshoe Bay and catching the Nanaimo ferry across the Inlet. It had taken three hours to navigate the twisting and terrifying Island Highway to reach the village of Tofino. There, feeling more and more as if she'd reached the end of the world, she'd chartered a floatplane to Ahousaht.

The isolated island village had both appalled and appealed to her. Sunshine shimmered on the water, bluegray mountains rose in the distance and thick forest surrounded the sprawling frame buildings. The only road was a rutted dirt track that snaked its way up island. If she'd wanted isolation, it didn't get any more remote than this.

The chief, council members and the nursing supervisor, Christina Crow, had greeted her warmly. They'd asked a lot of questions, including why she wanted to come to Ahousaht.

Without going into details, she'd told them her marriage had ended and that she wanted a complete change of scene. Her résumé spoke for itself, graduation at the top of her class and several years at St. Joseph's E.R.

They'd been touchingly honest about their community: the isolation, the lack of amenities, the unique customs of the First Nations people.

She'd admitted little knowledge of their culture, and

giving her two books, they'd left her alone with coffee and a plate of brownies. By the time they decided to hire her, the plate was almost empty, she knew a little about the history of the Nuu-chah-nulth people—and she was on a sugar high.

Jordan had accepted their offer on the spot.

Now, however, she wasn't so sure. She tried to suppress her apprehension as the distance from Tofino increased, but finally gave in and let her emotions run. Aware that the Tilley couple were watching her bawl, she turned her face to the window, pretending to be intent on the small islands rushing by.

"Be aware of what you're feeling. Don't censor it, don't struggle to subdue it," Helen had advised. "Allow the emotions to come and just watch them. Darkness can't survive when you let light in."

Back in Vancouver, Jordan had been certain that this drastic life change was right and good for her. But as the minutes ticked by, she began to wonder.

She'd sold her car and many of her belongings, making the trip from Vancouver to Tofino by plane this time. There really was no point in having a car on an island where the majority of the community was within walking distance. And they did have a rusted-out ambulance for emergencies.

The boat chugged along, rising up high and then slapping heavily down on the waves. The noise of its props and powerful twin-engine motor finally soothed her. Whatever lay ahead was out of her control.

The tension in her neck and arms gradually subsided and she relaxed. For these brief few moments, she could just be.

Half an hour passed. Ahead, the clouds began to dissipate, revealing blue sky in patches overhead.

The water taxi skirted a long finger of land and several crab boats before turning into an inside channel, bordered by a wild, rocky shoreline. A few houses came into view, gray and weathered against the thick evergreens.

The boat glided past a fish farm and then more houses on the left and a long brown building with the sign Motel and Restaurant.

They finally arrived at the ramshackle dock, where a purse seiner and a cluster of fishing boats bobbed in the waves. And just as Jordan was wondering what to do with her unwieldy suitcases and grocery bags, Billy hoisted them out of the boat.

"They're fine here," he told her. "You go ahead, we'll bring them up for you. You're living at the back of the medical center, right?"

"I am. Thank you so much." Carrying her medical bag and her purse, Jordan climbed out of the boat and walked slowly down the long pier and up the dirt road. A large sign nailed to a building read, Welcome to Ahousaht. Jordan looked around for Christina. The nursing supervisor had said she'd meet her, but she wasn't there.

Two small boys on bikes came ripping past. One of them did an elaborate wheelie for her benefit and then hopped off the bike. He was wearing a billed cap backward over unruly black hair, and he gave Jordan an enchanting, gap-toothed grin. His face was still round with baby fat.

"Hi," he said. "You're our new doctor, right?"

She smiled back at him and nodded. "And who are you, sir?"

"I'm Eli Crow—Christina's my mom. She told us to watch for you. She had to go see Auntie Elsie—she fell yesterday and hurt her foot, all the toes on the right foot are bruised."

"Hi, Eli." Jordan set her bag down and shook hands with Eli. She remembered Christina saying that she was the single parent of an eight-year-old. "Who's your friend?"

"He's Michael Nitsch. His mom is gonna make movies."

"Hi, Michael." Jordan held out her hand to the other boy. "So are you going into the movie business, too, when you grow up?"

"Nope. I'm gonna be a fireman." Michael took his time shaking her hand. "Should we call you Mrs. Doctor?"

"You can call me Doctor Jordan, how's that? I'm pleased to meet you both. You came along at exactly the right moment, too. The last time I was here somebody met me, and now I'm sort of lost. Could you guys get me to the medical center? And maybe help me carry those grocery bags?"

"Sure. We're really, really strong." One on each side of her, they hefted her plastic carryalls over their handlebars. Taking the job as guides seriously, they talked nonstop, pointing out the band office, the school and where they lived.

They informed the smiling drivers of two pickup trucks and a man out chopping wood that they were taking Doc Jordan to her new house. They told Jordan that the man chopping wood had a wife with six fingers, and that she'd let Jordan see them if Eli asked her and said please. Jordan quickly declined the offer.

"Maybe another time."

"Okay, whenever you like," Eli replied expansively.

Everyone called out a friendly hello. A woman pegging flowered sheets and diapers on a clothesline smiled and waved.

"That's Audrey. She's got a new baby," Michael confided.

"Yeah, and her daddy went to live with his other wife," Eli said with a nod. "Audrey won't let him in the door now."

Fascinating. This had a motorcycle escort beat all to hell, and Jordan felt pretty much like an informed VIP by the time her young heroes had delivered her safely to the apartment. She gave each of them two dollars and their dark eyes lit up.

"Thanks a lot, Doctor Jordan," said Michael.

"You need anything, just call us," Eli added. They sped off on their bikes to spend their reward money.

Jordan's apartment was at the back of the medical center. Using the key she'd been given, she tried to open the door, only to find it was unlocked. Inside, it smelled of fresh paint, and Jordan had to smile.

Christina had made good on her promise. The walls were a warm, light color somewhere between lemon and cream, and the apartment had improved drastically since Jordan had last seen it on her first visit.

That day, these walls had been a nauseous institutional green.

"Can you tell this was where the cops stayed overnight before they got their trailer?" Christina had groaned. "They must get this paint free from the government. I think a nice warm lamb's wool shade for these walls, don't you?"

"What color's lamb's wool?"

"I dunno." Christina had shrugged and shot Jordan a wicked grin. "I'm just trying my damnedest to impress you. I saw it in a Martha Stewart magazine."

Jordan smiled now, remembering. There was an exuberance about Christina that made her irresistible, and obviously Eli had inherited it.

The paint made the small area welcoming, but the place was still strange to her, and she was suddenly achingly homesick for the familiarity of the Kitsilano apartment she and Garry had shared.

But not homesick for Garry. She shivered. Over the past few weeks she'd had to alert security at St. Joe's, and she'd called the police and threatened to get a restraining order when he had turned up at the door of the motel one night.

Cancel, cancel. No more depressing thoughts. So she had no idea how to make a fire in the iron cookstove. She'd learn. The hot plate she'd ordered in Tofino wouldn't be delivered for a couple days, but she'd brought a lot of cereal and apples. It wouldn't do any harm to fast a little.

She walked around, taking stock of her new home. It was clean, sparsely furnished but adequate, with mismatched furniture and an odd but generous assortment of dishes in the kitchen area. A distinctive and colorful native painting hung on one wall, and someone had obviously hand-carved the two beautiful wooden bowls on the counter.

She opened the door wide to get rid of the smell of paint, hung up her jacket on a wooden peg and began unloading the groceries. When Billy arrived with her suitcases, she'd unpack and add her own small touches to the decor, like the soft turquoise silk shawl her brother Toby had sent for her birthday.

She'd use that as a table cover. And she had an old black-and-white photo of her and Toby when they were little to put on the bedside table. One of her mother, as well.

It would soon feel like home, she reassured herself. This wasn't the same as when she was a child, shuffled from one home to the next, sharing bedrooms and sometimes even beds with other foster kids.

This apartment was hers alone. It had been her choice to come here, and she'd do her best to turn this little place into a sanctuary.

FROM A WINDOW in the band office, Silas watched the new doctor walk past with Eli and Michael. He'd honored his promise to Christina; although he was a member of the council, he'd deliberately been absent for the initial meeting with the doctor. Instead, he'd hiked up island to visit an elderly couple recovering from a severe bout of the flu, but he couldn't deny he was curious. Ahousaht was a small, close-knit community. The addition of someone from Away always had repercussions.

Jordan Burke was tall, maybe five-nine or ten—or maybe she only looked that tall because she was long-legged and very slender. Her thick chestnut hair, down past her shoulder blades and silky straight, was parted in the middle and tied simply at the base of her neck with a blue scarf. She was wearing faded jeans, brown boots and a hooded blue sweatshirt. She carried a navy rain jacket slung over one long, slim arm.

Eli and Michael were hoisting her grocery bags and talking a mile a minute, and he saw her smile at them. Her smile transformed her narrow face with its aristocratic long nose and full lips from almost plain to—he thought pretty and then changed his mind to beautiful. But only when she smiled.

She looked foreign. Pale, exotic, fragile. Silas made a dismissive sound in his throat and turned away from the window.

She wouldn't last long. He'd bet the council would be hiring another doctor within six weeks. Strength and endurance were essential in this wild, remote location. Fragile flowers didn't thrive in Ahousaht.

JORDAN HAD JUST FINISHED hanging her jacket in the small closet and was assessing how much space the drawers of the rickety chest gave her when she heard a knock at the door. She hurried to open it, hoping it was Billy with her suitcases, but Christina stood there, navy shirt accentuating the dramatic angles of her high cheekbones.

"Welcome, Jordan," she said with a wide smile. She handed her a bouquet of wild roses in a glass canning jar.

"Hey, Christina, thank you so much. Come in. I met your adorable son and his friend. Thanks for sending them to escort me from the boat."

Jordan put the flowers in the middle of the table.

"I wanted to be there myself, but there was a minor emergency. Did the boys give you the rundown on the entire population?"

"Only their immediate families and everyone we passed. I can't wait to pump them for more."

"They're nosy little demons. I just hope they never find out about blackmail."

Jordan waved an arm at the walls. "Thanks for the paint job, I love the color."

"Lambskin duvet, just like I promised." Christina glanced at the grocery bags. "I hope you didn't make lunch yet. Mom wondered if you'd like to come and eat with us?"

Jordan glanced at her watch, suddenly aware that it was past noon and nerves had kept her from having anything but coffee that morning.

"Thanks, Christina. I'd love to, but I'm waiting for Billy to bring my suitcases. He should be here any minute. Can you wait?"

"Sure. No rush. Mom's serving stew, it'll keep."

"Please, sit." Jordan gestured at the brown tweed couch. "Do you want to call her? I have my cell phone—"

Christina grinned and shook her head. "Mom's pretty easygoing. She'll expect us when we get there."

Jordan sank into a stuffed armchair across from the couch and then gave a startled squeak when her bottom almost hit the floor. The springs were gone.

"Oops." Christina put a hand over her mouth and giggled. After a moment of stunned silence, Jordan began to laugh too, and then she couldn't stop. Tears rolled down her cheeks, and she pressed her fists against her mouth, willing herself to regain control, losing it more with each passing moment.

CHAPTER FIVE

CHRISTINA GOT UP after a moment and knelt in front of Jordan.

"Let it come," she said in her soft, slow voice. "Let it out, it needs to escape now." She laid a small hand gently on Jordan's head and stroked her hair.

Ashamed, but too far out of control to do anything about it, Jordan wailed, gulping out strange guttural noises.

"That's the way," Christina encouraged her. "Let 'er out."

It took what felt like forever before Jordan regained control.

Christina went to the bathroom for a tissue, then pressed it into Jordan's hand.

"Oh, dammit, I'm so sorry," Jordan said when she could speak again. "What an idiot, having a meltdown like that." She blew her nose hard and tried for a smile. "And I'm supposed to be the doctor. It's enough to scare you, huh?"

Christina shook her head. "You're a woman first. Women need to cry, it keeps us healthy."

A knock at the door signaled the arrival of the suit-cases.

"Oh, no, I'm a wreck." Jordan hated the idea of any-one else witnessing her breakdown.

"Go in the bathroom and run some cool water. I'll tell Billy to put the suitcases in the bedroom, okay?"

"Thanks." Jordan hurried into the bathroom and locked the door. She was shaking.

"What the hell is wrong with you?" she whispered to her bleary image in the mirror over the sink. "You'll need to go back on medication if you keep this up."

She washed her face and held a cold washcloth over her swollen eyes. She could hear Christina's calm voice directing Billy, and then the sound of the door closing behind him. Grateful that she'd already put the small cache of cosmetics she carried in her purse on the shelf above the sink, Jordan used eye drops and touches of concealer, then an eyelash curler. A critical glance told her that no one with normal eyesight would be fooled; her cheeks were flushed, her eyes still bloodshot, her face puffy.

She took a deep breath and opened the bathroom door.

Christina studied her. "Well, it looks like you either have one hell of a hangover or you've been on a major crying jag," she said.

"Let's be optimistic and think hangover."

Christina grinned. "Okay, let's go eat. Food fixes damned near anything. I'm starving."

"Me, too." That in itself was amazing. Jordan's appetite had been on sabbatical for weeks, but at this moment she was voraciously hungry.

"That's gonna make my mother one happy woman. She loves feeding people. It's a wonder I'm not three hundred pounds." Christina waited while Jordan locked the door, and then they set off down the gravel road.

The wind was up—it smelled of the sea—and it cooled Jordan's burning cheeks and smarting eyes.

"Where'd you train, Christina?" She liked the other woman a lot. She'd only ever had a handful of women friends, and she'd lost touch with them since marrying Garry. He'd taken all her attention.

"Edmonton, nine years ago," Christina said. "I followed my high school sweetheart there. David got a job in the oil fields and I enrolled in nursing. But he was killed when a generator blew up. I was two months from graduating and four months pregnant. We were getting married the day after graduation."

Lordy. All of a sudden, Jordan's life didn't seem so desperate.

Christina was matter-of-fact about it all. "I got my degree and came back here so Eli could grow up with family and friends."

Family. Friends. The words left a hollow space in Jordan's heart. She'd grown up in foster homes, struggling to make top grades, too busy to have time for friendship. And then somewhere along the line, she'd learned not to trust other women. And yet here was a woman, on an island in what at this moment felt like the outer edge of the known world, who made Jordan think friendship was not only possible, but likely.

They left the road and headed up a slight hill to a wooden frame house indistinguishable from every other they'd passed. Each had a stack of firewood outside, and many of the yards were cluttered with discarded bathtubs, broken high chairs, rusted motors, old tires— even bed frames.

Some had electrical lines leading to them, but many didn't. The one Christina headed for was tidy and well kept. The pile of firewood was neatly stacked, and wooden tubs of flowers flanked the walkway. Christina led Jordan up the sturdy stairs and opened the front door.

"Mom, hey, we're here!"

Mouthwatering cooking smells greeted them, along with Elvis singing gospel on a boom box. A plump, very pretty woman hurried down the hall to greet them, wiping her hands on a striped apron tied around her ample waist. She was smiling, and her dark eyes were almost buried in her round apple cheeks.

"About time. I was about to send out a scouting party."

"This is Jordan Burke, Ma. Jordan, my mother, Rose Marie Crow."

Rose Marie took both of Jordan's hands in a warm, welcoming clasp.

"You're a pretty one," she commented. "But way too skinny, we'll have to feed you up, eh?"

Jordan's smile took effort. Her skin felt shrunken from crying, and she was suddenly shy. "It smells wonderful in here," she managed to say. "Thank you so much for inviting me."

"We're not fancy, come and sit in the kitchen and I'll serve the stew. Christina, Eli came by and said he's eating at Michael's house. Wanda's making them KD."

"Kraft Dinner," Christina interpreted. "They'd live on the stuff if we let them."

Rose Marie led the two women to the large kitchen at the back of the house. Sliding doors opened on to a deck, where the yard below was mostly garden. Green plants in a variety of pots lined the deep windowsills.

The kitchen was warm and inviting, counters lined with baskets of food and a wood-burning cookstove in the corner like the one in Jordan's apartment. Except this one sent out waves of warmth. Its gleaming surface was crowded with pots, and a large, sturdy basket beside the stove held a good supply of firewood.

Rose Marie deftly lifted the lid with an iron utensil and thrust another log into the firebox, slamming the lid back in place. The big square wooden table in the middle of the room was set for four with sea-green place mats and colorful Fiestaware.

Christina indicated a chair, and Jordan sat.

"Where's Grandmother, Mom?"

"She went back home to get something but told us not to wait for her."

Rose Marie began filling huge bowls with stew. Slicing up a loaf of freshly baked bread, Christina filled a wooden platter, and set it on the table along with a wooden bowl of glistening salad greens.

"Dig in," Rose Marie ordered, taking her place beside Christina.

Jordan, suddenly ravenous, did as she was told. Her first bite confirmed that Rose Marie was an exceptional cook who knew her way around a seafood stew.

"This is *sooo* good," she sighed.

Just as Jordan was sampling the crusty bread—irresistibly still warm—the deck door slid open and a short, very old woman with long black braids came in. Almost as wide as she was tall, she moved with an assured dignity and grace that belied her years.

Christina got up and gave her a hug and a peck on the cheek. "Hey, Grandmother Alice, this is Jordan Burke, the new doctor. Jordan, this is Alice Sam."

"How do you do." Alice set down the plastic bag she was carrying and came over to take Jordan's hand. Her gaze seemed to penetrate beneath the skin. "It's a pleasure to meet you, Jordan Burke."

"And you, Mrs. Sam."

"Grandmother, everyone calls me Grandmother."

"Sit," Rose Marie ordered. "I'll get you some stew. Help yourself to salad and bread."

While Elvis sang "Amazing Grace," they ate the food, simple and delicious.

After a long silence, the women began to discuss the weather and the garden and someone's new baby. Jordan didn't feel excluded, but rather, relived they didn't make her the focus of the gathering.

She sensed they were giving her a chance to get to know them, to feel at home with them—and to recover from whatever had made her eyes red and bloodshot.

She felt relaxed and peaceful, sitting in the bright kitchen with these kind and tactful women.

"I made Nanaimo bars," Rose Marie said when everyone was finished eating. "You drink coffee, Doctor? Or I can make tea, herbal or regular, whatever you want."

"Coffee's fine." A jolt of caffeine would help get her through the afternoon.

The Nanaimo bars were decadent—layers of sweet custard, coconut and smooth dark chocolate. Between the sugar and caffeine, Jordan was soon wide-awake again.

"I read that now they think chocolate is actually good for you," Christina said. "What's your professional opinion, Jordan? You can lie—we'll all be grateful."

They all turned to look at her.

"Women have always known chocolate's good for them," she said, munching a second slice. "We didn't need scientists to prove it."

The others smiled and nodded, and then fell silent. Waiting politely for her to tell them something about herself. But she couldn't. She'd learned to talk to Helen, but she still couldn't let others into her private space. "You're an amazing cook, Rose Marie," she said. "I'll have to learn to cook, too. I've gotten way too used to eating out and ordering in."

"Here, we don't have much choice," Alice said. "And

most of us don't have the money, even if there was somewhere to go besides Mabel's."

"Working in Emerg, you probably came home too tired to do much cooking," Christina said in her defense. "You're gonna find life a lot slower here."

"I'm looking forward to that."

"You got family on the mainland?" Alice asked.

"No." Jordan hesitated. "An ex-husband." The ex part was stretching the truth somewhat. "No kids," she added with a sense of regret. "I have one brother, but he's in Seattle. I don't see him very often."

"Your folks passed on?" Alice obviously believed family was very important.

It would be rude to avoid a direct answer. "My mother died when I was four," Jordan managed to say. "My father figured he couldn't take care of us on his own so he put my brother and me into foster care. He's still alive, but I don't have any contact with him."

"Too bad," Alice said shaking her head. "We all need family."

The women nodded.

"We have a saying," Grandmother Alice said, murmuring in her own language. "It means we are all related."

"Most of us, my generation anyways, we got separated from our folks, too," Rose Marie said. "They took the kids from the reserves and put us either with foster families in the city or in residential schools."

"I've read about that," Jordan said. "That had to be one of the most destructive things politicians ever did."

"Yeah." All three women agreed, but without any show of emotion.

"It was bad, getting taken away," Alice said, matter-of-fact. "And then it was real hard, comin' back."

"Culture shock comin' and goin'," Rose Marie agreed, and they all laughed.

"But now we got our own school, our kids stay here in Ahousaht."

Jordan recognized the pride in her tone. "When I saw the school the first time I came here, I was impressed. It's beautiful."

Rose Marie nodded. "And we got some really good teachers."

"Did any of them grow up here?"

"Three." Alice poured Jordan another cup of coffee. "There's two from Away, but they've been here two years now. Looks like they might just stay."

"Is that a problem?" Jordan asked. "Teachers leaving?"

"Oh, yeah, big-time," Christina said. "Last year we had some leave before September was even over. That young couple who came from the Interior—"

She was interrupted by a man in rough work clothes and rubber boots who opened the sliding door wide and stepped inside.

Rose Marie got up fast. "Peter, what's happened?"

"Louie's cut his leg damned near off with the power saw," he said, breathing hard. "I knew the new doc was comin' here for lunch—we called for the ambulance but it's got a flat tire."

"This is my husband, Peter Crow," Rose Marie said.

"We'd better hurry, Peter." Jordan got up quickly, adrenaline pumping. "I'll have to get my medical bag from the apartment."

"You go with Dad," Christina said. "Give me your key, I'll bring your bag." She turned to her father. "Where's Louie?"

"Down by the old wharf, he's bleedin' pretty bad, but Silas is there. He'll get it stopped. C'mon, Doc."

Jordan had to run to keep up with him. He'd left a battered green half ton running, and she climbed into the passenger seat, barely getting the door shut before Peter stepped hard on the accelerator.

A medical emergency. For the first time all day, Jordan felt confident that she was doing exactly what she was meant to do.

CHAPTER SIX

HER PATIENT WAS LYING FLAT on an old dock in a pool of coagulating blood. His right thigh, halfway between knee and groin, had been torn open in a crosswise cut. Someone had been smart enough to elevate the wound and apply a pressure bandage.

Jordan knelt and looked into the man's eyes, at the same time taking his wrist, gauging his pulse.

"Hi, I'm Doctor Burke. Can you tell me your name?" She knew it, but needed to ascertain his level of shock.

"Louie Adams." His voice was thin and reedy, but he was conscious and responding. *Rapid pulse, dilated pupils. Shock, but not bad. Considering.*

Louie was stoically silent, and an equally silent crowd had collected around him. Someone had draped a jacket over his chest and shoulders, possibly the lean man who knelt beside him. He was talking to Louie in a low tone, his shoulder-length black hair partially hiding his face.

The man's hair had a dramatic white streak, although he looked young. His black leather jacket was well-worn, open to reveal a white T-shirt with a picture of an eagle in full flight. His jeans fit like a second skin, molding to his long, strong thighs. He looked up, meeting Jordan's eyes. His were clear and cool, a surprising pale green with specks of gold, and for an instant she had the disconcerting feeling that he could see into her mind.

"I'm Silas Keefer," he said in a deep, soft voice. He didn't smile.

"Jordan Burke. Hi." She'd heard that voice before, she thought, turning back to her patient. "Okay, Louie, we'll get some fluids into you and then take you up to the medical center."

Although just how she was going to accomplish that without any medical supplies or an ambulance—

"It's slowing down now, Silas. I'll have it stopped in a minute." Louie's glazed eyes looked to the man beside her.

Obviously he was in shock. Silas leaned over her patient and murmured something close to his ear. Jordan couldn't make it out.

From somewhere nearby, she heard Christina. "I've got your bag here, Jordan, and the medical pack from the ambulance. The first-aid guys are bringing a stretcher. We'll have to use a pickup to get him to the center—it'll take too long to fix the damned tire. You want me to establish a line?"

Christina crouched beside Jordan, proving herself first-rate at finding a vein.

The flow of blood from the wound was much less than Jordan had expected, and there didn't appear to be

a severed artery or nerve damage. The saw had bit
deeply into the muscle, the fleshy part of the thigh.

Jordan supervised Louie's transfer first to a stretcher
and then to the back of the pickup truck that had backed
in close. Through it all, Silas Keefer helped without
once getting in the way. Jordan was aware of him the
whole time, as she was sometimes aware of electricity
in the air before a thunderstorm.

In the back of the truck, she crouched beside her patient, feeling a little like a pioneer doctor as she steadied the drip and kept tabs on Louie's pulse and
breathing. Christina and Silas Keefer rode in front beside the driver.

At the medical center, Jordan had to argue with
Louie, who refused to be airlifted to Tofino.

"What good's having a doctor here if you're gonna
send me to the hospital over there? Can't you sew me
up right here, Doc?"

Jordan considered it. It would have been impossible
if there was major nerve damage or arterial bleeding,
but Louie had lucked out.

"I'd have to give you a brief general anesthetic," she
warned. Christina had said she was qualified at anes-
thesia, but they'd never worked together. "Wouldn't
you feel safer having this procedure done in hospital?"

"Hell, no," Louie insisted. "You've sewed people up
before, haven't you?"

"Oh, yes." Jordan grinned. "One or two." She'd done
more than her share of minor surgery in the E.R.

"Then do it, Doc. I want you to patch me up here,

that way I can be home in a couple days, keep an eye on the kids for the wife. She works at the RCMP office."

Jordan hoped she was making the right decision. "Okay, that's what we'll do."

As she and Christina scrubbed, Jordan said, "That tall guy, Silas Keefer, who is he? He knew a lot about first aid, but he left before I could talk to him."

"Oh, that's my older brother."

"Your *brother?*" Jordan shot Christina a surprised look. Different surnames and no family resemblance. Even Silas's speech patterns were unlike Christina's slow, measured delivery.

"He's my half brother," Christina amended. "From Mom's first marriage."

"I see. Has he had medical training? He seemed to know exactly what to do."

"Not really." Christina concentrated on soaping her hands. "Silas does a lot of things. He's a writer, he's published a few books and he writes articles for various journals. He lives in the bush outside of town. He's not very social. I keep telling him thirty-six is too young to be eccentric, but he's determined to play the part."

"So he's your big brother." Jordan felt a familiar jolt of homesickness, thinking of her own big brother. "Is he married?" There was no real reason for the question—except that she very much wanted to know.

"Nope. He came close a couple years back, a nurse from Edmonton who spent a year up here. But she couldn't stand the isolation. She went home, Silas didn't follow, so that was that."

Jordan filed that information away and forcefully evicted Silas Keefer from her mind. She had work to do.

The surgery on Louie's leg took every ounce of Jordan's concentration. She was accustomed to an entire crew of nurses and aides, and far more sophisticated equipment. The clinic had the basics, but it was a strange experience to work with only Christina and an ambulance attendant standing by. Jordan was acutely conscious of being totally responsible for her patient's well-being, in a way she never had been at St. Joe's.

The wound was jagged and dirty, the flesh ripped by the teeth of the saw. Splinters of wood needed careful extraction, and there was heightened danger of infection from the dirt and oil off the blade of the saw. She heaved a sigh of relief when the procedure was finally over, shocked to learn that the afternoon had faded into evening.

She talked to Louie's wife, Roberta, and then to his mother, Angie. A long string of concerned relatives and friends dropped by the clinic, and Christina was kept busy reassuring them.

Louie came out of the anesthetic in record time, and within an hour was asking for something to eat, which astonished Jordan.

He had to be in severe pain. She'd ordered five milligrams of morphine every hour to keep him comfortable, and she couldn't believe he was actually hungry. "Food's not a good idea," she warned. "You may be nauseous, I'd recommend only liquids until tomorrow."

"C'mon, Doc," Louie wheedled. "I cut my leg, not my stomach. Can't I at least have some soup?"

"Okay, then. I'll see if I can find a tin of clear broth," Jordan offered doubtfully, thinking of the woodstove she had no idea how to light. She felt more than a little nostalgic about St. Joe's, where one call to housekeeping took care of these kind of details.

"Oh, you won't have to make anything. I think somebody left a pot of soup back there in your kitchen," Christina said with a mischievous grin. "I unlocked your door so the donor could get in. I hope you don't mind."

"Mind? What are you, nuts?"

Jordan went through the connecting door into her apartment, and stopped dead at the kitchen. The cookstove was giving off waves of heat. Not only was there a pot of soup simmering, but on the table someone had laid out three kinds of salad, a tray of sliced beef, what looked like a meat pie, along with jars of pickles, relish and berries. On the counter, she saw another pie, chocolate cake, oatmeal cookies—and homemade bread.

Jordan studied the bounty, and for the second time that day, tears burned at the back of her eyes. For several long moments she couldn't contain them.

Get a grip, for God's sake. It's only way too much food. But there was something about women welcoming her by bringing gifts of food that touched her deeply.

"Louie's hungry," she said aloud to no one, blowing her nose and studying the feast. She filled a small bowl with broth from the potato chowder, poured a glass of apple juice and, folding paper towel into a napkin, used a battered cookie sheet as a tray. Then she took it all to the room where Louie was stretched out, his heavily bandaged leg elevated and IV firmly in place.

Roberta was there with him and she took over, putting the tray on a bedside stand, spooning the soup into her husband's mouth.

"You and Christina go have some supper," she suggested. "I'll take care of Louie. Nothin' to it, I been doin' it for ten years already. He's an awful baby when something goes wrong." But the glance she and Louie exchanged was tender.

"I dunno about you, Jordan, but I'm starving," Christina said.

"Have I got a dinner for you." Jordan took her back to the kitchen, and together they filled plates and sat on the rump-sprung couch to eat.

"I'll have to give some of this away or it'll go bad. There's enough here for twenty people," Jordan said.

"We can put some of it out in the clinic for a free lunch tomorrow. There'll be a crowd around—everybody will want to size up the new doc."

That should have unnerved her, but Jordan was far too tired. By the time she'd finished a slice of blueberry pie, she was yawning.

"Excuse me," she apologized, and then yawned again.

"Why not go to bed?" Christina gathered up their dishes and stacked them in the plastic dishpan in the sink. "These'll keep till morning, dirty dishes always do. We'll just stow the meat and salad in the fridge— I'll take Roberta a plateful. I'm gonna set up a cot for her beside Louie's bed. That way she can keep an eye on him for us during the night. I'll check the drip and make sure there's no bleeding."

"Bless you. I'm absolutely wiped out. It must be the sea air."

"Or it could have something to do with a major emergency your first day on the job. I meant to ask, are you planning on having office hours every day? A couple of Roberta's relatives were asking."

"Every day except Sunday. I didn't come here to laze around, I'm used to the pace in the E.R. I'll put a sign on the door with the hours. What do you think is reasonable? Eight to twelve, and then two to five?"

"You can try that." Christina laughed. "People here don't go much by the clock, we run on what we call Indian time. That means people will turn up when it suits them. But they also don't mind waiting, so it evens out. There's also a lot of extra stuff that won't fit into rigid office hours. Like the well-baby clinic once a week and Community Care where we go out to whoever needs us. There's also a drug education program for teens and a prenatal group. You sure don't have to attend all those things all the time, but it would be great if you'd come once in a while."

"I wish now I'd gone into general practice. Until I get the hang of it, I'm going to have to rely on you to keep me on track."

"It shouldn't take that long, you strike me as a reasonably bright woman."

"Gee, thanks."

They both grinned. Today they'd worked together as a smooth, efficient unit. As if they'd done it for years.

"We'll grab time tomorrow to work out a sort of timetable," Christina said. "You go on to bed. If anybody needs you, they know where to come."

"Thanks, Christina. For everything. And tell your mom thanks for the lunch, I sort of ate and ran."

"No kidding, I wonder why? I'll tell her."

After Christina went back into the clinic, Jordan covered the remaining food, turned out the lights, and made her way into the bedroom. Groaning when she realized her suitcase had been flopped onto the double bed, she wrestled it to the floor so there'd be room for her to sleep. She put on the worn flannel nightgown she'd had since her intern days, and after a quick wash in the bathroom, tumbled into bed. She'd unpack in the morning.

The mattress was firm, the sheets soft, and Jordan burrowed into the fluffy comforter. The window she'd opened let in the smell of the sea with a distinct tinge of pine, mingling with wood smoke, maybe from her own kitchen stove.

She really had to learn how to light that thing— she'd probably even have to learn how to use the oven.

Unless the women took pity on her and kept bringing food, she'd also have to learn to cook. There was so much for her to learn here. It felt as if she'd been catapulted to a different planet. One where Garry couldn't find her.

But it wasn't Garry's face that came to mind as she began to relax. It was the lean, hard-edged features of Silas Keefer.

You're out of it, Burke. You're so tired you're hallucinating.

With a sigh of exhaustion and something closer to contentment than she'd felt in a long while, she closed her eyes and fell asleep.

LESS THAN A MILE AWAY, Silas slumped in front of his laptop, struggling with the lengthy article he'd agreed to write on ideological differences toward healing between native and white culture. It was for the University Press, to be included in a book on many diverse healing modalities. It had been assigned by a professor he'd come to respect during his student days, and Silas was being well paid for it—the main reason he'd taken on the contract.

Living in Ahousaht was definitely a low-rent proposition, but even the simplest lifestyle required an income.

He ran a hand through his hair. This wasn't going well at all, and it should be a piece of cake. He knew the material, he *lived* the material.

He deleted a couple of paragraphs, scowling at the

screen. Why couldn't he keep his mind on what he was doing?

Because I'm thinking about the blue-eyed doctor. The answer surprised him. He hadn't been consciously thinking about her, but she was definitely there, just under the surface, distracting him.

His body had reacted to her today. He'd tried to pretend it hadn't, because he liked to believe he was in control of himself, his thoughts, his responses.

He'd been celibate for a long time—by choice. Several attractive women in the village had made it plain they'd welcome him in their bed. And he'd been tempted. It would be a lie to say he hadn't.

But he wanted someone to share his ideas with, a woman he could trust enough to open up to, dream with, laugh with—and, yeah, take to his bed. He was strong and healthy, with a hale and hearty libido. He was also solitary, preferring to watch people rather than engage with them. It wasn't a trait that endeared him to women when the lovemaking was over, and there hadn't been many who intrigued him enough to risk sharing more than sex with them.

The problem was there were no secrets on this island. Everyone would know before noon who he'd bedded. Not that there was anything wrong with that, either. But as a healer, he had a certain status. He wasn't obliged to embrace celibacy, except during the periods of purification necessary for certain ceremonies. But there was a personal moral code he felt obliged to sustain.

"And now you're laughing at me, Grandmother," he whispered. He could almost see Sandrine in the corner of the room, as she used to be, sitting in the rocking chair she'd given him long ago. "You're right, I'm a stuffed shirt. I take myself way too seriously. You always told me I needed to laugh at myself more."

"Love more, too. The opposite of man is woman, and we all need to know our opposite and embrace it. You will only find the other half of yourself in another person, Grandson. It's the only way we ever really see ourselves."

He turned and looked directly at the chair.

"Help me, Grandmother." He wasn't sure what he meant, exactly. He only knew that he suddenly felt vulnerable.

But Sandrine wasn't there.

He had to escape outside. He saved his document and got to his feet, grabbing his jacket from the wooden peg by the door.

Outside, the woods were alive with night sounds. Silas stood and listened, separating them, naming them. Owl. Coyote. The scurrying of a small animal, maybe a marmot. The twittering of birds, settling in for the night. The faint scent of skunk, somewhere off to the west. The tang of the evergreens, the salt of the sea.

He'd deliberately built in the bush so he wouldn't have to see any lights at night except the moon and stars. Looking up, he watched as the clouds opened up to reveal Venus and Orion.

There was only a sliver of moon, and a cloud obscured it after a moment, but it was enough. The vastness of the night sky put everything into proportion, as it always did. The world was very small compared to the universe and there were more worlds than this one.

His eyes had adjusted to the darkness, and he made his way effortlessly and silently along the path. Usually he went down to the water, but tonight he headed to the village.

There'd been an AA meeting at the school, and it was just breaking up as Silas drifted past. He heard Lily's distinctive belly laugh, and Sam saying something about the coffee being too strong.

"Strip the rust right outta your pipes," he rasped. "Hey, there. How's it goin' Silas?"

The healer nodded to them but didn't stop to talk. His long stride carried him up the slight incline to the medical center. There was a soft light coming from the treatment area, where Louie was resting. The living quarters at the back were dark, the screened window to the bedroom open as far as it would go.

He imagined her sleeping there, curled under the blankets. It must have been an exhausting day for her. Silently, he walked around the building, bending over to hush a dog that came loping out of nowhere. Pausing a moment outside her bedroom window, he imagined he could hear her breathing softly, in and out.

Going in the front door of the center, Silas headed for the room where Louie slept deeply. Roberta was lying on a cot close beside her husband's bed. Her eyes opened and she started to get up, but Silas waved her back down again and made a sign for silence.

He stood beside Louie and put a hand gently on the top of the man's bandaged leg. Closing his eyes, he hummed softly, a healing prayer, one of the first Grandmother Sandrine had ever taught him.

Louie slept on, and Roberta nodded her thanks.

Silas left as quietly as he'd come.

CHAPTER SEVEN

SILAS HEADED DOWN to the water. Just out of reach of the incoming tide, he stopped and crouched down on his haunches.

He felt disturbed. This woman wasn't for him. The culture she came from was the same one that had almost destroyed him. Tonight he needed to remember that, as much as he usually needed to forget it. He wanted her, but he could control his desire.

The ebb and flow of the water slowly quieted his mind, and after a while it felt as if his blood were flowing in rhythm with the ocean's current. He began to hum, a monotonous deep thrumming in his chest, clearing away the emotions that swirled in his bloodstream like fireflies. The sound centered him, connected him to the earth and water, the wind and sky, and at last a measure of peace touched the place where his hunger raged.

JORDAN WOKE TO THE SOUND of crows waging a territorial war outside her bedroom. Her bedside clock said

6:00 a.m., and the thin curtain covering her open window did little to keep out the light and cool, fresh air.

There was no confusion about where she was; ever since her intern days she'd come out of deep sleep fully alert. This morning, her first thought was for her patient. Surely she'd have been awakened during the night if anything had gone wrong, but she wanted to check for herself, right now.

In under ten minutes, she was showered and dressed in jeans and a T-shirt. Shivering, she pulled on a hoodie. Her kitchen was chilly, the fire long burned out. The food on the counter and the dishes in the sink made the room look like the day after a party, deserted and lonely. She made her way through the connecting door.

"He slept like a baby," Roberta reported with a smile, coming out of the bathroom. "He woke up just once and I gave him a drink of water. I checked the bandage—it's clean and dry. That stuff dripping into his arm's going down, though. Christina said she'd come by and change it if you didn't wake up by seven."

Louie was still sleeping, but he woke when Jordan said his name. Rolling the sheet aside, she removed the bandage to check her handiwork. The wound was pink and healthy looking, with far less seepage than she'd expected. Miraculously, it was already beginning to heal.

"I've seldom seen a wound heal this fast," she told Louie and Roberta. "You must be incredibly healthy, Louie. I'll put on a fresh dressing and, if it continues to improve this way, we can soon do away with the IV drip."

"And then I can go home," Louie said with a wide grin.

"Not for a few days. You'll have to be able to make it to the bathroom on your own first. You can't expect Roberta to empty bedpans."

"You got that right." Roberta rolled her eyes at Jordan. "Yuck. Mind if I go make some coffee?"

"You'll have to light the stove first." Jordan added an automatic coffeepot to the list of things she was going to order from Tofino. "Maybe you could teach me how, while you're at it."

"Glad to." Roberta led the way into Jordan's kitchen. "This here's a damper, you gotta make sure it's open before you start or you'll smoke yourself out. You've got some kindling—that's a good start. And paper." Popping crumpled newspaper into the stove, she laid thin strips of alder on top.

"Matches." She lit one from a tin container hanging on the wall. The paper flared and the kindling caught. "Then you just add wood, starting with small stuff and moving up to logs. When it gets going good, you move the damper a little this way—" she demonstrated "—so all the heat doesn't go up the chimney. Easy as anything."

"Yeah, about as easy as brain surgery." Jordan groaned.

Roberta laughed, emptying last night's dregs from the enamel coffeepot, deftly filling it with water and measuring out spoonfuls of coffee from a tin. Lifting the stove lid, she added more wood. "You never cooked on a woodstove?"

"I never cooked much on any sort of stove."

"Then I'll fix you some breakfast."

"You don't have to do that. There's cereal in the cupboard, and juice."

"No bother." Roberta had found a black iron skillet, and eggs from the fridge. "Louie'll want eggs, if I know him. And you oughta have something hot under your belt, it's gonna be a busy day. You might not get a chance to eat again for a while. Everybody's been savin' up their bellyaches because they knew you were comin'."

It was a prophetic statement.

When her cell rang late that afternoon, Jordan glanced at her watch and couldn't believe the time. It was past five, and there were still six people waiting to see her. She'd already treated eighteen. Roberta had been absolutely right, everyone had been saving up their ailments—but more out of curiosity than real need. In any case, the day had passed in a blur.

"Hello?"

"Hey, squirt, how's it going out there in the boonies?"

"Toby." A wave of love and loneliness swept through Jordan when she heard her brother's deep, gruff voice. "Oh, damn! I said I'd call you as soon as I got here, didn't I? I'm so sorry. Things got a little hairy here."

"No sweat, I just wanted to make sure you got there safe and you're getting settled okay."

"I did and I am. Hold on one minute, it's not too private here."

She went to the open door, motioned at the phone

and held up a finger signifying a moment's delay to her next patient.

The elderly woman nodded and smiled. Everyone else nodded, as well, and Jordan shoved the door closed. Leaning against it, she shut her eyes and visualized Toby's ruggedly handsome features, his slate-blue eyes two shades darker than her own, his tall, thin, deceptively strong body.

"Everyone's so friendly," she said into the phone. "The entire village seems to be cooking for me—pies, cookies, even a roast. They've made me very welcome."

"Home cooking, huh? Got a spare room?"

"Absolutely." She knew he was teasing, but she jumped at the chance to see him. "When can I expect you?"

"Maybe when this yacht gets done," he said with a sigh. "I need a holiday. The stress is getting to me."

"Are you feeling okay?" The last time they'd talked, Toby had mentioned migraines and sore muscles. "More headaches?"

"Mostly a pain in the ass. The owner's got more money than patience, and he keeps changing his damned mind. So I'm grinding my teeth and putting in long hours. But once I get the bulkheads in, he's going to have to take it the way it is, no more changes."

"And then you'll come?"

"I'll try. You didn't really say much the last time we talked, except that you were leaving Vancouver—and Garry. I'm worried about you. Did you leave St. Joe's because of him? The asshole's not giving you a hard time, is he?" When she didn't answer, Toby cleared his throat apologetically. "I guess it's no surprise that I never liked the guy."

"No surprise, no." Toby had only met Garry once, and there'd been raised hackles on both sides. Garry had made it plain he had no use for Jordan's brother. And Toby, bless his heart, had simply never mentioned her husband.

She was going to have to lie a little—either that, or Toby might pay Garry a visit. Her brother was a physical man.

"He wasn't exactly thrilled that I was leaving the marriage, but no. No real hassles, and I've got a good lawyer."

She hadn't told Toby why she was leaving Garry, and she wasn't about to now. She couldn't handle any more conflict in her life.

"He's a bully, you watch out for him. You need anything, you let me know right away, okay?"

"I will. And I'll phone you next time."

"Great. You think you're going to like it there in Ahousaht? I looked it up on the Net—it sounds pretty isolated to me."

"It is isolated. It's too soon to say for sure how well I'll adapt, but I'm committed for a year, so I'll give it my best shot."

"They're lucky to have you."

"I'm grateful for the job." She was, too. She'd felt like her old self today, listening to lungs and tapping backs and examining kids' ears.

"I miss you, Toby."

"Me, too. I love you, kid. By the way, I heard from Dad last week. He's moved into a care facility and he's got a phone now. You want the number?"

Suddenly the tenderness between them was gone, and Jordan resented the loss. But it wasn't Toby's fault. It was her father's.

"Nope. I don't really have anything to say to him."

Toby sighed, deep and long. "He's getting old, Jordan."

"Mike made his choices a long time ago."

"He's old and sick, Jordan. And he's lonely."

"I'll keep on sending you money for anything he needs—as long as he never knows it's from me. But he's just going to have to learn to live with loneliness. The same way you and I did." Her voice was hard. "He's got the advantage there—he's an adult, with choices."

She'd been four when their mother died; Toby six. After a scant month of trying to care for them on his own, Mike—a logger—put them in foster care. At first, attempts were made to keep them in the same foster home. But by the time Jordan started school, she and her adored big brother had been moved twice, and visits between them arranged by the social workers petered out.

It hadn't taken long for Mike to drop contact with his children altogether. The only stability in Jordan's life during those years was school, and she'd compensated by excelling academically.

Toby quit school early and ended up in serious trouble. She'd been lucky enough to eventually find wealthy foster parents who helped pay her way through university.

And yet it was Toby who now said, "Life's too short to carry grudges, Jordan."

"It's not a grudge, Toby." She'd convinced herself of that. "It's simply a case of indifference. I really don't have any feelings for him. He wasn't there when I graduated, not high school, not university, not when I became a full-fledged physician. I gave up on him, the way he gave up on us."

"God knows I hated him myself for years." Toby's voice was subdued, the earlier lightness gone. "But all that did was sap my energy. And when he turned up, he was so damned old and sad. I just don't have it in me to hate him anymore."

"I don't hate him. But I don't want anything to do with him." And she didn't want to talk about it anymore, either. "I really should go, Toby. I've got a lineup of people still waiting to see me, and there's some sort of meeting tonight I have to attend. I'll give you a call in a couple of days and tell you how it's going, promise."

"Sure, squirt. I've got to get back to work myself. Talk to you soon. Love you."

"Love you too, Toby."

She hung up, feeling bereft. Toby sounded tired, and she had a sizeable knot in her stomach from talking about her father. Why did her brother have to spoil every conversation by bringing up Mike? Didn't she have enough to cope with, being married to a drug addict? She'd convinced herself long ago that she'd made peace with the past, moved beyond the powerful emotions Mike used to arouse in her. Trembling a little as she opened the door, it took effort to force a smile as she called her next patient.

THE NEXT FEW DAYS flew by.

Jordan was accustomed to the orderly pattern of hospital timetables, shifts on and then scheduled time off. But here there wasn't the same division between work and leisure. Sometimes the clinic was empty for hours, and other times there weren't enough chairs.

The Nuu-chah-nulth people were nothing like the patients she'd treated at St. Joe's. Here, no one ever seemed to mind waiting for her. They talked softly with one another, drank the coffee and tea Christina made, ate the homemade cookies that appeared in a steady stream, and seemed grateful when at last their turn came.

She soon learned that she was never really off duty. If someone had a medical problem outside of clinic office hours, they simply came and knocked at the door of her apartment. Jordan began to suspect that it wasn't always a medical emergency that brought the visitors— their problems were often very minor, ranging from sore toes to toothache to a pain in one shoulder.

Christina confirmed her suspicions. "They're curious about you," she told Jordan. "That's why they come to your place."

"But they don't ask me questions or say anything."

Jordan shook her head, puzzled. "Yesterday an elderly man came over late in the afternoon. He said he had an aching in his legs and wrists, so I suggested an herbal remedy for arthritis and that he should come to the clinic for tests. Then he just sat in my kitchen for forty-five minutes without saying anything. I tried asking him questions, but finally I just sat there, pouring tea and feeling like a dweeb."

"It's our way," Christina said. "Particularly with the elders. They like to listen to what people don't say, to the silences between the words. It's a mark of respect."

"I need to learn so much more about your culture," Jordan admitted. "I read the books you suggested, but they focused on the history."

"History is what we're trying to get back to, because life worked for us back then. But it ain't easy. The world has changed so much. Listening to the stories our elders tell is the best way for you to learn. There's a dinner at the community hall Saturday night, lots of food and conversation. You should come, everybody will be there."

"What time?" She saw the look on Christina's face and laughed. "Just give me a ballpark figure."

Christina shrugged. "Come when it suits you."

"You're a big help."

"Probably around six-thirty or seven would be good."

"Thanks, I'll be there."

"My brother Silas has written a lot of articles about our ways. He'd be a good person to talk to. He understands both cultures. See, his father's white. Silas lived with him in Vancouver from when he was little until about six years ago."

"You said he's a writer." Jordan had seen Silas several times these past few days, at the small grocery, walking along the dirt road through the village, in the clinic talking to Louie. He'd nodded politely, but he never made a point of talking to her the way others did.

"Yeah." Christina hesitated, and then added, "He's also a healer."

"He's a healer?" Jordan was amazed. "I know he comes by to see Louie often, but I had no idea, I mean he must…does he…he probably resents the fact that the council hired me."

"Not at all." Christina shook her head. "He believes, as I do, that there's a need for all types of healers in the community."

"He's not very—" Jordan stopped herself from adding *friendly*. She was talking about Christina's brother. "He seems to keep to himself. I'd love to talk to him, compare notes on medical techniques."

"Silas is a loner," Christina said. "He's caring and compassionate, but growing up half-and-half was hard on him. He doesn't trust easy. It took a long time for me to establish the sister-brother thing. We had to get to know each other as adults."

"Why do you think he came back?" Jordan knew she was being nosy, but she couldn't help herself. The man interested her.

"He didn't plan on staying, I know that much. He was doing research for his Ph.D. thesis on modern science's approach to medicine versus indigenous healing, and he spent a lot of time with Grandmother Sandrine. She was an amazing healer. Anyhow, he spent the winter here. In the spring he went back to Vancouver for a couple days, but he's been here ever since. He hardly ever goes as far as Tofino."

"This would be a good place to hide out, if you wanted to." Which of course was exactly what Jordan was doing. "Is your grandmother still alive?"

Christina shook her head. "Grandmother Sandrine passed two years ago. Ninety-six. She was sharp right up until the week she died. An amazing storyteller."

"I'm sorry I never got to meet her."

"I'm sorry she's gone—I miss her like crazy. She was so much fun. Silas wrote down some of her stories—he might let you read them."

"That would be wonderful." Jordan suspected it would never happen. Silas didn't exactly seem like a big fan of hers.

"Why don't you ask him? He's coming to the dinner Saturday night."

"Why don't you ask for me? I'm scared of him—he never smiles."

"I'll tell him you said that."

"Don't. I'll ask him myself."

"Good. Nothing ventured, nothing won."

"Do you do a lot of counseling? Because your technique could use work."

Christina stuck out her tongue.

THE DINNER HAD BEEN FANTASTIC. Seated between Rose Marie and Grandmother Alice, Jordan was enjoying watching the villagers as they mingled over coffee and dessert. And then she saw Silas making his way toward her through the crowd. Suddenly she felt a tinge of nervousness.

She'd seen Christina buttonhole Silas a few minutes before. Now she understood that Christina had laid down the law.

Go be nice to the doctor.

Silas moved with a quiet grace, and because of his height he stood out in the crowd. He stopped beside Jordan. His long hair was neatly parted and caught back in a leather tie, the white streak standing out dramatically.

"Doctor Burke." He inclined his head in a brief nod. His voice was deep and soft. "We met before, I'm Silas Keefer."

"I remember." *As if I'd forget.* And what was the polite term for addressing a healer? Jordan had no idea. Uncomfortable with him looming over her, she pushed her chair back and got to her feet. She came just past his shoulder, which made him a good six-four or -five.

"Nice to see you again." Smiling easily—she hoped—Jordan held out her hand.

"Doctor." He took her hand and held it.

"Jordan, please." His grip was firm, his hand dry and slightly rough. She was shocked at how hot his skin was. Waves of heat seemed to radiate from his palm to hers. She drew her hand back and folded her arms, feeling awkward and aware that everyone in the immediate vicinity was trying too hard not to look at them.

"Christina says you'd like to read Grandmother Sandrine's stories."

"Yes. I'm trying to learn as much as I can about the First Nations people."

"I'll drop them off for you."

"That would be great." She could sense that he was about to turn and walk away.

"Christina tells me you're a healer," she blurted, with all the finesse of a Mack truck. "I thought—that is, I wondered—would you like to talk sometime?" She was stammering. She was an idiot. "Talk about healing," she amended, heat scorching her face.

Oh my God, did he think she was coming on to him? A relationship was the last thing in the world she wanted. Garry was one relationship too many. She honestly did just want to talk about their approaches to treating patients. Didn't she?

He was looking into her eyes and for the first time since she'd known him, he smiled. An enigmatic smile that revealed wonderful strong white teeth. That made him unusual among the adults of Ahousaht, since the village had no dentist.

Here she was with the most physically attractive man she'd seen off the silver screen, and all she could think about was his teeth?

And Garry. Whatever physical response this man

stirred in her reminded her of the husband she'd loved—and grown to hate. She'd heard about rebounds, and she wasn't about to go there.

CHAPTER EIGHT

"WOULD YOU LIKE SOME COFFEE, Jordan?" Silas gestured to two huge urns set up on a side table. "I'm heading over that way, you want to join me?"

"Thanks." She fell into step beside him. "Louie seems to be recovering amazingly well. He's up already, getting around on crutches."

Brilliant, Burke. As if the entire village doesn't already know that.

"I've never seen anyone heal that quickly. He must have an extremely strong immune system. Or else the air here should be bottled and sold as an elixir."

"Nah, you just did a great job sewing him up."

They'd reached the coffee machines, and he filled a mug and handed it to her. "Cream? Sugar?"

"Black, thanks." He took his the same way. "You've been treating him, as well, though." It was just a hunch, but the more she thought about it… "Maybe that's the reason he's breaking records."

"Or maybe Roberta's driving him nuts and he can't wait to get back to work."

His expression didn't change, and it took Jordan a

second to realize he was making a joke. My God, the man had a trace of humor. She pretended to consider his words, and nodded.

"Yes. We really do need more study into the effect of negative incentive on recovery."

"My thought exactly." He motioned to two empty chairs, and they sat across from each other at an empty card table. Jordan sipped at her coffee, propped her chin on one hand and decided to take a chance.

"You do know that you have me totally intimidated, Silas Keefer. You write books, you cause wounds to heal practically overnight, you probably paint master-pieces and design rocket ships in your spare time."

"Only very small ones. Working undercover for the government doesn't leave a lot of time for hobbies." He was smiling again, his deep-set green eyes twinkling. His lashes were enough to make any woman sick with jealousy. "And what do you do when you're not being Doctor Burke, Doctor Burke?"

"You mean for fun?" Helen had asked her that in their last session. It had been so long since Jordan had done anything except work and worry about Garry.

"I read a lot. I used to love swimming. And paint-ing. Years ago, I took some art classes in watercolors— not that I'll ever be an Emily Carr. At the moment, I'm trying to learn to cook on my trusty woodstove. Rose Marie has promised to give me lessons."

"Mom's a good teacher. And she's an excellent cook. She taught me, teaching you'll be a snap after that. Boiling water was a big milestone for me."

"I've gotten as far as lighting the stove, that was a major hurdle. By the way, where do you buy kindling? I'm running out."

For the first time, she actually heard him laugh out loud. "I'll order some for you, they're a specialty item. I take it you've never had a personal relationship with a woodstove before."

"I grew up in the city. Flip a switch, turn on a burner, cancel the above and pick up the phone, which I'm adept at."

He shook his head. "Not skills that're going to stand you in good stead in Ahousaht. It takes a little while, but pretty soon you'll get used to doing things the hard way. And the surroundings make up for it. Done any exploring yet?"

"I haven't had time. Christina told me there's a wonderful trail with routes to three beaches. I thought I'd give that a try soon, maybe on Sunday, if nobody needs me and it's not raining."

Too late, she realized that he might misconstrue that as an invitation.

He nodded. "The Wild Side Trail. It leads through miles of old-growth forest. Some of the women got together a few years ago and bullied the government into funding it. Attracts lots of tourists. You'll probably be called on to treat more than a few sprained ankles and strained ligaments before the summer's over, maybe even a broken leg."

"That strenuous, huh? I'd better get in shape before I tackle it."

He made a quick up-and-down survey of her chinos and blue T-shirt. Apparently this Renaissance man was also a typical male. Startled by his obvious appreciation, she looked away.

"You'll manage fine. But the wooden planks are slippery when wet. Warning signs are posted—people just don't pay attention."

"I'll keep that in mind. I'm not exactly an athlete, myself." She was relieved that he hadn't offered to come with her, yet disappointed when he drained his coffee and got to his feet.

"Good luck with the cooking classes." He shrugged into his battered black leather jacket, gave her a half salute and was gone before she could say goodbye.

Jordan sat for a few minutes while her heartbeat slowed. She wasn't prepared for the way Silas made her feel. The man was a walking aphrodisiac. And here came Christina, with a younger version of the same. She sat in the chair Silas had just vacated. The tall teenager hooked a spare chair, spun it around and straddled it, cowboy-style.

"I want you to meet my baby brother, Patwin Crow. Patwin, this is Doctor Jordan Burke."

"Hi, Patwin, good to meet you." Jordan smiled at the young man.

"Pleasure," Patwin said with a polite nod.

Jordan studied him. There was a lot about the boy's appearance that reminded her of Silas: shining long black hair tied at the nape of his neck, sculpted cheekbones, aquiline nose, strong indented chin. His eyes were black instead of green, but he had the killer lashes. There was something about his sullen expression and the set of his jaw, however, that made Jordan think he wasn't very happy at the moment.

Christina said something in their language, and he responded in a deep, soft, uninflected voice. Shaking his head, he got to his feet.

"Nice to meet you, Doctor."

Before Jordan could answer, he was moving away.

"Your brothers don't have a whole lot of time for small talk."

"Oh, usually you can't shut Patwin up. I just said something that made him good and mad. I saw you talking to Silas. He said he'd get Grandmother's stories to you, did he tell you?"

"He also just warned me about broken legs and muscle strain…."

But Christina wasn't listening. She was staring after Patwin, a frown creasing her forehead. He'd stopped to talk to a group of young people near the door of the hall, and Jordan could hear them laughing at something he'd said.

"Is Patwin still in school?"

Christina shook her head and sighed, turning toward Jordan.

"Don't I wish. He's just turned seventeen, he's got a brain on him, *but.* He got out of the youth detention center in Vancouver last week, so at least for the time being he's clean."

"Drugs?"

"Yup. He's a disaster, our Patwin. He ran away to the city at fourteen and each time Dad brought him back he ran again. I just hope this time he stays here. Mom and Dad worry about him so much. Silas has tried to straighten him out, I've tried. Patwin doesn't listen."

"I'm sorry, Christina." Jordan understood all too well. "If there's ever anything I can do—"

"Thanks, Jordan. I hope he's being straight with me when he says he's gonna stick around. Dad's told him he can work with him taking out fishing charters, but Patwin's not too keen on the idea. I was asking him what the hell else he's gonna do if he doesn't work with Dad." She glanced around. "Mom and Grandmother Alice must be in the kitchen cleaning up. I should go help."

"I'll come, too."

"You'll get bossed around. They're tyrants, that kitchen crew."

"I can take it."

The kitchen was a hive of coordinated activity. Women's voices rose and fell in an intricate singsong punctuated by bursts of laughter. It seemed to Jordan that everyone was talking and no one listening, while at the same time, things were getting accomplished with little wasted effort.

Christina raised her voice over the hubbub. "Okay, you have two more bodies here, what can we do?"

The woman with her hands in dishwater at the sink was more than happy to turn the task over to Christina. Jordan was handed a fresh tea towel by a tiny, older woman.

"Grandmother Bertha, this is our new doctor, Jordan Burke," Christina said.

When the elderly woman moved away, Jordan whispered, "How many grandmothers do you have?"

"A whole parcel," Christina said, laughing. "It's our custom to call all elders grandmother and grandfather, or auntie and uncle—out of respect."

"So Grandmother Alice isn't related to you?"

"Not in the sense you mean. Dad's mother, Grandmother Katchina, died before Sandrine. Kids here are lucky, they have a whole lot of grandmothers to fall back on when one leaves for the spirit world."

"That's more than luck, it's a blessing. I never had even one grandmother." She hadn't had a chance to even get to know her mother.

"It is a blessing. The elders are always willing to help, but a lot of the young folks think the old ways are out of date. Like my smart-ass kid brother."

"Maybe he'll change his mind as he gets older. Silas must have…?"

Christina nodded. "But Silas wasn't as much of a bonehead. That kid is stubborn and pigheaded. He thinks he knows it all."

"All young people nowadays think they know everything," Grandmother Bertha said in her singsong voice from behind them. "They make it hard on themselves. When I was a girl, we got that knocked out of us at the residential school."

Jordan dried a dented pot. "Were you sent away to school?"

"No, in those days we had a school right here in Ahousaht, run by the United Church," Bertha said. "We lived there, though. The first one was built in 1903—my father went there, too. We had to stay at school even when our parents went away hunting and fishing. We used to be so happy when summer came, because then we got to go with them."

Jordan dried two more pots and exchanged a wet tea towel for a dry one. She listened, spellbound as Grandmother told stories about her youth.

"When the whole school came down with measles, there was only one teacher and a couple of older girls who didn't get it. They took good care of us."

"Didn't your own medicine man—or woman—also treat you?" Jordan was thinking of Silas, wondering what the protocol was in those days between native healers and allopathic medicine. "What methods did they use?"

Grandmother Bertha pursed her lips. "Healers weren't allowed in those days," she said shortly, hurrying into a story about salmon fishing at Megin River. Several of the other women joined in, recounting their own childhood experiences in the fishing camps.

As she wiped away at the pots and pans, Jordan wondered why Grandmother Bertha wasn't comfortable discussing healers. Her mind strayed to Silas.

Had Silas forbidden it? Why?

JORDAN WAS STILL WONDERING about that two days later. It was a warm, balmy summer evening. There'd only been two patients in the afternoon clinic, both with minor problems. But one of them mentioned an ovarian tumor that she said a healer had taken away. When Jordan quizzed her about it, the woman changed the subject.

Jordan came home and made herself a cheese sandwich for dinner, eating it outside sitting in a battered lawn chair Michael and Eli had brought her. Restless, she decided to get some exercise, changing into cutoffs and a pair of runners. At the last moment, she grabbed a heavy cotton sweatshirt.

She'd learned that a hot day here could turn surprisingly chilly, thanks to the ocean. She tied the arms of the shirt around her waist.

The wooden pathway that led into the forest was a revelation. Meticulously constructed, just wide enough for easy walking, she wandered along it, marveling at the magnificent old-growth timber. Birds sang their evening songs, a woodpecker hammered at a dead tree, a stream gurgled below her as she crossed a wooden bridge.

Soon she was deep in the forest where rays of sunshine trickled down through giant pine trees, scattering like golden dust. A sense of peace came over her.

Coming to Ahousaht had been a good thing. Before she left Vancouver, Jordan had set up a series of telephone appointments with Helen, the next one early tomorrow morning. She'd be able to tell the psychiatrist that finally—finally—the low-grade anxiety that had plagued her for months was easing. She felt confident that soon it would disappear altogether.

She walked briskly for about twenty-five minutes, laughing a little at the unpredictability of the pathway as it led up and around and down again. It was a game, following the twists and turns.

At one particular spot where there was a sturdy railing, Jordan stopped and leaned against it, looking down at a deep, stagnant pool and wondering if fish could live there. Small, delicate purple and pink blossoms poked up out of the mossy bank and in spite of the clouds of mosquitoes hovering over the water, the idyllic scene looked like a drawing from a book about fairies Jordan had loved when she was a little girl.

It seemed a perfect spot to sit a while and dream in the quiet evening—if the mosquitoes didn't eat her alive.

Impulsively, she bent over and slid one leg and then the next through the gap in the railing, reaching with her toes for solid earth.

Damn, the walkway was higher than she'd thought.

Grunting, she let go and landed badly off balance. Lurching sidewise down the sharp incline, for an instant she was certain she was going to end up in the water. The ground that had looked so solid was actually marshy, and her right leg slid out from under her at a sharp angle. Pain tore through her upper thigh and groin, and she let out a loud yelp.

She fell, hitting the ground hard.

CHAPTER NINE

JORDAN LAY STILL for a long moment, dizzy and half-sick with pain. When she tried to ease herself to her feet, she realized she'd torn muscles and tendons. The pain shot through her thigh, her groin and up into her abdomen. Gasping, she crumbled back down on the damp ground.

"*Dumb,*" she muttered. "*Dumb, dumb, dumb. Idiot. Silas warned you—*"

This wasn't helping. She lay still, trying to think what she should do. What she *could* do. The answer was not very much. It was going to be dark soon.

Her pulse began to hammer. She'd never been out in the woods at night in her life, and the thought terrified her.

She did her best to suppress the fear, trying to figure out whether there was any way she could get back up on the walkway. If she could use the handrail for balance, maybe she could hop along on one foot.

Yes, and you can hop for half an hour on one leg? Hello, Wonder Woman.

At least she could get to higher ground. Here, the

earth felt soggy and damp. Gritting her teeth, she tried to stand again, but there was nothing to use for balance. The pain took her breath away.

Scrap that idea, she thought when she got her breath back. Which left what? There was no chance of getting back up on the walkway, much less making her way back to the village. She was already a mosquito magnet, slapping frantically as they landed on her.

She hadn't told anyone where she was going, either.

It's okay, she assured herself, trying not to panic. People use this path all the time. Someone probably walked along here not long ago on their way to the beach to watch the sunset, and they'll come back before it gets really dark.

But she hadn't passed anyone, and she couldn't hear any voices. She hollered a few times, just in case, but all she heard was the echo of her own voice. And the birds had stopped singing for the night.

Don't panic. Try to pull yourself up again. Put on your shirt so the bugs can't eat you alive.

Drawing in a deep breath, she dragged herself backward, using her arms for leverage. Clawing her way up the slope, she cursed out loud at the agony of it. But at last, puffing hard, she reached a place where the ground was dry and collapsed, moaning.

After a while she struggled her way into her sweatshirt, swearing viciously when every movement hurt.

Her hands and legs were filthy, her cutoffs and pale yellow shirt stained and grubby, her hands scraped raw from trying to break her fall. She was already thirsty, and she half wished she'd crawled down instead of up, although the scum on the pond wasn't inviting. But it was water. Her mouth was dry, her throat parched, and she knew it wasn't only thirst. The truth was, she was scared out of her skull at being out here alone in the dark.

Maybe someone would need medical assistance and come to her apartment to get her… But unless it was a dire emergency, it was unlikely they'd raise the alarm before morning. Why hadn't she thought to bring her cell phone?

Because you wanted an hour's peace, an hour totally to yourself.

She hollered another half-a-dozen times, but the light was fading fast, and she had to face the fact that no one would come along tonight.

Her heart began to hammer, and it was all she could do to stop from crying. She, Doctor Jordan Burke, was about to spend an entire night in the woods alone, injured, with no shelter, food or water. What a story that would make for the gossip mill at St. Joe's.

She tried not to think about cougars and bears and whatever other wild animals hunted in these primitive woods.

She looked at the watch on her wrist. It was already past nine.

What time did it get light? Five? Five-thirty?

Eight solid hours of darkness before dawn came again.

She rolled into a ball, closed her eyes and began to

recite the Latin names for the muscles of the body, but
the image of Silas Keefer kept intruding. Where the hell
was a healer when you needed one?

SILAS MOVED SILENTLY through the forest, making every
step a prayer. He'd fasted all day, aware of the spirit that
had been calling to him. He walked swiftly until at last
he reached the sacred spot deep in the forest.

Stopping inside a ring of alders, Silas made a ceremonial offering of a pinch of tobacco to the spirit of
the place. He arranged his sleeping bag on the ground
and sat, watching the last of the color fade from the sky.
He waited, softly chanting the words Sandrine had
taught him. Dusk became deep darkness, and hours
passed before the ego barrier slowly dissipated and his
mind became peaceful and open to guidance.

The vision came as it always did for him, in pictures
that flickered across his mind like stark images in a
black-and-white film, silent phantoms clothed in sym-
bols.

There was the raven, the messenger, the symbol of
change. And there was his friend, his personal totem,
the bear—except that in this vision, the bear was female, with a cub. And the cub was in danger. He saw
fear and monumental love. And death.

When the vision faded, Silas stretched his aching
legs, his heart heavy with foreboding. Death in a vision
didn't necessarily mean physical death. It could be an
indication of profound change, an ending and a new beginning.

Sleep was slow in coming. When it did, he dreamed of his father, Angus Keefer. But in the dreams Angus was no longer angry at Silas. No longer angry that he had abandoned everything Angus valued.

Instead, Angus was very old and he was dying. He was holding out a gold wedding ring. "Take it, please," he begged Silas. "It's the ring of truth—it's all I have to give you. It will heal the two parts of your spirit."

But Silas shook his head and walked away. He heard his father weeping, and his heart ached with the sound of the old man's pain, but he didn't turn back.

He wanted nothing from his father. Angus gave nothing for nothing.

If you have a choice between being right and being kind—be kind. Sandrine's voice, chiding him.

The next dream was vivid, sensual—and unnerving.

It was dark. He was immersed in water as warm as blood. It covered every inch of him from head to toe. And yet he felt no need to breathe. Inside the circle of his arms was a woman, facing him. He couldn't make out what she looked like, but her skin was as familiar to him as his own. Their legs were entwined, their naked bodies pressed tightly together. His erection was urgent, demanding, and she whispered, inviting him, urging him, to come into her.

His intense desire warred with fear. If he entered her, he would lose something, some part of himself he needed to survive.

In the dream, the feeling he had for her went far beyond desire, far beyond love. It was as if he held the other half of himself, but his fear was overwhelming, and he fought to escape, gulping in lungfuls of the water, suddenly aware that he was drowning—

He bolted upright, heart pounding. It was the deepest hour of the night, the hour before dawn when the stars and moon were gone and light seemed only a distant memory. He heard the echo of the terrible sound he'd made, the lost and desolate cry that warbled back to him in the darkness.

He didn't sleep again. With the first gray light, Silas rose, willing the unsettling dream out of his mind. He meditated instead on the vision, trying to figure out whom or what the bear cub might represent.

The voice came to him, very faint and far away, and at first Silas thought it was an animal in pain. But then he realized it was human—too distant to tell whether it was a man or woman. He heard the urgency. Whoever was calling was in need.

He turned in the direction it came from and quickened his pace.

THE BLACKNESS HAD BEEN thick and deep, when exhaustion finally claimed her. Jordan had fallen into a kind of stupor, far from sleep, but not really awake, either, when she heard the animal snuffling and grunting. An instant later she smelled it.

The odor was pungent, and she could smell it growing stronger from where she huddled, trembling and curled into a tight fetal position. Shaking, she could hear herself making tiny whimpering sounds she couldn't control.

It seemed an eternity passed while she waited for the thing's jaws to clamp on her body or claws to rake through her flesh. Her eyes were wide open, straining to see into the thick darkness. Finally, she saw something. Two small bloodred eyes staring down at her.

Bear.

She'd witnessed death, at times horrible death, and now she faced her own. She'd often wondered whether she'd find the fortitude to be brave when the time came. Now she knew she wasn't brave at all.

The bear's head was moving from side to side, close enough that Jordan could've reached out and touched it. She could smell her own fear as the perspiration trickled down her sides. Surely the animal could smell it, too.

With one last grunt and snuffle, the bear moved. Jordan caught the full odor of its foul breath and gagged. Bile burned her throat and she shut her eyes tight, knowing it was the end. Time stopped, and she never knew afterward how long it had taken for her to understand that the animal was gone.

For the first time all night, Jordan had slept, exhausted and drained and dreamless.

When she woke again, it was beginning to get light, and she propped herself on an elbow and started calling for help.

She was thirsty and stiff and bone weary. Mosquitoes had bitten her face, neck, wrists and legs.

Someone had to rescue her soon. It was just a question of time. She fantasized about a mug of steaming strong coffee, a hot shower, painkillers—a toilet. She had to pee really badly, and she couldn't figure out how to accomplish it. The pain in her groin had gotten much worse overnight. There was no way she could get her shorts down and squat.

She let out a long, drawn-out, hopeless moan and closed her eyes.

"Hey, Jordan, where are you hurt?"

"Silas?" She opened her eyes and saw where he stood on the walkway, looking down at her. Trying to sit up, she flinched and cried out. "God, Silas, I'm so glad to see you. I've pulled a muscle in my groin, I can't get up."

The relief and gratitude she felt was overwhelming.

"Oh, Silas, it was so dark, and there was a bear! I know it was a bear. It was so close to me I could smell its breath—it was awful, I really thought it was going to kill me...."

"A bear?" He stood motionless. "Did it speak to you?"

"*Speak* to me? Silas, I thought it was going to *eat* me. It was this huge thing, making a sort of grunting noise." She shuddered. "And it stank so bad, and it moved its head back and forth, swaying—God, I thought it was going to attack me. But then it walked away." She waited. And waited. Why wasn't he hurrying to help her?

Instead, he just stood there and stared. At last he said in a conversational tone, "How did you manage to get down there, anyhow?"

And that's when Jordan began to get irritated.

CHAPTER TEN

"I SLIPPED OFF THE WALKWAY last evening and fell," she said, doing her best not to snap at him. The man was only trying to understand. And she knew as well as anyone that doctors were impossible when something was wrong with them. "I've been here all night. I can't walk, I can barely move."

He grunted. "Hurts like hell, pulling a groin muscle."

Nothing like stating the obvious. She tried to shift position so she could see him better and grimaced. "*Ouch*. Damn it to hell, *owowoww. Yes,* it hurts, it hurts like fury, Silas. Now could you *please—?*"

He was giving her the strangest look. Why the hell didn't he do something instead of just standing there as if she were a macabre exhibit?

She was getting dangerously short-tempered.

Finally, in one lithe, easy motion he swung down beside her. He took the pack off his back and pulled out a water bottle, crouching down beside her. Handing it to her, he surveyed of the ground, probably looking for bear tracks to make sure she wasn't hallucinating.

She tilted the bottle up and gulped again and again,

not stopping until the water was gone, at which point her thirst was slaked, but her bladder was really going to burst.

"Not much for sharing, huh?" He raised an eyebrow. "Good thing I'm not thirsty."

She ought to be grateful, but instead she just felt angry at him for being so damned casual and good-natured and—and *fit*.

"Guess we better get you back to the village. Exactly how did you do this again?"

She scowled at him. "I *said*, I accidentally slipped down from the walkway and my leg slid out from under me in the mud. Now, please, *please*, get me out of here."

The question was how. Jordan looked up at the walkway. He'd have to hoist her up and over the railing, which would take brute strength on his part and a disgusting amount of pain on hers. The very idea made her cringe. She didn't do agony well at all.

"I could radio for a helicopter."

"Oh, could you do that, please?" Just for an instant, she thought he was serious. His teasing grin told her otherwise.

"If I had a radio, that is."

"I don't exactly find this funny," she snapped.

"Neither do I." But he was still smiling. "I'm gonna have to pack you out, not a cheering thought. I hope for the sake of my back you don't weigh a lot heavier than you look."

She glared at him. "Why not just go and get help?"

Although the thought of spending another hour here by herself brought her to the edge of hysteria.

"Let's give this a try first." Settling his pack on his shoulders, he slid one arm under her thighs and the other around her back. She tensed in anticipation of pain, and the embarrassment of being carried like a child.

He paused. "Try to relax, you're stiff as a board. And hold on to my neck."

She did, and discovered that his neck was as muscular as most men's biceps. She squeaked as he lifted her, and he grunted. It didn't hurt as much as she'd anticipated, and he didn't seem to be straining too much with her weight once he was on his feet. He bounced her a little, adjusting his grip, and that did hurt.

"Ow! Go easy, *please.*"

"Your wish is my command. Low pain threshold, huh?"

"Yeah."

She could feel the hard, sinewy muscles in his shoulders and his arms underneath her legs. Her bare, bitten, muddy legs, which she hadn't shaved for a week.

"You been here all night, you probably have to pee, right? Do you want me to help you—?"

She was a doctor, and bodily functions were pretty much taken for granted, but something about Silas propping her up as she yarded down her shorts made her decide she'd rather die of a burst bladder.

"I think I can make it back to the village, thanks."

"Let's just hope I can, and I don't even have to go."

He let out an exaggerated grunt and made his way down the slope, circling the pond. "Good thing we're going down instead of up."

"What are you doing? Aren't you going to use the walkway?"

"It's too hard to get you up there from here. There's a path through the bush, it'll connect back up where the ground's closer to the walk."

He moved into the woods with assurance, and sure enough, there was a path of sorts. For all his seeming nonchalance, she noticed that Silas was careful not to let branches slap her face or snag her feet. He moved cautiously, without a single misstep.

"I really appreciate this," she said through gritted teeth. It was the anticipation of pain that kept her on edge.

"I hope so." He pretended to groan. "I'll be lucky if I don't end up in traction."

"Oh, for God's sake, aren't you supposed to be an outdoorsman? And don't you think I feel stupid enough without you complaining about your back every second minute?" And why was she snapping at him like this? He was doing his best to help her.

"Doesn't hurt to feel stupid once in a while. It's good medicine for subduing the ego." He laughed, and then grunted again as the ground slanted uphill. "So you were out all night, huh?" He was puffing a little, and she could feel his body giving off heat from the exertion.

"Pretty tough to just slip off that walkway by accident. Unless you were drunk?"

"Of course I wasn't drunk." She knew he was teasing, but her good humor was on sabbatical. "I wanted to take a closer look at those little orchids growing beside that pond."

Her face was very close to his throat, and she breathed in his sweaty, smoky, male odor. She probably stank of nervous perspiration. If they didn't hurry, she would also reek of urine.

"We call those little orchids lady's slippers. They're an endangered species now, along with most everything else."

He sounded pragmatic rather than bitter.

"I wasn't going to pick them. I just wanted to have a closer look."

"We believe we have a responsibility toward all plant life. That they should be picked only for food or healing."

"They look like fancy little shoes, don't they? Fairy shoes."

"You believe in fairies?"

"I used to. I guess most little girls do."

"Not ever having been a little girl, I wouldn't know. Little boys are more prone to frogs and worms and fish." He was puffing. "Okay, I'm going to just set you down here for a minute, take a breather—"

They'd reached a point where the path he'd followed intersected the walkway without much difference in height. He slid her under the handrail and onto the planks. He was gentle about it, but she couldn't help grimacing in pain.

"Sorry. Take deep breaths." He jumped up on the wooden pathway beside her and reached out to steady her. His hands were long-fingered, strong, with short clipped nails. Prominent veins snaked their way up his forearms.

After they had both caught their breath, he lifted her again. "Not much farther now."

She prayed he was right. She was on the verge of a bladder accident. "It's still really early. Were you out for a walk when you found me?"

He didn't answer for a moment. "Something like that."

"You don't have a gun, so you weren't hunting, right?" She hated the thought of killing anything, for food or for sport.

She could feel his chuckle, deep in his chest. "I hate to spoil an illusion, but Indians aren't all hunters. I barely know one end of a gun from the other."

"I thought it wasn't politically correct to say Indian. I read that First Nations was the proper term in Canada."

"We can call *ourselves* anything we want. It's when others label us that we get politically correct about it."

They were on the outskirts of the village. To Jordan's relief, everyone appeared to be still sleeping. She felt as if hours had passed since Silas appeared on the walkway.

Several scruffy dogs came running over, barking and sniffing at Silas's pant legs, but he made a guttural, growling sound in his throat and they stopped barking immediately. The dogs slunk away.

"How did you do that?" Jordan had been besieged by the dogs ever since she arrived. "I've taken to bribing them with scraps. It would be a lot easier to deal with them your way."

"You just have to talk to them in language they understand."

She expected to hear laughter rumbling in his chest at the joke, but when she glanced at his face, he wasn't even smiling.

"And you speak dog?"

"Not fluently, but enough to get by with." Now he did smile, but it was an acknowledgment.

"You are one very strange man. Strong, though, thank God."

He laughed. They were nearing her apartment. "And you are getting to be one very heavy lady."

"Only a few steps more. The door isn't locked." She'd given that up the first few days she was here. It seemed no one locked their doors in Ahousaht. She leaned down and turned the knob, and then they were inside.

"I've never been this glad to get home in my life. Thank you more than I can say, Silas."

"No problem. Want me to take you straight into the bathroom?"

"Oh, yes. *Please.*"

He left her between the tub and the toilet, balancing on one leg, and somehow, she managed. The relief was enormous. She was wondering how to deal with a shower when he tapped on the door.

In a panic, she hauled her shorts up before he opened it.

"I called Christina, she's on her way over." His smile flashed. "I figured you'd prefer having her help you clean up."

"Thanks." She had a quick mental image of him taking off her clothes and blushed.

"Here, let's get you on the couch." He slipped an arm around her, supporting her weight, and again she was conscious of him on a disturbing and visceral level.

When she was settled, he put his hands on his hips and studied her. "I know you're the doc, but don't you think you ought to have ice on that strain?"

"Yes, I should. That's a good idea." She leaned back on the sofa, watching him as he took an ice-cube tray out of the tiny freezer portion of her fridge. He moved like an athlete. He went into the bedroom and came out with one of her tube socks, which he filled with ice. Knotting the top, he handed her the makeshift ice pack and then laughed when she shrieked at the shock of the cold against her tender inner thigh.

"I've always heard that the very worst patients are doctors," he commented.

"Really?" Her eyes were wide and innocent. "I can't see that, can you?"

"No comment." He laughed again. "I'll light the stove, it's chilly in here. And you could probably use some tea."

"There's an electric kettle over there." She pointed again and he found it and filled it with water.

Now that she was safe, Jordan was beginning to assess her injury and the ramifications of the accident. She'd be able to work, but she'd be on crutches for a while. Groin tears took a long time to heal, and there wasn't much to be done for them, apart from icing, painkillers and physio. For that, she'd have to travel to Tofino.

Silas was peeling strips off an alder stick for kindling, and she admired the efficient, easy way he got the stove going. He fed in more wood after a few seconds.

"What sort of treatment would *you* use for a groin injury, Silas?"

"Ice first, same as you, right?"

She nodded, watching him as he rinsed the teapot and dropped several tea bags in. "Then herbal poultices to help the healing. A tea to ease the pain."

"I've got Tylenol in my bag over there. Could you—?" She gestured and he brought it to her. He filled a glass with water and she swallowed two tablets and then downed the rest of the water, aware now of her raging thirst. He refilled the glass.

"I'd like to try your herbal poultices, please." She didn't have any real faith in herbal medicine, but this seemed like a good way to build a bridge between native methods and her own. And at this moment, her groin hurt so much she'd gladly try anything if it meant getting rid of the pain.

And getting to know Silas better? She squelched the thought.

"Sure." He filled the teapot from the boiling kettle. "I'll come by later and bring some of Grandmother's stories for you to read, as well."

When the tea was steeped, he poured her a cup, adding a generous spoonful of sugar. Hot, sweet tea; a tried and true remedy for shock and hypothermia. Not that she had either one, but it tasted wonderful all the same.

"Don't you want some?"

"Not just now." He handed her the cup just as Christina came in the door.

She nodded at her brother and then turned to Jordan. "Hey, Doc. What the heck happened to you?"

"Well, I spent a night roughing it and came closer than I ever want to again to meeting a bear," Jordan explained. While she was telling Christina the rest of the story, Silas gave them both a silent salute and slipped out the door.

"Silas rescued you, eh?"

"He came along just at daybreak. I've never been as glad to see anyone," Jordan said. "He carried me all the way home—he's incredibly strong. I'm not exactly a lightweight."

Christina laughed. "You're nothing but skin and bone!" She stripped off Jordan's shoes and socks. "You look like you could use a bath. I'll go run a tub of hot water, and then I'll cook you some eggs and toast, how does that sound?"

"So good it brings tears to my eyes."

"Let's get this show on the road, then, before you get all wet."

SILAS HURRIED through the village, greeting the few early risers but wanting to be alone. He needed to be in his cabin so he could go over the morning's events and look at them from the context of his vision.

The hydroelectric service from the village didn't extend as far as his cabin. He'd installed solar panels instead, so there was hot water even though the woodstove was out. He stripped off his clothes and stood under the shower faucet, ritually cleansing his hair and body with a bar of handmade soap one of the aunties had given him for a healing ceremony.

Sandrine had taught him that it was important to cleanse before and after a vision quest, before breaking fast. Healers traditionally cleansed in the ocean, and he'd planned to swim, but that was before he'd found Jordan.

Jordan. He closed his eyes and remembered the sweet warm weight of her in his arms. Her hair had smelled faintly of lemon. The scent of her skin, the proximity of their bodies was arousing. No question, the persistent ache in *his* groin was lust.

But lust was a thing of the body. The spirit had shown him something else, something confusing. The bear in his vision was familiar, but a real bear had visited Jordan at almost the same exact time. He'd seen the tracks, and just as she had said, it had been very close to her.

So was hers, like his, also the powerful bear totem— the spirit of the West Wind, who leads the way into the dream world? And whom or what did the cub represent?

What was the connection between him and Jordan? Whatever it was, he didn't want it. Relationships took too much and gave back too little.

Alone was uncomfortable at times, but he'd chosen to be solitary and he wasn't about to change. He was too damned—old? Selfish? Lazy?

Scared, Grandmother cackled, but this time he ignored her.

He climbed out of the shower and toweled off. Pulling on old sweatpants and a threadbare shirt, he broke his fast with herbal tea and thick slices of Rose Marie's wheat bread layered with tomato and goat cheese.

He'd had enough practice holding his center, he could continue in spite of this unnerving attraction to the doctor. And then he smiled at how easily he lied to himself. He'd tried his best to avoid her, but the spirit had a sense of humor, literally tossing this woman into his path. And now he wanted to see her again. He needed to know what went on behind that beautiful, sad smile.

He'd make Jordan an herbal poultice and take her Sandrine's stories, but first things first. He climbed the ladder to the sleeping loft and crawled into his nest of blankets and pillows. Right now he needed to sleep. He murmured a prayer of thanksgiving and slid into oblivion.

"YES, THANKS. I'm sleeping really well, Helen." Jordan settled herself against the pillows and adjusted the angle of the cell phone at her ear. "I thought last night this stupid groin thing might keep me awake, but I lay down at eight and didn't open my eyes till half an hour ago." Jordan glanced at the clock. It was seven-thirty-eight. She'd slept almost twelve hours, which was some kind of miracle. Although the painkillers she'd swallowed probably had something to do with it. She'd called Helen the moment she woke to apologize for missing their appointment.

"What about the anxiety attacks?" Helen asked, and Jordan thought about it for a moment.

"You know, spending a night out in the woods by myself and being sniffed over by a bear puts anxiety into perspective. Right now my concerns over Garry and the divorce seem pretty puny."

"I can see how that would work," Helen said, and Jordan could tell she was smiling. "Are you making any friends? Anyone you feel comfortable talking to, confiding in?"

Jordan hesitated. Strangely enough, the first person who came to mind was Silas, which was ridiculous. "The nursing supervisor, Christina, is great. And so is her mother, Rose Marie. They came over yesterday, after I finally made it home. They're so thoughtful— they brought food and made sure I was okay. They're very—" Jordan was stuck for a word for a moment "— very nurturing women. It makes me a little uncomfortable. I'm not used to having anyone do things for me."

"Enjoy it. You deserve some TLC. You've been on the flip side way too long."

The call ended, and Jordan heaved herself out of bed and onto the crutches Christina had found for her.

It took what seemed forever to get through a shower and struggle into clean sweats.

She was drinking a cup of tea and eating cereal when Silas knocked once and then opened the door.

CHAPTER ELEVEN

HE SMILED AT HER. The man had a killer smile when he chose to use it.

"Morning, Hop-along." He came over to the table and set a fat yellow folder down. "Grandmother's stories. How's the groin this morning?"

"Sore as blazes, but I'm keeping the pain at bay with liberal doses of Tylenol." She wished she'd injured another part of her anatomy, like her ankle or her shoulder. Talking about her groin was somewhat awkward, especially with Silas.

Get a grip, Burke. The man's only interest in you is as a healer.

"Want some tea? There's lots in the pot."

He shucked off his black leather jacket, and she admired his broad shoulders as he filled a mug. He sat across from her at the table. "Large doses of Tylenol can be hard on your kidneys, you know."

"So I've heard." That sounded sarcastic. The guy was just trying to be nice. And even though she was a doctor, it was good to be reminded of medicinal side effects. "I'm a coward when it comes to my own pain, so

I'll swallow whatever it takes. I guess your herbal preparations don't have any side effects, right?"

"They can. They're powerful medicines—they can react badly in the wrong combinations, just like any other drug."

"How did you learn to use them?"

"Grandmother Sandrine taught me, and I also studied herbalism from books."

"Christina told me it was Sandrine who taught you to be a healer."

She just hadn't said why Silas had agreed to learn, and Jordan was curious.

"Yeah. My grandmother was a fantastic teacher."

"Did you always want to be a healer?"

He laughed and shook his head. "No, it wasn't high on my list of careers. My chosen field was research."

"What area?"

"Medical."

He was anything but a blabbermouth. Jordan wasn't about to let him off the hook. "From medical research to hands-on healing…?"

He looked at her for a long time before he answered. He seemed to study every angle of her face, and she forced herself not to glance away. Finally he said, "I was working on a Ph.D. thesis. I came here to observe my grandmother."

"And you stayed."

"There's something about Ahousaht that's addictive."

His words made her smile. She waited to see if he'd reveal anything else.

He swallowed a mouthful of tea. "Got anything sweet to eat?"

So much for revelation. "There's half an apple pie in the fridge, if you like. Roberta brought it over yesterday."

He got a plate and cut himself a piece. "Want some?"

She started to refuse but then nodded. "Not that much, though."

He cut her a piece.

"I don't think I've ever eaten apple pie for breakfast before."

They ate in silence.

He still hadn't answered her question, and Jordan really wanted to know. "So why give up on research to study healing?"

He chewed and swallowed. "Because of my mother."

"Rose Marie?" Jordan had expected him to say his grandmother, Sandrine. "How so?"

"When I was still a baby and we were living with Angus in Vancouver, she got sick with a rare blood disorder called TTP. Fatally sick. She was covered in bruises, her white-cell count was down to something like thirty-five, and she wasn't expected to live. My father made sure she had the finest specialists, but she got worse. Finally Sandrine came and abducted her, bringing Rose Marie to Ahousaht in a wheelchair."

Jordan whistled between her teeth. "Thrombotic thrombocytopenic purpura, that's a bad one. I'm familiar with the condition, but it's pretty rare. Until the past few years when plasma exchange became a possibility, the survival rate was very low, less than twenty percent. And there were almost always serious side effects."

"Well, as you can see, Rose Marie survived without any. Sandrine treated her and she got better. Six months later Mom married Peter. Five years later she had Christina, and then much later, Patwin. She's stayed healthy."

"Sandrine cured her."

He shook his head. "Patient and healer form a partnership from which each of them benefits, so it's not accurate to simply say Sandrine healed Mom."

"And you're certain Rose Marie wasn't just misdiagnosed?"

"I dug up the medical records. There was no doubt about the diagnosis."

"But Sandrine must have done something specific. What medicines did she use?" Jordan was fascinated. She'd heard of spontaneous remission and so-called miracle cures, but she'd never known anyone who'd personally experienced such a thing—if that's what this was. "Herbs?"

"Among other things." Silas shrugged. "Our treatment is always a combination of methods. Sandrine used herbs, sure. She also used massage, counseling, prayer, song. Vision quests, sweat lodges. Lots of different treatments, and she called on other healers to help."

"Did you know how sick your mom was?"

"I was too young. I didn't know about it until I came back here as an adult. Even then, I didn't believe it until I saw the medical reports."

"So you stayed, and your grandmother taught you?"

"Yes."

"Are you happy living here?" The moment the words were out of her mouth, she wished she'd never said them. What right did she have to ask about happiness? It was something that had eluded her most of her life. "Sorry," she mumbled. "Way too personal."

"I read somewhere that happiness is a choice we make every morning. Sometimes I remember to choose, sometimes I forget." He swallowed what was left of his tea. "What about you? Are you happy, Jordan?"

"I'd be a lot closer to it if my damned leg didn't hurt so much."

"Try this poultice." He drew a packet out of his pack, something pungent sewn into a cheesecloth. "Steep this in just enough hot water to get it moist, let it cool just enough to tolerate, and then bind it to where it hurts."

"Thank you." She eyed the compress suspiciously and then wrinkled her nose when she sniffed it. "It smells unusual. What's in it?"

"Willow leaves, which are anti-inflammatory. Comfrey root. Arnica."

"I'll give it a try, thank you."

"If you need any help fastening it to your groin, just ask."

"Thanks, but Christina is handy that way."

"How come I never get to do any of the fun stuff?"

She gave him a look. "You know, Silas, the first time I talked to you I had you pegged as a cranky old eccentric."

He raised an eyebrow. "The old part really smarts."

"You answered the phone when I called about the job, and you were so abrupt I thought you had a reason for not wanting me to come."

"I'd forgotten about that. I was just in a rush to make it to a welcoming ceremony for a new baby."

"So you had no objections to me being hired?"

He hesitated. "Not exactly. I just figured you wouldn't stay. It's tough on the locals. They start to rely on a service and bingo, it's gone."

"Do you still feel that way about me?"

"Yes."

The simple admission surprised her. He was certainly honest, but it made her defensive.

"And why is that?"

"You're from the big city. It's isolating and lonely to be in a place where the customs aren't what you're used to." He flashed that devilish grin. "The natives are friendly, but they're still natives."

"I can learn and adapt. I've had more practice than most at blending into other people's lives." She thought of the foster homes she'd lived in before she finally settled into the last one. And even there, she'd been constantly on trial.

"Why did you really come here, Jordan?"

She wasn't ready to bare her soul. "I needed to get away from the city. I *wanted* to get away from the city," she corrected herself. Dammit to hell, she wasn't about to share the story of her failed marriage with him. "I don't know how it'll be long-term, but so far I like it here," she said. "Well, I didn't like communing with bears that much, but then I'm not going to make a habit of falling off walkways. Apart from that one little slip, I'm settling in. I think I'll be very—" she almost said happy "—content living here. The women in your family have made me really welcome, and I appreciate that."

His expression told her he wasn't buying it. "You're a highly qualified E.R. doctor. Apart from the odd mishap with a power saw, this job isn't going to challenge you. You'll get bored, miss the adrenaline rush of the E.R."

"I thought of that, and yes, I probably will miss it at times."

He nodded. "A year is a long time."

"I guess it can be." Whatever intimacy they'd shared was gone. She glanced at the clock. "And it's ticking past. Right now I've got to hobble over to the clinic. I have patients to see this morning." She put a hand on the compress. "Thank you for this, and for the stories. I can't wait to read them."

He was on his feet, putting on his jacket. "When that groin heals enough so you don't need a crutch, maybe you'd like to sightsee with a qualified guide instead of blundering around on your own?"

The man always caught her off guard. First he clearly let her know he didn't approve of her being here, and in the next breath he—was he asking her out on a date? If so, his technique was rusty.

"What did you have in mind?"

"You've heard of the hot springs?"

She had. Christina had told her about the natural mineral springs on the island, and that tourists flew over from Tofino or took a boat from the village to visit them. "I've heard they're breathtaking."

"They're healing. The mineral water is excellent for muscle stress. Except we can't go until you can walk. We'll go by boat, and then we'll have to hike in for about twenty minutes. Whenever you're up to it."

So it wasn't a date. He was a healer simply thinking of ways to help her recover. Why did she feel disappointed?

"Sounds good, Silas. I'll look forward to it."

"We're better off not going on the weekend, too many tourists. Can you get away midweek for an afternoon?"

"Barring emergencies, I don't see why not."

"As soon as you can hike up a hill, we'll go."

He drew a plastic baggie out of his pocket. "Oops, almost forgot this." He tossed it on the table. It contained dark green-and-brown herbs. "Boil the herbs in a kettle full of water about twenty minutes and then drink a half cup at a time. It'll ease the pain."

"Thanks again."

"I'll come by this evening and see how you're doing. If you're not busy?"

"I'll check my day timer—I do have this frantic social life. But somehow I believe tonight is free."

"Yes, I heard the symphony got canceled. Bummer." He smiled and gave her a small salute and then he was gone, leaving Jordan wondering what the heck to make of him.

Was he coming on to her? The sexual teasing had made her think so, but then he retreated behind the role of healer.

Silas was complex. And she was out of her league, because really, what did she know about men? The only male she'd ever had a satisfactory long-term relationship with was her brother, and she didn't see Toby that often. She'd thought she knew Garry, and look how wrong she'd been there. There had to be some weakness, some fatal flaw in her that had drawn Garry to her. She'd said that once to Helen.

"We all have wounds in our psyche that need to be healed," the psychiatrist had said. "I believe we attract the individual who has the most potential to help us heal those wounds. Sometimes it's through negative lessons, as it's been for you with Garry. Sometimes it can be positive, but the potential for healing is always there, on both sides, in any relationship."

It sounded rational, but Jordan hadn't really understood it. And she didn't have time to dwell on it. Grabbing her crutches, she hobbled off to work.

CHAPTER TWELVE

THAT AFTERNOON, Silas was busy at the computer when he heard a tap at his door. He opened it and smiled at the girl standing there.

"Hi, Mary." Mary John was about seventeen. Her long, thick hair and wide dark eyes set off a pretty heart-shaped face.

Silas knew her the way he knew most of the villagers. He also knew she'd been dating his brother Patwin, and that she'd quit school before her final year and now helped run the guest house, which catered to overnight visitors to Ahousaht. Usually vivacious and good-natured, today she looked pale and tired.

"Silas, will you help me?" As was customary, she made the request formally and held out an offering that would count as a consultation fee. It was a small hand-made willow basket, beautifully woven and filled with tiny, jewel-like wild strawberries, the seaside strawberries prized by the Nuu-chah-nulth.

Silas ceremoniously accepted the offering and thanked her. Accepting the initial gift sealed a contract between them. It meant that Silas would ask the spirit for help not in curing Mary, but in healing her in a much broader sense.

"Come in. Would you like some tea?" Silas gestured to the couch, as he stirred up the fire and heated water. When the tea was ready, he handed her a cup and took a seat across from her in a straight-backed chair. He waited silently for her to speak.

A couple of tears slipped down her cheeks. She hung her head. Finally, Silas said gently, "Tell me what's making you unhappy, Mary."

"Patwin dumped me yesterday," she whispered. "He said we were getting too serious." She mopped at her cheeks with her sleeve like a child, and Silas handed her tissues.

"How do you want me to help?" Mention of his brother made Silas uneasy. Patwin had a well-earned reputation as a stud among the girls. He was the proverbial bad boy, and he could have his pick of companions. But this wasn't about Patwin. It was about Mary.

"I'm so tired all the time," she sighed. Voice trembling, she stammered, "I'm s-sick every m-morning."

"How long have you felt this way?" Silas was *sensing* her as they talked, getting a feeling for the psychological and spiritual components to her illness as well as the physical ones. Even though he had a good idea, he said, "Do you know what's wrong?"

"Yeah, I think so." Mary gulped and started to cry. "I think I'm pregnant. With—with—Patwin's baby. And I'm scared the drugs will hurt the baby."

"What drugs?"

"The ones Patwin took. Before. I heard they can make the baby deformed."

Silas kept his expression neutral, but his heart sank. Patwin was seventeen, unreliable as hell, with a history of running away and drug use. Definitely not good father material. Mary was hardly more than a child herself. And from what he knew of Mary's family, they wouldn't be much help. At least he knew the Crows would do everything they could.

"Do you know for sure you're pregnant?"

Mary shrugged. "I'm pretty sure, yeah. My period's late and I'm sick in the morning."

"Have you gone to the doctor for tests?"

Mary shook her head. The tears were now running freely down her cheeks.

"Have you said anything to your mother? Or to Patwin?"

Mary shook her head again. "I was scared to tell Patwin, and now he doesn't want to see me anymore."

"If you are pregnant, do you want to keep this baby, Mary?"

She didn't hesitate. "Yeah, I do. Patwin's gonna be really mad at me, though. He's gonna say it was all my fault."

"It takes two people to start a baby, Mary. Patwin's just as responsible as you are." Another thought struck him. "Are you scared of Patwin, Mary? Are you afraid he'll hurt you?"

Silas hated having to ask that question about his

brother, but youth detention centers weren't gentle places.

Mary shook her head. "He wouldn't hit me or anything. But he might go away again when he finds out, back to Vancouver. There's lots of drugs and bad people there, he'd get into trouble again. I—I really love Patwin, Silas."

"You need to think of yourself. And the baby."

"I guess." Mary's pretty face was a mask of misery. "You remember my brother, Adam?"

Silas nodded. Adam had died in a boating accident two years before. He was fourteen. Mary's father had started drinking heavily and finally left the family— Silas didn't think Mary's mother, Josephine, was coping well at all.

"I want to have this baby so my mom will have something to cheer her up. She still cries every day about Adam."

Mary's words were heart-wrenching. Silas wanted to tell her that having a baby for someone else's benefit wasn't smart. Instead, he searched for more positive advice.

"It should have been me that died. Dad wouldn't have left if it had been me."

Silas felt such sympathy for the girl. "Why do you say that?"

"It's what my mother thinks."

"Has she said that?"

Mary shook her head. "I just know it."

Silas struggled to keep his personal feelings at bay.

They wouldn't help Mary, and that was what he wanted to do.

"Do you know your totem spirit, Mary?" Silas had caught a glimpse of it in her eyes.

He gave her time, and after a while she said hesitantly, "Maybe a mule deer? There was one that used to come right up to me. I'd feed it lettuce from my hand."

"A deer symbolizes flexibility and inner beauty," Silas explained. "Part of your spirit left for the afterlife when Adam died because of your belief that your mother didn't value you. The deer moves between the ordinary and spiritual realities. She represents the power you have lost. We must ask her to help you reclaim it."

Silas got the deer hide someone had tanned for him and made into a throw. He asked Mary to lie on it, to honor and invoke her spirit helper. He lit tapers and smudged with sage and cedar, purifying his patient and himself to create an atmosphere that invited healing energies.

He prayed and sang a deer honoring song. Then he sang two healing songs, and visualized the lost parts of her soul returning to her body. When the ceremony was over, he taught Mary the songs and told her to keep the image of her deer helper in her mind and to express gratitude to it every day. He asked her to keep track of her dreams, to write them down whenever she awakened in the night. He gave her a small container of juice made from herbs he'd gathered, and told her to mix it with a little water and drink some every day until it was gone. "It will help the sickness, and strengthen your body so the baby has a safe place to grow."

Mary thanked him. "Should I come back for another healing?"

"Ask your mother if she would come with you."

Mary hesitated and then nodded. "I'll ask. But I don't think she'll do it, though."

"She must decide that for herself. And if you want to come on your own, that's okay."

"Thank you, Silas." She put twenty dollars on the table, but Silas shook his head and tucked it back into her hand. Normally he accepted whatever fee the patient offered, but this was a special case, a family matter.

"Before you come back, I want you to go to Doctor Burke. If she confirms your pregnancy, you must talk to Patwin. This is his responsibility as much as yours. He has to know. Then, if you want to, come back and see me."

When she was gone, Silas meditated, asking for the best outcome for everyone. By the time he opened his eyes again, it was dusk outside. The healing had taken all afternoon. He was always surprised at the passage of time when he was involved in a ceremony; hours passed like minutes.

He smudged the house, clearing it of negative energy. Hungry, he decided to walk to the medical center to see if Jordan needed something to eat. It was tourist season, and Mabel's would be open for dinner. Next to his mother, Mabel Smith was the best cook he knew.

He washed and put on a fresh checked shirt and clean jeans, trying to put the disturbing meeting with Mary out of his mind.

It was hard not to be furious with Patwin. The boy seemed to create heartbreak at every turn, and now there would be an innocent child as a result of his carelessness. Patwin wasn't able to care for himself, never mind take on the responsibility of a child. Financially and emotionally, it would be the Crow family who shouldered the burden.

Over the past several years, Silas had run the gamut of frustration and anger and impatience with his young half brother. He'd done his best to help Patwin in every way he could devise. But as always, the only person who could change Patwin was Patwin. And so far, there was no sign that the boy wanted to change.

In the meantime, this powerful energy drew Silas toward Jordan Burke. And he knew that resisting energy was fruitless.

SITTING ACROSS FROM JORDAN at Mabel's half an hour later, he watched her study the hand-lettered menu and wondered what those full lips would taste like. He could smell her perfume, light and woodsy.

"What's bannock?"

"Indian bread. Flour, water and baking powder. It's how it's cooked that makes a difference in how it tastes. It's best made on a sandy beach. You build a fire and put the dough under the sand. When it's cooked, you take it out, brush off the sand and break it into pieces. It's good."

"Sand, huh?" She wrinkled her nose. "What are you having?"

"Baked salmon." It wasn't much of a decision. The only real choices were between the salmon and shepherd's pie. There were burgers, of course, but Mabel kept things simple with dinner menus.

"It comes with greens and bannock," he explained. "And dessert, whatever Mabel felt like making today."

"Okay, I'll have the same."

Silas gave the order to Mabel's daughter, Grace, and their meals arrived almost immediately.

Mabel made her own dark basting sauce, and Silas had to smile as Jordan took a tiny, suspicious forkful of the salmon. She looked across at him with a surprised look on her face. "Wow, this is absolutely great."

He figured that the simple café with its mismatched tables and chairs wasn't exactly the sort of place Jordan was used to going on a date.

"Mabel used to cook at logging camps," he explained. "You have to be exceptional to get hired, loggers are really fussy about their food."

"It's such a relief to know there's somewhere I can come for a decent dinner. After working all day, lighting that stove and making something seems overwhelming. Don't tell Rose Marie I said that, either. She's been busting her butt teaching me the basics. And thanks for the kindling and the wood, by the way. Eli and Michael brought two wagonloads over this afternoon. I gave them each three dollars—I hope that was enough?"

"You weren't supposed to pay them anything."

"Nonsense, the poor little kids were sweating by the time they got it all unloaded."

"Those poor little kids have you pegged as a soft touch. If you must pay them, fifty cents a wagonload is more than enough. And what's this about them selling you bread and berries?"

"Michael's mother, Wanda, sent a loaf over and it was so good I asked him if she'd supply me with one every couple days. Eli's been bringing me those lovely little strawberries, he deserves a good tip for going to all the work of picking them."

"I buy them from him, too. The going rate is a quarter per pint."

"Really?"

He could see from her guilty expression she'd been handing over considerably more.

"Your nephew has a promising future as an entrepreneur, Silas."

"More likely a gossip columnist."

Jordan laughed. He loved to see it. She had a sadness about her that disappeared when she laughed. "All the news that's fit to print, and some that isn't."

"True. Getting back to school will be good for those little gossipmongers."

"I'll miss them."

"Me, too."

"By the way, I drank some of that tea you gave me. I can't believe how well it worked. The pain hasn't been nearly as bad. It's got pharmacy painkillers beat all to heck."

"Good." He concentrated on the food for a few moments, noticing that she hadn't tasted the bannock. He broke off a chunk, smeared it with butter, and held it out.

She leaned forward and took it from his hand. The fleeting contact of her fingers on his sent heat coursing through him.

"Yum." She swallowed, and gave him a slow smile. "You can't even taste the sand, can you?"

"I think Mabel uses an oven."

"It's delicious."

He nodded agreement. "Were you busy today?"

"It was quiet in the morning. But this afternoon we were immunizing babies, so it was a little hectic. Fun, though. The babies are so cute, even though they hate me for sticking them. How did you spend your day?"

"Writing. One article is overdue, there are several others I'd like to finish."

"I've always wondered what it would be like to be a writer."

"Tedious. You sit at a keyboard until blood comes out your fingers."

After a dessert of bread pudding with thimbleberries, they walked home—slowly, because of Jordan's crutches. "I saw a patient today who told me you'd been treating her for chronic fatigue syndrome," Jordan said casually.

"That would be Zweena Watts."

"Yes. Chronic fatigue syndrome is a difficult condition to treat, and she's so young to have developed it. Have you treated anyone else for it?"

Silas hesitated. He suspected this was going to lead to controversy.

"Probably, but I don't label illness the same way you do," he said after a moment. "Our healing teaches that it's best not to give a condition a name, because by naming it we are inviting its presence, making it more real than it already is. So we deal with symptoms, with energy patterns and avoid saying yes, you have this or that."

"But how do you know what treatment to prescribe if you don't diagnose the disease?" They were almost at the clinic. The evening was soft and warm, and the sky was just beginning to darken. The sun had set while they were having dinner.

"We rely more on interpretation of the patient's story. How and when did the illness develop? What does it symbolize in the patient's life? Is offering a therapy in harmony with everything else? Timing is all-important, since a medicine offered at the wrong time may make the symptoms worse instead of better."

They were at Jordan's door. She motioned to two lawn chairs on the small patch of grass. "Would you like to sit and talk? Or will we get eaten alive by mosquitoes?"

"You need a smudge fire to keep them away." He steadied one of the chairs as she set her crutches aside and lowered herself into it.

"I have a candle thing someone gave me that's supposed to keep the bugs away—citronella. It's just inside, on the shelf where the books are."

He went inside and found it. Outside again, he set it on a stump of wood and lit it with a match.

"Thanks, Silas. I hope it works. I'm going nuts scratching the bites I got the other night."

"Rub them with the inside of a banana peel, it'll take the sting out. An old man told me that mosquito bites represent the little irritations we carry around with us."

"I must have a ton of them." She scratched in silence. "The way you describe your healing technique is very holistic, Silas. I met a naturopathic doctor in Vancouver, and your approach sounds similar to hers."

Relieved at her open attitude, he sat beside her, stretching his legs out in front of him, and noticing the long, lean lines of her body. She had a natural grace, a way of moving, even with the crutch, that he found intensely attractive.

"Indigenous cultures around the world have developed healing techniques that work, and in many cases they're almost identical."

"So can you tell me exactly how you treated Zweena, or is it confidential?"

"Sure, I can tell you." Some areas of the treatment were confidential, but most of it was pretty general. This was where he'd find out how open-minded she really was about alternative therapy.

"Getting the person to talk is always critical. I listened to her words, but at the same time I paid attention to her energy. I could feel that there were psychological and spiritual components to what was bothering her. I could see a desperate child inside the woman, and I knew the child had to be addressed before we could go further. I helped her identify her spirit totem, and then we used its power to ask for help. It helped me see her soul, trapped inside the child and not allowed to grow to meet its potential. Using visualization, I performed a ceremony to help her free that part of herself, to help her spirit return to her body."

Jordan had been listening intently. She waited, and when he didn't say anything else, she shook her head, puzzled. "I don't understand. Didn't you give her any herbs or—or whatever it is you use?"

"I gave her juice derived from herbs." He wasn't surprised at her emphasis on tangible medication, and her dismissive attitude toward the other, subtler healing techniques. There had been a time when his reaction would have matched hers.

"Herbal medicine is being recognized more and more in scientific studies. I read in a medical journal that yew bark is effective for a wide range of ailments."

Silas nodded. "My people have always used it. Over seventy percent of all western drugs have come from isolating the active ingredients in plants and animals that the world's indigenous people have used for centuries. Fortunately, yew bark's still widely available. Other plants and herbs are disappearing—destruction of the forest and land."

"I had a chance to read some of Sandrine's stories, about the summer camps and fishing for salmon, and the rigorous training the young women went through. To me, it sounded as if things went steeply downhill after the missionaries came."

"You've got it." Silas laughed. "Sandrine used to say that in the beginning we had the land and the white man had the Bible. Now all we've got is the Bible and the white man has the land."

Jordan said softly, "The way you transcribed Sandrine's words made her world come alive for me, Silas. I'm sure things weren't easy in those days, but they sound idyllic compared to now."

"It was a different life." There was sadness in his tone. "A different time. We're trying to reclaim the best things about our culture, but it's tough."

"It must make you very angry."

He shook his head. "Sad, yes. Mad, no. Sandrine taught me that balance is integral to healing. Anger knocks you out of balance. Illness is an imbalance. You can't give what you don't have."

"Physician, heal thyself?"

"Exactly."

"Easier said than done."

He looked up, into her eyes, wondering what had caused her such deep unhappiness.

Jordan reached for her crutches and struggled to her feet. "It's getting late. I should go in. Thank you for my dinner—I loved it. And I've really enjoyed our conversation." Turning, she tripped over her crutch and let out a shriek. Silas grabbed her before she fell, but instead of letting her go drew her close, tight against him. She felt fragile in his arms, and familiar. He'd learned the shape and weight of her.

"Is it all right if I kiss you?"

She caught her breath. Instead of relaxing, he felt her stiffen in his arms.

He was prepared to release her when she nodded, just the faintest inclination of her chin. She closed her eyes, and put her hands on his shoulders.

CHAPTER THIRTEEN

SILAS TOOK HIS TIME. He touched her mouth with his in the gentlest of kisses. When she relaxed just a little, he teased at her lips, nibbling and caressing until she began to respond.

He made an appreciative sound deep in his throat and went on kissing her until the final bit of tension left her body and she allowed him to gently draw her in, so that the contours of her body matched his. Supporting her with one arm around her waist, he put a hand at the back of her head, sliding his fingers into her thick, silky hair.

She slid her arms up and around his neck, and now the kiss spiraled out of control. The force of his desire caught Silas by surprise and his whole body shuddered.

SWEET HEAVEN, but the man could kiss. Jordan was grateful for his strong arm supporting her, otherwise she knew she'd slither to the ground—and it wouldn't be a wound in her groin this time. Pain in that region gave way to a desperate ache that had nothing to do with injury and everything to do with need.

Tightening her grip around his neck, she gave herself up to the sweetness of his lips and the intoxicating sensation of his strong body pressing against her. His erection made it clear how very much he, too, was enjoying this.

But she wasn't about to take the next step. She wasn't free. She was still married to Garry, and theirs had been a strong emotional bond. She no longer loved her husband, but she couldn't forget that she *had* loved him.

She wasn't ready for Silas. For her, making love required commitment and familiarity. She didn't really know him well enough, and still it took every ounce of her willpower to pull away.

"My crutches," she said in a shaky voice. She'd dropped them. "I really need to go in now."

"Sure." Reluctantly he let her go, steadying her as he found the crutches and handed them to her. He used his knuckles to tilt her chin up so she was looking into his eyes. "There's strong energy between us, Jordan Burke."

Her heart attested to that, as well as her libido. "There sure is."

"What do you want to do about that?"

"What do you mean, do about it?"

He looked amused. "I think it's called having sex. I'm asking you if you want to make love with me."

Jordan didn't know how to answer. Talk about straightforward, this guy was an arrow. She looked up at him and shook her head. "Nothing subtle about you, you go straight for the jugular."

He grinned. "Think lower down. And I guess I don't know any way except direct. I'm out of practice at the mating dance."

"Is that what this is? A mating dance?"

He shrugged and looked at her with those clear green eyes. "It's whatever you want it to be."

She had to look away.

"Are you going to be okay now? No more throwing yourself at me?"

"I'll try to restrain myself."

"Night then, Falling Down Woman." He gave her his characteristic salute and walked off into the dusk.

Jordan snorted. "Falling Down Woman? What's that about?" she muttered, going inside. "I'll give him Falling Down Woman."

Silas Keefer was one of the strangest men she'd ever met. He was also one of the most vital. He made her laugh, he made her want to tear her clothes off and jump his bones. He made her feel alive again, as if she'd recovered from a long illness. When she was with him, she hardly thought about Garry, or her past life at St. Joe's. When she was with Silas, there was only the present, the moment. *Now.*

It had been so long since she'd felt like a desirable woman, so long since a man had kissed and caressed and admired her.

The physical relationship had ended long before she finally admitted Garry had a drug problem. She'd made so many excuses—both of them were busy, she worked shifts, Garry hadn't recovered from the accident. Like so much else, she hadn't been able to face that an important part of her marriage was dying.

Which was why she had to consider carefully whether it would be a mistake to make love with Silas. Physically, she was more than ready. She wanted Silas as her lover. Emotionally, she wasn't as certain.

THE TEA WORKED LIKE MAGIC on her muscles, and in a little over a week she was barely limping. On a warm Wednesday afternoon, she and Silas set out for the hot springs.

The boat he'd borrowed was a smaller version of the one that had brought her to Ahousaht.

"It belongs to my cousin, Earl Lucas," he told her as he helped her aboard. "It's his fishing boat."

"I probably could have guessed by the smell," Jordan said, wrinkling her nose as she hastily stowed her backpack in the tiny cabin. She hurried back up on deck to stand beside Silas. He looked exotic in dark wraparound sunglasses, his hair tied back at the nape of his neck. His white T-shirt clung to his torso, and his ragged cutoffs emphasized the powerful muscles in his thighs. He had great legs, long and well shaped.

It was a windy, blue sky day, and the water was choppy. Silas turned the tiller into the waves, and Jordan laughed as the water thumped under the boat's bow.

"Like that, do you?" He managed the tiller with one hand and looped the other arm around her shoulders as the little boat bounced along. "It can blow pretty big along this coast, you don't want to be out here when it's storming."

"It's not going to storm today, though, is it?" Jordan squinted at the expanse of sky and ocean and relished the feeling of his bare arm against her skin.

"No. I checked the weather. Perfect sailing."

Jordan felt lighthearted. It had taken some arranging to break free for a few hours. She'd put a sign up several days ago announcing that she'd be away for the afternoon, and then had to do some fast talking to get out of saying exactly where she was going. Her patients had no qualms about quizzing her.

Christina was the only one who knew, and she'd promised to keep the information to herself. But Michael and Eli had been down at the dock when she and Silas set sail. By now the news would be spreading like the flu.

Jordan had her cell phone in her pocket, in case some dire emergency arose at the village, but she was really hoping for a quiet afternoon.

"I finished Sandrine's stories last night. You're going to publish them, aren't you?"

"The University Press is interested, but I haven't decided. Grandmother's yarns have always belonged to her people. It's hard to let them go."

"Christina said that Michael's mother is trying to talk the grandmothers into taping them."

"Wanda's creative. I think it's a good idea."

"So do I. They're powerful and moving, anyone could relate to them," Jordan declared. "I cried when

Sandrine described how she hid when they came from the residential school to take the children away. I can't believe the government sanctioned something so barbaric."

That story had touched Jordan deeply. She remembered clearly the day the authorities had come and taken her and Toby into custody.

Silas turned the wheel of the boat to steer it across the waves. "Sandrine never did go to the residential school. Everyone said she'd died, and the authorities believed them because so many died from the measles. And then Sandrine was taught by the elders, in the old ways. Her grandfather was a powerful healer, and he understood that Sandrine would be a healer, too."

"And she taught you."

"I didn't have the benefit of learning from an early age, though, the way Grandmother did."

"Why not, Silas?"

"I was born here, but my father was white—an anthropologist who came to study the poor natives." He pressed his lips together.

"And he fell in love with Rose Marie?"

"He married her, took her with him back to Vancouver, probably because I was on the way."

"And then your mother got sick."

"My father kept me with him when Rose Marie was brought home. He wanted me to have a good white man's education." Silas pronounced each word very clearly. "Rose Marie fought for custody, but he had good lawyers and plenty of money."

"Didn't she have visiting rights?" But Jordan knew all too well that having them and using them were two very different matters. Mike had had visiting rights.

"The agreement was that I'd spend summers in Ahousaht and the school year with him in Vancouver."

"Sounds reasonable." Imagine having two parents who actually wanted you with them, Jordan thought with a pang of jealousy.

"I hated it. I didn't fit in here. I was a half-breed. In Vancouver, Angus sent me to boarding school as soon as I was toilet-trained. I was a half-breed there, too." There was no self-pity in his tone. He sounded almost amused.

"So…what are you now?"

"A half-breed." He turned and smiled at her. "But I'm a damned well-adjusted one." He squinted at the shoreline. "Look, can you see the deer over there, just beside the cedar tree? She has a fawn with her—he's tough to see because he blends in so well with the foliage." He was steering the boat in a parallel line to the wild, thickly timbered coastline.

Jordan squinted through her sunglasses. At first, she couldn't see the animal and then suddenly it was obvious. She could just make out the smaller shape, half-hidden behind the doe.

"Oh, she's so graceful. And her baby's small, a real Bambi."

"She's welcoming you, Jordan."

"That's a nice thought."

"See that wharf up ahead? That's where we're heading."

In another few moments, he'd pulled the boat alongside the floating dock and tied it securely. Shouldering his pack, he jumped out of the boat and held out a hand to Jordan. She rescued her belongings from below and then took his hand. Her groin was pretty much healed, but it was still tender, and she winced a little as she clambered up beside him.

The route to the hot springs was well marked, a wooden pathway that led through the woods and up, built like the one she'd followed on her ill-fated hike the week before. It wound through evergreens and firs, eventually opening on to a small clearing on a point of land with a view of the ocean and islands.

"People have had campfires here," Jordan noted.

"It's a common place to come and camp," Silas explained. He pointed to a spot where warm water was bubbling up out of the ground. "That's where the springs originate." The water trickled to an embankment where worn stones formed a natural stairway down the gently sloping cliff face.

Silas took her hand and showed her to the first of four pools in a deep, narrow cleft in the gray stone. Steaming water poured from a height of six or seven feet into a shallow pool.

"Oh, Silas, isn't this beautiful?" Jordan stood and stared. The rock face was open to the ocean below, and she could see the waves rolling in breaking on the shore.

"We're lucky there's no one else around today," he said, taking off his hiking boots and socks. He unfastened his belt and shinnied out of his cutoffs. "Weekends there's always hordes of people." He lifted the hem of his T-shirt over his head. His bathing suit was a loose boxer style, and it shouldn't have been sexy at all. But it was.

Clothed, Silas was impressive, but nearly naked he took her breath away. Ridiculously wide shoulders tapered to a narrow waist, flat hips and strong, long legs. He had very little body hair, and his smooth, glowing skin was a light, gleaming copper. His long white-streaked black hair cascaded in a mass down over his neck and shoulders.

Jordan realized she was staring. But the man was magnificent. Looking away, she concentrated on getting her own clothes off. She'd worn her blue one-piece bathing suit under her shirt and shorts, and now stripped down to it. It was a simple tank, cut high on her thighs and low on her breasts. She could feel Silas's eyes on her as she stepped out of her shorts, and she felt a little self-conscious as she waded into the pool, gasping when the blood-warm waterfall beat down on her head and shoulders.

"Hoo-weeee!" She closed her eyes and turned slowly, letting the water envelop her. Her eyes popped open again when Silas caught her in his arms. He slid an arm under her thighs and lifted her, spinning them both in a circle under the waterfall. She grasped his neck and squealed with delight. It was intoxicating, being held like this in his arms with the water churning around them.

After a short time—too short—he set her down and

they played like children, splashing each other, hollering, enjoying the warmth of the sun and the water cas-
cading down.

"Let's move down to the next pool," Silas suggested.

"Sure." Jordan shoved her wet feet into rubber san-
dals and followed him. The second pool was slightly
cooler than the first, and she lowered herself gingerly
into the water, sitting on the bottom. The water covered
her shoulders, and Silas sat close beside her.

Side by side with their legs stretched out, they rested
against the rock face. Silas took her hand, folding her
fingers in his, and they listened to the water, the splash
of the surf below them, the birds in the nearby trees.

It took time for Jordan to identify the feeling that
stole over her.

"I'm happy," she said, surprised. "I actually feel
carefree, isn't that amazing?"

She expected him to laugh, but he didn't. "If this is
all it takes to remove the sadness from your eyes, we'll
set up camp here."

"Don't I wish."

"When was the last time you were this happy, Jordan?"

She really had to think about that. "I think it was
when I was a little girl. I have this memory of being
with my mother in a field. I was picking dandelions and
she was braiding them into a crown for me."

"How old were you?"

"She died when I was four, so it must have been before that."

"And after she died? What happened to you then?"

Jordan hesitated. She didn't have a lot of practice at talking about her childhood, but Silas had confided in her.

"My father was a logger, he worked out of town a lot." She took a breath, wondering how much to reveal. "He—he was also a drunk."

Silas waited.

"He couldn't take care of us, so he put my brother and me into foster care. We were supposed to be placed together, but of course that didn't last long." She could hear the bitterness in her voice, feel it in her heart. "Toby was labeled difficult, and finally they split us up."

"That's hard. It's happened to a lot of my people, too."

Jordan nodded. "I only saw Mike a half-dozen times after he abandoned us. He didn't make it to any of my graduations, high school, university, med school. Eventually I heard that he'd left Vancouver."

"Do you know where your brother is?"

"Yes. Toby had it rougher than me. I was finally placed with an older couple who couldn't have children. They wanted to adopt me, but Mike would never sign the papers. They paid for my education."

"And your brother?" he said gently. "Toby?"

"He wasn't so lucky." Jordan felt angry whenever she thought about her brother's childhood. "Toby got bounced from one foster home to the next. He quit school at sixteen, ended up in a juvenile detention center charged with break-and-enter. But his parole officer took a personal interest in him and helped him find a job as a carpenter's helper at a shipyard. That fueled Toby's passion in boat building." She was aware of the pride in her voice. Silas smiled at her.

"He has a business in Seattle designing and building small pleasure boats."

"And your father?"

Jordan shrugged and turned her head. "I hear he's back living in Vancouver." Her voice was hard. "I haven't seen him in years, and I don't intend to ever see him again." She shot him a challenging look. "I suppose that seems hard-hearted to you."

"No, not at all. It gives us something in common. Except it's my father who doesn't want anything to do with me."

There wasn't any discernible emotion in his tone.

"How come?"

"He's an anthropologist, an academic. He had high hopes for me, envisioned us working together. When I chose to come and live in Ahousaht and study healing with my grandmother, Angus disowned me. He wanted me to forget that I was half First Nations."

"But he and your mother were married. He must have cared about her, accepted her heritage?"

"I'm not sure about that. I think he thought that if he just got her to Vancouver, she could pass as white. I tried that for a while, but I was made to see how false it was."

Jordan knew from experience that it took a powerful emotional event to instigate change. For her, it had been the night Garry was brought to the E.R. She shivered, remembering.

"It began with the conflict between the government and my people over land claims and fishing rights," Silas said. "My father was considered an expert because he'd spent time here. To him and the politicians, it was a matter of who owned the rights to the land. The First Nations understand that we are only caretakers of the land and water. No one can own them."

"So you got involved?"

He smiled. "Oh, yes. I shot my mouth off a lot. My father got royally pissed."

He was thoughtful, looking past her to the ocean. "I came back here out of rebellion against Angus, not from any deep-seated curiosity about healing methods. But when I got here, my grandmother outsmarted me. She'd decided when I was very little that I was born to be a healer, and nothing was going to change her mind."

"So she taught you."

"In spite of myself. Sandrine reclaimed my soul."

Jordan shook her head. "I don't understand."

"I was at war with myself, rejecting both sides of my heritage. She helped me see that I needed to go where my heart led. To please my father, I had denied the part of me that belonged here. She helped me past the guilt."

"Sounds as if Sandrine was a gifted psychologist." *You have to reclaim the part you gave away to Garry.* Helen had told her that. "Someone once told me it's not good to give your power away."

"That sounds like something Sandrine would say."

He stood and pulled her to her feet. "C'mon, let's go down to the next pool."

Jordan shivered a little when they were once again settled side by side in the cooler water of the third pool. She could see the sun, sparkling on the surf, but the cliff walls were too steep for it to shine down this far. Silas was still holding her hand, his fingers laced between hers.

"So I gave my power to my father," he said softly. "Who did you give yours to, Jordan?"

"My husband…my ex-husband," she corrected herself. That wasn't technically true yet, but she hoped it would be soon. She wasn't comfortable, talking about Garry with Silas. The whole disaster was too recent, too humiliating, too painful. Before he could ask anything else, she added, "Have you ever been married, Silas?"

"No." He tipped his head back and squinted up at the blue sky. White frothy clouds scudded along its surface. "It's not something I'd be good at."

"You're a wise man to know that about yourself." Too bad she hadn't had as much insight. This time it was Jordan who got to her feet and tugged at his hand. "Come on, three down, one to go."

"Okay, but just remember, this was your idea."

They had just settled in the lowest pool when a gigantic wave came rolling in, forcing its way into the narrow opening at the bottom of the gorge and foaming up until it spilled icy ocean water over both of them.

Silas laughed as Jordan screamed, sputtering and gasping.

"You sadist," she accused him when she got her breath. "You didn't even warn me."

"I wanted to surprise you," he said with a grin, as another wave dumped more icy water over them. This time, he let out a wild yell and half dragged her back up the steps.

"Don't surprise me again, I may not live through it," she cautioned. Shivering, they scrambled back up to the top pool, immersing themselves in the water, which now felt hot in comparison.

Panting, Jordan relaxed beside him, and gave herself up to the warmth and the peacefulness of their surroundings. They sat silently, up to their shoulders in water, for what seemed a long time.

After a while he held her fingers up and studied them. "You're puckered. Maybe we should get out now? I brought lunch. Are you hungry?"

"Starving." Reluctantly, Jordan stood up. "I hate to move, but you're right, I'm totally waterlogged. Shriveling up as we speak."

He studied her deliberately. "Just a little wrinkled around the edges. Nothing a kiss won't fix."

Touching only her hand, he gently touched her lips with his. He tasted of salt and the sea. Both wild and familiar.

CHAPTER FOURTEEN

JORDAN SHUDDERED. The blood-warm water and hot summer sun enhanced a raw sensuality between them.

"Come," he said. "I know this private dining room."

"Is this a shirt-and-shoes sort of place?"

"Shoes, yes, the ground's rough. And you might want to pull on a T-shirt over your bathing suit, your skin's so fair it's going to burn."

In the clearing at the top of the springs he led the way into the woods. There was no path, and he was careful to hold back the foliage so it didn't scratch her bare arms and legs. The evergreens were taller here, and he led her along some invisible track, deeper and deeper into the forest, turning this way and that until Jordan was thoroughly lost.

"Here we go." He pushed through what appeared to be an impenetrable mass of vines and branches, and suddenly they were in a small clearing. Silas slipped off his pack and set it on the ground, crouching to open it.

Jordan admired his strong back before looking around. The earth was cushioned with pine needles, and it was absolutely quiet. There was a small pile of stones underneath the largest tree, the top stone flat and darkened by fire.

"What's that?" She pointed at it.

"It's an altar. We call that tree a cedar, but actually it's an alpine fir. The needles are burned to help clear energies that inhibit visions." He was setting out food—smoked salmon, bannock, blueberries—and plastic bottles of water. "This is a sacred place."

Nervously, Jordan glanced around again. "Should you have brought me here? If it's sacred?"

He laughed. "Somehow I don't see you bringing busloads of tourists."

"Gee." She widened her eyes and pretended to think about it. "Well, the thought did cross my mind. But I was born without a sense of direction, so I might have a hard time finding this spot again."

"There you go. It's safe." He spread out a small blanket and motioned to the food. "Come and sit. Eat."

She did. She was ravenous. "Mm. This fish is so good."

"Indian candy. It's our special, secret recipe for smoking."

"Did you smoke it?"

"No, I traded for it. I pretty much run on the barter system. I help somebody out and they pay me with what they have. Harold gave me the fish in return for helping him get better after a car accident."

"I envy you. No government forms to fill out." She chewed and swallowed bannock, and they ate in silence.

What was it about simple food and fresh air that

was so intoxicating? What was it about Silas that was so intriguing? Besides his killer body. And his strange, clear eyes.

Sometimes, like right now, she had the feeling he could see straight inside her head. She hoped not. Her thoughts would definitely betray her.

When they'd both had enough to eat, Silas crumbled the remaining bannock and scattered it for the birds. Jordan leaned back on the blanket, watching him, entranced by the focused attention he paid to whatever he was doing. What would it be like to have that intense concentration aimed her way?

She shut her eyes, letting the sun warm her skin, blurring images inside her closed eyelids.

She felt him kneel beside her. His shadow blotted out the sun as he put a hand on either side of her shoulders, and leaned down to kiss her.

"Jordan Burke. Beautiful Falling Down Woman."

She opened her eyes and squinted up at him. His hair, still damp from the water, hung down on either side of his face, tickling her skin. His cheekbones were sharp and high, his nose straight, his jaw angular and firm. And those clear green eyes were like laser beams, staring into hers.

"Tell me that you want me."

Her heartbeat accelerated. "I want you."

"Making love here in this sacred spot must be a committed act by both of us," he said. "Otherwise it transmits negativity to the earth."

"The earth is safe with me."

With that, Silas pulled her T-shirt up and over her head. In that concentrated, unhurried and intense fashion she found so seductive, he kissed her mouth, her nose, her eyes, her chin.

He ran his tongue along her jawline, tasted the hollow at the base of her throat, growling in low approval when she shivered, using her hands to learn the shape of his back. She moved her splayed fingers down the smooth slide of his backbone, long bones, long muscles, relishing the sun-warmed skin that led to firm buttocks, narrow hips. There she traced his ribs, found his flat nipples, teased them erect with her fingernails.

She felt the tremor that ran through him. She heard him catch his breath, intensifying the desire that had been simmering since—when? Five minutes after she'd first met him?

"This suit just slides down?" He was peeling the straps from her arms, using his mouth on every inch of newly exposed flesh as if there'd be a penalty for missing a single scrap.

"Lycra's amazing that way." She felt the tremor in her throat as she spoke. When the suit cleared her breasts, he paused and his mouth covered her right nipple. She couldn't have articulated two sane words if her life depended on it. Her body bucked in sharp reaction, and a moan of pleasure escaped.

God, he was slow. It drove her nuts. He was thorough, rolling the suit with maddening patience down and down, marking territory with his lips and tongue and teeth as he went. He made her entire body sing—

fingertips, toes, but most of all, between her legs. She'd almost forgotten how powerful it was, this drive to completion.

His tongue circled her belly button, lapping at her stomach for what seemed forever, and she couldn't stand it another instant. Taking handfuls of his hair, she pulled him up. She wriggled out of the bathing suit and then slid fully beneath him and wrapped legs and arms around him. Hunger. Anticipation.

"I need you inside me," she said, holding his eyes with hers. "I need you now, Silas. Please?"

He wasn't the least bit slow about getting rid of his own swimming shorts. He balanced above her, blocking out the sun. And when he lowered himself to her she felt the shocking heat of him, the way his bare skin seemed to burn hers wherever it touched.

"Jordan." The way he said her name was a song that touched her heart. And then in one long, smooth glide, he was exactly where she needed him to be.

Lust and intention came together in an explosion that ricocheted from her core, bringing life to a part of her that had been sleeping. And when she arched and shuddered and cried out, he lost gentle and civilized. He became savage, pinioning her arms over her head and driving himself into her in a frenzy that caught her in its wake, pulling her with him up into orgasm that left her stripped of all but sensation.

THEY LAY SIDE BY SIDE, spoon-style, half on the blanket and half on pine needles. Sunlight filtered down and birds chirped in a syncopated chorus. In the warmth and stillness, Silas's hand was curled around her breast, the long-fingered hand so familiar to her now.

"So where do we go from here?" His voice was low and rumbling, close to her ear.

"Back to the village, I'd say." She deliberately misunderstood him, because she absolutely didn't know. "It must be getting late." She squirmed out of his embrace, rummaged in her pack. Yanking on her panties and cutoffs, she said in a phony chipper voice, "At least my cell phone hasn't rung."

He was watching her, not moving. The man had a gift for stillness. It made her nervous. The sheer raw force of their joining made her nervous.

"So that's how you want it, huh? Mindless sex."

She pulled her blue sports bra on and then let her shoulders slump in defeat.

"No," she said with a sigh. "That's not what I want." But maybe it was. All of a sudden she was so confused she couldn't figure anything out.

"L-look," she stammered, trying to work it out as she went along, "I haven't been with anyone for a long time. No dates, no one-night stands, nothing. Before I was married, I wasn't exactly a party girl. And even when I *was* married, sex wasn't—well, very satisfactory. I have to say, this—" she waved a hand at him, at the blanket "—this totally blew me away."

Helen wouldn't have let her get away with that. She would've forced her to examine her emotions.

Yes, but how does that make you feel?

Not the sex, but Silas himself. How did Silas make her feel?

Confused came to mind. Overwhelmed. "Like you said, the energy is powerful between us. And I guess it sort of…the truth is, it scares me, Silas."

"Sex with me scares you?"

"No." She gave an impatient wave of her hand. "Not just sex. This whole complicated thing, the whole man-woman thing. I'm not good at it."

"Maybe you just need some practice."

His matter-of-fact assessment made her laugh. "It's a lot more complicated than that."

"It doesn't have to be. The only thing we have to bring to each other is honesty. How long were you married?"

"Two years." He'd told her what she'd wanted to know about his life. She owed him some insight into hers in return. "Garry was a lawyer, I met him when a patient decided to sue the E.R. staff for negligence. His firm was hired to represent the employees."

"And you fell in love?"

She hesitated. "I thought so at the time. Although it was probably as much Garry's family as him. His mother and father welcomed me with open arms, treated me like a daughter." She shuddered, remembering how they'd accused her of not trying hard enough when they found out she'd left their son.

"Garry was—weak." Even now, even though she knew he'd understand, she couldn't bring herself to tell Silas about the drugs. She was too ashamed—she still couldn't believe that she'd written Garry prescriptions for drugs for as long as she had. It showed such poor professional judgment on her part. She knew Silas would think so, too—and above all she didn't want him to think her a fool.

"He had a car accident. He…he got better physically, but emotionally he never really recovered."

"And so you went from being wife to being care-giver?"

That damned, unnerving *focus* of his made her uneasy.

She nodded. "Pretty much." It was so much more than that, but for the moment, it was as much as she felt comfortable talking about.

"How long have you been divorced?"

"Not long enough." The truth would require an entire new set of explanations.

"Do you still have feelings for him?" His voice was so casual. She glanced over, gauging his expression. It was neutral.

She struggled to put her complex feelings into words. "I feel sorry for him. I pity him, I guess." And she was angry with him. Angry? Hell. She was bloody furious. She resented the things he'd done, the scenes he'd created, the private and professional embarrassment he'd caused her. It had taken some time for her to unearth that rage, but with Helen's help, it had surfaced, frightening Jordan with its magnitude.

Helen said it was healthy. Jordan, on the other hand, hated feeling so out of control. Anger frightened her, it always had. Again, she didn't feel she could tell Silas about it.

"And now you're afraid to trust someone again?"

God, the man was worse than Helen, picking away at her psyche.

"I wouldn't say that." But she wasn't sure. "I'm just a lot more cautious than I used to be."

"That's probably a good thing."

He got up and started pulling on his clothes. Pants first, no underwear. Then he thrust his arms into a gray T-shirt, pulled it down over his head, scooped his dark hair out from under it. She watched, fascinated. She'd seen more than her share of naked male bodies, but not one of them had been this perfectly formed.

"Do you trust me, Jordan?"

"You ask really tough questions, you know that?"

"Being honest is something that was hard for me to learn. I try to practice it so I never forget how it goes."

"Trust is a complex thing," she said slowly. "It has a lot of layers. For the most part, yes, I do trust you."

"But there are gray areas?"

She hesitated and then nodded. "It's because I don't know you that well yet, I suppose. It takes time to really know someone."

"Ahousaht's a small place, and I'm not going anywhere. You say you'll be around for a year. I'm available if you want to know me better. While you're here."

He reached out a hand and pulled her up. "Let's get back to the boat before the tide changes. And then I'll show you where I live."

"I'd like that." She understood. He was offering what he had to offer, what he was willing to offer, a place to be with him away from the village, a friendship that included sex. A time limit so she knew exactly what the rules were.

It suited her, she decided. It suited her very well.

SILAS'S CABIN, like the man himself, was fascinating. A little mysterious, multifaceted.

It was built from logs in a small clearing amid tall evergreens. The main floor consisted of one large room, with a tidy corner kitchen that contained the inevitable wood-burning cookstove and a small refrigerator. There was a bathroom with a sink, a shower and the strangest looking toilet she'd ever seen. There was no flushing mechanism, and amazingly, no odor, either.

"It's a composting toilet," Silas explained when she asked. "I don't like to be dependent on anything. It doesn't need water, and it's environmentally friendly. It does need electricity, but I use solar collectors on the roof to provide and store enough energy for the toilet, my hot water—and to recharge the battery for my laptop." He pointed to a corner opposite the kitchen where an old door on two sawhorses formed a large desk. It was cluttered with books, loose papers, a computer and printer. "I have a generator for backup, but I don't use it much. Only when it rains for days on end in the winter."

Upstairs was a sleeping loft with a homemade king-size bed of rough logs, set squarely in the middle of the room right under a skylight. The bed was covered with what Jordan considered a museum-quality handmade comforter. It was a patchwork scene, and the workmanship was exquisite, depicting a stylized hawk and bear against the background of the village.

"This is truly beautiful," Jordan said, running a hand over it. "It's a work of art. Who made it?"

"Grandmother designed it. A group of her friends helped her put it together." He sat on the comforter and wrapped his arms around her waist. "You could stay here tonight, sleep under the blanket, watch the stars through the skylight."

"I'm tempted." She put her hands on his hair, loving the rough texture, the thickness, the shape of his skull. "But I can't," she finally decided. "Everyone will know we're sleeping together if I stay, and it's too soon for that. For me, it's too soon."

He gave her a look and then he laughed. "I hate to disillusion you, but I'd bet everyone is jumping to conclusions this very minute. We went off in the boat and we were gone all afternoon. Eli and Michael waved us off. Harold saw us at the dock when we got back. And Sara Smith and her sister passed us on our way here. Sorry, Doc, but I'd say we're *so* busted." He rested his head on her breasts. "So what d'ya think? Will you stay?"

She reached down and unhooked his hands from around her waist. "You must have quite a reputation, if everyone assumes it only takes you one afternoon to get me in the sack." She felt suddenly irritable.

He took her words literally.

"I'm no stud. The last woman I was involved with moved away seven months ago. And I haven't wanted to form an intimate relationship with anyone here, so I'm celibate. Or I was, until today."

She bristled at the implication. "Why's that? Why's it okay to have a sexual relationship with me, but not with someone who lives here?"

"Because there's no one here I'm attracted to this way."

"Oh." He was attracted to her. "Don't you mind everyone gossiping about your personal life?"

"I value my privacy, that's why I live away from the village. But I've accepted that people are curious, and that very little goes on that everyone doesn't know about. It's not malicious gossip, at least not usually."

"I hated the gossip that circulated at St. Joe's," she admitted. "In most cases, it was destructive." She had reason to hate it. Garry's actions had been the fuel for plenty of talk, and so had her breakdown. How many times had conversations stopped abruptly when she came in, and whispers followed her on the way out? It had made her final days at St. Joe's painful.

"There's two choices around here, Jordan. Either you put a lot of time and energy into trying not to let people know what's going on, or you live your life freely. Gossip never stays fresh long, there's always something new to talk about."

She knew he was right. But she needed time to get used to this whole idea of having a lover.

"If I don't stay tonight, do I get a rain check?"

"Absolutely. Like I said before, I'm not going anywhere."

"I should be getting back, then. It's going to be dark soon."

"I'll walk with you."

"Thanks, I'd appreciate that." She hesitated, and then confessed, "I have dreams about that bear from the other night."

Silas narrowed his eyes. "What kind of dreams?"

"Weird ones. I'm alone in the clinic, and the bear walks in. I scream, but it never seems to be threatening me. It wants me to go with it, of all things."

"Why don't you do that? Next time, see where the bear leads you."

"I'm too scared. I wake up sweating, with my heart hammering."

"Next time, try to follow him. Maybe he wants to show you something."

"And maybe he wants to eat me."

"I don't think so. He could have done that already."

She was still thinking about that when, nearly back to the village, Jordan's cell phone rang. She dug it out of her pocket, amused. She was so relaxed that for a moment she hadn't known what the strange noise was. But her smile faded when she heard the tension in Christina's voice.

"Jordan, come to the medical center right away. Hurry. My brother Patwin just tried to hang himself."

CHAPTER FIFTEEN

JORDAN STOPPED ABRUPTLY, her heart rate accelerated. "Is he breathing?"

"He's having a rough time. My dad found him and the ambulance brought him here. If Silas is with you, can you tell him to come, too?"

"We'll be right there." She turned to Silas.

"It's Patwin," Jordan said. "He's alive, but he attempted suicide by hanging."

Silas swore and grabbed for her hand, helping her move as fast as her injury allowed, the rest of the way. Silas had much longer legs, and Jordan was winded when they burst through the door. Her brain was going over the various potential injuries caused by neck trauma.

The most serious were permanent spinal-cord damage and brain injury, but there was a horrible list of other things such as laceration of the jugular and perforation of the larynx, trachea or esophagus.

She could hear Patwin straining to breathe the moment she came through the door. The ambulance drivers had used an oxygen mask and put him in a C-spine, but he was fighting the restraints. Peter Crow was trying to calm him down.

Rose Marie hovered close, her hands over her mouth, tears streaming down her cheeks. The two volunteer medics were also standing by.

"Okay, let's have a look here."

Straining hard against the restraints, Patwin was making a horrible guttural choking sound. His throat was black, bruised in a circle around his neck.

"He's panicking because he's in pain and he can't breathe." Knowing he had a history of drug abuse, she still had no choice except to use morphine. Jordan gave the injection, and then turned to Peter.

"Tell me exactly what happened and where you found him."

"He was in my workshop, in the basement," Peter said. The big man's hands were trembling, as was his deep voice. "I was working on my boat and I forgot some tools. I came back for them, thank God." He wiped his forehead with the tail of his shirt. He was sweating profusely.

"He strung a rope over a beam, stood on a toolbox and kicked it away just as I came in. The rope had some give to it, so his feet were barely off the floor. I cut him down. I was gonna give him mouth-to-mouth, but he was breathing. He was awake."

Jordan put a comforting hand on Peter's arm. "Do you know if he lost consciousness at all?"

Peter shook his head. "I don't think so. Like I said, I came in just as he kicked the box away."

"Good." She turned back to Patwin. "By struggling, any spinal damage is going to increase," she warned him in a stern tone. "Dying is one thing, but going through life in a wheelchair is quite another. So try your best to lie still, okay?" The morphine was already having an effect, and as Patwin gradually relaxed, she did a quick but thorough assessment.

From the way he'd been moving his body, it was a pretty fair bet that at least there hadn't been any damage to his spine. Patwin's eyes were swollen and bloody looking because the strangulation had caused tiny blood vessels to burst.

"He's going to have to be medevaced to Tofino for X-rays," she told the family, and Christina hurried away to make the emergency phone call.

"My guess is he's escaped without major or permanent damage to the spinal cord, but we have to make absolutely certain. He's going to need to be on oxygen support for a couple days, and he'll need painkillers."

As Jordan went on with the examination, she thought that the young man must have a busy guardian angel. Somehow, against the odds, Patwin seemed to have escaped paralysis, suffocation and major neck hemorrhage.

As far as Jordan could determine without X-rays, there seemed to be only bruising to the spinal cord. There were no discernible breaks, and no other damage that she could find. She left the ambulance men to watch over her patient, and took Silas and the Crows into an examination room and closed the door.

"Physically, it seems as if he's come off very lucky," Jordan told Patwin's family. "The X-rays need to confirm it, but I don't think there's any serious damage to his spine. Too early to tell if he's permanently harmed his larynx or suffered brain damage. I've had to give him morphine, despite his history of drug use. He may have to go through detox all over again."

"Thank God he's alive." Peter put an arm around his wife, and the other around Christina. "Thank God he's okay."

Jordan met Silas's look. They both knew that Patwin was a long way from okay.

"The question now is what to do next," she went on. "I need the family input here. I can request that he's taken from Tofino to Nanaimo and committed for psychiatric assessment. Attempted suicide is a clear call for help."

"He hates being confined," Rose Marie said. Her voice was steady, but tears were still rolling down her cheeks. Peter dug a red handkerchief out of his pocket and tenderly mopped her face. "If we send him away, he'll find a way to escape, and then who knows what he'll do?"

"Do any of you have any idea what might have precipitated this?"

"It's my fault." Peter Crow's face twisted with anguish. "I gave him hell this morning—I told him he had to get a job or move out of the house."

Peter's broad shoulders slumped. "I found out Patwin's been hanging around with that no-good Johnny

Swann again. He's trouble, that Swann kid, everybody figures it was him and his friends who broke into Mabel's last month. Stole the float from the cash drawer and went on a rampage in her kitchen." He turned to his wife. "Patwin got in trouble before, hanging out with Swann. I'm sorry, Rosie. I didn't want Patwin in trouble again."

"I know." Rose Marie patted her husband's arm. "I got after him, too. He's been drinking a lot and not coming home. I bawled him out this morning, I was really mad at him."

"You can't blame yourselves." Christina's face was flushed, her voice angry. "It's time Patwin smartened up. It's not like he hasn't had support from everybody, the little shit." Her face fell. "I can't believe he'd do such a stupid thing."

Silas put his arm around Christina's shoulders and turned to Jordan.

"I'd like to go with Patwin to Tofino. Let me talk to him alone, before you make any arrangements to send him to Nanaimo. If he's willing, maybe I could help him this time."

Jordan said, "You've tried before?"

Silas nodded. "It didn't work, because Patwin didn't really want help. Maybe this time it'll be different. Will you agree to let me go with him?"

Ordinarily, Jordan would have accompanied her patient.

"Absolutely. I'll phone the Tofino hospital and speak to the doctor who'll be treating him. But I need Patwin to give me a no-harm commitment, an assurance either verbally or in writing that for twenty-four hours he promises not to harm himself."

Jordan made the call to the Tofino hospital, and was assured by the attending physician, Doctor Magrath, that they'd be expecting Patwin and that as soon as the tests were completed, Jordan would be notified.

Back in the examination room, Patwin was quiet, his eyes closed. His breathing was still erratic and obviously painful, but the morphine had calmed him.

Jordan took his hand in hers. When he looked up at her, she explained that Silas would accompany him to Tofino, and added that she could request he be taken to Nanaimo for psychiatric assessment.

Patwin was obviously disturbed by that. He tried to say something but grimaced in pain. His eyes were bloodred now, and dark bruises were beginning to pocket beneath them.

Jordan quickly explained about Silas and the no-harm commitment, and Patwin wriggled his fingers as if writing in the air. Christina brought a pen and a pad; Jordan scribbled a promise and released the restraints enough so that Patwin could scrawl his name.

Following the ambulance attendants, they made their way to the school's playing field where the helicopter was already waiting.

A crowd had gathered, silent as Rose Marie kissed Patwin. Peter bent and pressed his lips to his son's forehead, and when her turn came Christina bent over him.

Jordan heard her say, "You bloody fool. Do you

think I changed your diapers and babysat just so you could go and do something like this? I'd like to kill you myself, you damned idiot." Her tears dripped down on her brother's face. "I love you, we all love you, don't you know that?"

Patwin was still strapped on the C-board. He couldn't hide the tears that rolled from the corners of his eyes and dripped into his hair. His hands were strapped down, but his fingers were free. He lifted one to Christina in a silent salute as the stretcher was carefully loaded on the helicopter.

"I'll take care of him," Silas promised his mother, giving her a hard hug. He did the same to Christina, then he and his stepfather clasped hands. Turning to Jordan, he put both hands on her shoulders. "I'll call you later tonight and let you know what's happening." And in a quick featherlight caress that took her by surprise, he bent and touched her lips with his. Then he climbed into the helicopter beside the pilot.

Jordan was stunned. In front of his family and probably half the village, Silas had made a statement about their relationship. If they hadn't guessed already, they certainly knew now. She should have been furious with him, but instead his gesture touched her heart.

They all watched the helicopter lift steeply up and turn toward Tofino, where an ambulance would be waiting.

Rose Marie came over and put her arms around Jordan, giving her a hug. "Thank you for helping my son." She threaded her fingers through Jordan's. "Come and have something to eat with us now, okay? Food always helps at a time like this."

"Yeah, Jordan," Christina seconded. "Come home with us for a while."

Jordan, who'd been looking forward to going to her apartment, shutting the door and taking quiet time to assess the various events of the day, opened her mouth to refuse. It was late, and now that the crisis was over, she felt drained.

But the expression on Rose Marie's face stopped her. The older woman needed reassurance, and Jordan guessed that maybe she needed to talk about her son.

She smiled at them and said, "Thanks, I'd like that."

Jordan had stopped being surprised at the way food appeared in an emergency in Ahousaht. When she and the family trooped into the Crows' house, it was almost ten, but two neighborly women were in the kitchen, taking hot biscuits out of the oven and putting freshly baked salmon on a tray. On the table were mashed potatoes, salad and crumb cake.

With a few words of comfort, the women slipped away, leaving Jordan and the Crow family to eat the food.

No one had much of an appetite, though. Peter filled his plate and then set down his fork.

"I keep thinking, what if I hadn't needed that damned socket for the spark plug." His kind, scarred face, usually smiling, was pale and grim.

Rose Marie wasn't eating, either. "I'd gone over to Auntie's, it was our evening for sewing circle. I didn't even know Patwin was home. He hasn't been around much these past few days."

"Dumb-ass idiot." Christina was still angry. She jabbed viciously at a biscuit, breaking it into crumbs. "He got better marks than I did in school—he won every scholarship award there was before he got mixed up with a bad crowd. He could have been anything he wanted—doctor, lawyer, teacher…. But instead he quit school in grade ten. It's one disaster after another with him. And now he goes and tries this." She burst into tears. "I still can't believe he'd *do* a thing like this."

Jordan reached over and drew Christina into her arms. "It's such a scary thing when someone tries to take their own life."

"Did you see many attempted suicides, when you were working at the E.R.?" Rose Marie asked.

"Yes, unfortunately we did." Jordan didn't add that many survivors ended up severely damaged. "Like I said, it's a cry for help, and the great thing here is that I think Patwin came out of it without serious side effects. And he's going to get help. If he won't let Silas work with him, then we'll find another way." She studied Rose Marie. "Tell me about Patwin. What was he like as a little boy, what did he most enjoy?"

"Christina, go get the album."

Christina blew her nose and hurried off, and Rose Marie said, "Patwin wasn't an easy child, not like Christina." She smiled a little and shook her head. "I didn't think I'd ever have any more kids, and then I got pregnant with Patwin. I guess we spoiled him bad, being the youngest."

Christina came back with an armful of albums, and Rose Marie selected one and opened it to a photo of a younger Peter holding a cherubic small boy under one arm. Patwin's face was split in a wide, happy grin.

"I remember that day," Rose Marie said, tapping a forefinger on the photo. "Patwin was three there, and he got away on me. He went down to the docks looking for his daddy." She looked up at Peter. "You remember how many times we had to go looking for him? He was the worst kid for running away, from the time he could first walk. Peter built a fence around the yard to keep him contained, but Patwin would always find a way out. He needed to explore, to experience everything firsthand."

"Is this Silas?" Jordan was looking at a black-and-white photo of a somber boy in short pants, standing on the dock, holding a suitcase.

"Yeah, that's him," Rose Marie confirmed. "He was about eight in that picture, coming to stay for the summer. I used to look forward so much to him coming home, but he wasn't happy about it. Look at that face." She rubbed a finger lovingly over the picture. "It was hard for him, living in two worlds. Funny, I always worried more about him than Patwin."

"It must have been hard on you, only seeing him in the summer."

"It was really hard." Rose Marie nodded. "I think when he was little he didn't know why I'd gone away and left him. I just didn't have the money for lawyers, plus I was sick at the time. That's partly why when Patwin came along, I couldn't help spoiling him—I wanted him to have the security Silas missed out on."

"Did Silas ever run away, the way Patwin did?" Jordan was curious about him, about what kind of baby he'd been, what kind of little boy.

Rose Marie shook her head. "No. Silas wasn't like Patwin that way. Silas was a quiet boy, but did he have a mind of his own. There was no reasoning with him if he got an idea in his head."

"He also had a ramrod up his ass," Christina said. "Thought he was too good to play with us when he was here in the summer. So the other kids and I used to play mean tricks on him. Grandmother Sandrine always caught us and gave us hell for it."

Rose Marie clicked her tongue. "And well she should. In those days Silas was used to a different sort of life. And I think he was jealous because you had a big family around all the time. He spent most of his life at boarding school."

Rose Marie turned a page in the album. Here were photos of Christina graduating from high school, then nursing school, of Patwin receiving an award for scholarship, and one blurry newspaper photo of Silas in mortarboard and gown, graduating from university.

"I wanted to go so bad," Rose Marie said softly. "But he said no. That was when he didn't want anything to do with us."

Jordan studied the pictures, thinking of her own

graduations. The best one had been from medical school. Toby had been there for her that day. She'd given up on Mike long before, but some small part of her had still hoped he'd appear. Had Silas missed his mother, in spite of telling her to stay away?

She turned the pages of the album. "What sort of things does Patwin like to do? What are his hobbies?"

"Drinking," Christina snorted. "Driving us all bonkers."

"He used to like to build things out of wood," Peter said. "When he was twelve, he and I built a small boat for him to sail. Remember that, Rosie? He was never interested in fishing, but he liked sailing."

"He'd get along with my brother," Jordan commented. She told them a little about Toby, confiding the early problems he'd had and the fact that he'd done jail time and was now a successful boatbuilder. Patwin's family needed to hear that other people had similar problems and came through them all right. Besides, it was easier to talk about Toby than confide in them about Garry. "Toby's coming for a visit as soon as he finishes this yacht he's been contracted to build."

When Jordan's cell phone rang, everyone waited quietly as she talked to Doctor Magrath at the Tofino hospital.

The news was good. Just as Jordan had suspected, there was no real damage except bruising to Patwin's spinal cord, and his voice was already beginning to come back. With Jordan's approval, Patwin would be released the following morning in Silas's care. She reported all of that to the Crows, but she didn't repeat what else the doctor said.

"These native kids get thinking there's no way out for them except suicide," Magrath sighed. "I wish we could help them before they become that desperate. Patwin's brother seems to be a stable guy, maybe he can help this kid get a handle on what's bothering him."

Relief that Patwin was physically okay made everyone relax. Rose Marie made coffee and Christina served the crumb cake. As soon as the meal was over, Jordan headed home.

She'd just walked in the door when her cell rang again.

Jordan answered eagerly, knowing it was Silas.

And froze when Garry said, "Hey, Jordie, how's it going?"

CHAPTER SIXTEEN

SHE HAD TO SWALLOW HARD before she found her voice.

"Garry, how did you get this number?" On her lawyer's advice, she'd had it changed so he couldn't contact her.

Tone playful, he said, "Now is that any way to greet your husband? I'm just calling to say hi, how are you. No reason for you to be so snarky, Jordie. And phone numbers, hell, I'm a lawyer. I know how to find numbers—and missing persons, too. You can run but you can't hide, babe." His laughter spiraled out of control, and Jordan knew he was high.

It was unlikely that he knew exactly where she was, but her stomach began to churn, and it was tough to keep her voice even.

"What do you want, Garry?" Dumb question. There were only two possibilities. One was drugs, and the other money.

"That matrimonial hotshot you hired just served me with divorce papers, honey pie. You really think I'm going to sit back and let you dump me like a bag of garbage?"

Jordan was shivering, but her hand clutching the phone was damp with sweat. There was no point in trying to reason with him. Instead, she waited for whatever he'd say next.

"I don't want a divorce. If you do, it's gonna cost you, Jordie. Any judge I know is going to be sympathetic to a guy who was seriously injured in an accident only to get dumped by his rich doctor wife."

"I'm far from rich, Garry."

"You have medical insurance, and you owe me, bitch."

So that's what this was about. But how had Garry lost his own insurance coverage? Jordan didn't want to know.

"I don't think I do owe you, and neither does my lawyer," she said in as cool a voice as she could manage. "So from now on, call Marcy instead of me. You and I no longer have anything to say to each other." She disconnected, and didn't answer when the phone rang again almost immediately.

It rang consistently for the next hour, and Jordan finally shoved the phone under a pillow on the sofa and closed herself in the bathroom to run hot water in the tub.

"Tomorrow morning, I'll just get a new number again," she promised herself as she lowered her body into the steaming water. And when he found that number, she'd do it again. And again. Panic began to settle over her, and she struggled with it. She'd moved beyond these feelings, she didn't want to go back there.

And the afternoon she'd so enjoyed now seemed to have taken place a very long time ago.

SILAS DIALED JORDAN'S cell number for the third time, and for the third time her recorded voice asked him to leave a number, which wasn't possible. He was calling from a pay phone in the hospital. He could have left a message, but he wanted her, not a machine.

Frustrated, he gave up and went back to Patwin's room. The doctors had finally finished their testing, and the results were exactly what Jordan had predicted. Physically, Patwin would recover. Emotionally, the jury was still out. With all the activity, there hadn't been a chance to talk to Patwin alone.

His brother lay immobile on the high hospital bed, eyes shut, throat swollen and bruised an ugly purple. On oxygen support, his breathing was easier. Silas had heard him whisper a response to a nurse's question, so his vocal cords were beginning to recover.

The doctors told Silas exactly the same thing Jordan had— that Patwin could either be transferred to the psych ward in Nanaimo or, with the consent of the psychiatrist who'd see Patwin the following day, he could go home with Silas.

They'd agreed to let Silas stay in the room for the night. A pretty blond nurse had even wheeled in an oversize chair that made a makeshift bed and found pillows and a blanket to make him comfortable.

It was time to find out whether his hunch was right. "You awake, bro?"

Patwin's eyes opened, bloodshot, with huge black bags under them.

"Did you do this—" Silas touched Patwin's neck with a featherlight forefinger "—because Mary told you she was pregnant?"

Patwin's eyes revealed his torture. He started to shrug only to grimace in pain. "Partly," he whispered, his eyes watering with the effort the simple word caused. He picked up the paper and pen beside him on the bed.

I'm a total fuck up, he scribbled, pen digging into paper. *How can I take care of a kid? I can't get own shit together. Wanted to run, but if I leave… Can't go to prison again, rather die!!*

Silas nodded. "Did Mary mention marriage when she told you she was pregnant?"

Patwin shook his head. *But I knocked her up, I marry her, right?*

"No point in getting married if it's not what you want, not what you can handle. But hanging yourself isn't the answer, either."

So what is? Patwin bore down so hard the pen tore the paper. *You and Chris—different, know what you want.* He tore off the sheet and began another one, his writing erratic. *All I've done is drive Mom and Dad crazy, fuck everything up. Now a kid.*

Silas read the note and started to laugh.

Patwin threw the pen at him, and it hit Silas on the side of the head.

"Ouch." He rubbed the spot and then laid a hand on

his brother's arm. "Calm down, Patwin, I'm not laughing at you. I'm laughing because I can't believe you actually think you're the only one who's ever felt like that. I don't know about Christina, but I've spent most of my life wondering who the hell I was and where I belonged. I spent years so jealous of you I used to fantasize about drowning you in the chuck."

The astonishment on Patwin's face made Silas laugh all over again.

"Think about it, little brother. You had parents who lived in the same place, a family the same color as you, a home where you belonged, where you lived all year round. I spent most of my time in boarding school and summers feeling like a stranger in a very strange land. But I'm not the one with the sore neck. How are we going to make sure you never feel so alone and desperate you have to do something like this again?"

Patwin waited.

"I asked you this before, when you were doing drugs, and you wouldn't make a commitment. I'm going to ask you again. I want to hold a gathering, with everyone in our family present, plus friends and neighbors, all of Mary's relatives, as well, and any elders who want to come. Everyone gets a chance to say how they feel, what's made them feel that way. No blame. Together, we'll come up with a plan that supports you and Mary and the baby. I'll hold a healing ceremony. Lots of the elders have been hooked on drugs, too, you know. They'll understand, and maybe give you some guidance."

Patwin didn't look convinced.

"Or you can be transferred to the psych ward at the hospital in Nanaimo." Silas hated using that as a lever, but his kid brother was one tough nut.

NO, Patwin scribbled. *I want to go home!*

"Then you agree to work with me?"

Patwin glared up at him. *OKAY. Tired now, want to sleep.*

Maybe almost dying would make Patwin more willing to change.

Silas could only hope.

"Sleep now." He took hold of Patwin's hand and gave it a squeeze. "I'll be here."

He waited until Patwin was snoring softly, and then he went down the hall to the telephone again. He dialed and waited while it rang, hoping she'd pick up. At last, her service came on with the now familiar words. "Jordan here, leave a message and I'll get back to you."

"It's Silas," he said. "Hey, pretty lady, I know you've heard Patwin's doing okay—the doc said he called you. He's agreed to a healing. I'll explain more about that when I see you." He paused for an instant, wondering what it was he really wanted to say. "I enjoyed our time at the springs. I appreciate your efforts on my family's behalf."

And then, surprising himself, he added, "I miss you tonight, Jordan Burke. I wish we were together."

AFTER A FITFUL NIGHT, Jordan forced herself to listen to her messages. There were four increasingly nasty ones from Garry, and one from Silas, which she played three times.

I miss you, Jordan Burke. The fact was, she missed him too.

Then she called the telephone service and requested a change of number, effective immediately.

"You can run, but you can't hide," Garry had sneered. With all her heart, she hoped he was wrong.

Two days later, Jordan was in a round-robin discussion with a group of pregnant women about the effects of cigarette smoke when she glanced out the window and saw Silas walking toward the medical center.

Her heart leaped. She apologized to the women and excused herself, heading out to the reception area to talk to him. Adrenaline pumped through her blood, and she realized she'd been waiting all day to see him.

"Hello, Jordan." He didn't touch her, but the warmth and low pitch of his voice felt like an intimate caress. "I know you're busy, I won't keep you. I just wanted to see you for a minute."

"Silas, I'm glad you're back. How's Patwin? Where is he?"

"At my mother's place, she's caring for him. He's still pretty weak and sore, but he's agreed to a healing circle tonight. Do you want to come?"

"I wouldn't be intruding?" She felt suddenly shy with him.

"Everybody concerned about Patwin will be there."

"Then absolutely." She had no idea what a healing circle was. "Do I need to bring anything?"

"Only good intentions."

"Where and when?"

"At the school gym, after dinner."

"I'll be there."

"Good." He looked at her for several moments, and then in a soft voice that she had to strain to hear, he added, "Afterward, will you come to my cabin with me? All I can think of is making love to you again."

She had to clench her fists to keep from reaching out and touching him. He was so stable, so strong yet gentle. She had the urge to tell him about Garry's phone call, how it had frightened her, and how she hadn't been able to get it out of her mind the past few days.

Instead, she settled for a quiet "I think that could be arranged."

"Phew." His smile was wide. "I was afraid you were still thinking about it. See you tonight, then."

JORDAN FELT NERVOUS as she approached the gym door. She had no idea what to expect, or what might be expected of her. She was also on edge about being either too early or too late; she still didn't understand what Christina called "Indian time."

Maybe she was getting the hang of it, after all, she decided as she came through the door. Several dozen people were sitting on folding chairs set in a circle in the middle of the room. The chairs were arranged around a large ceremonial drum where a woman Jordan didn't recognize was tapping out a repetitive rhythm. Everyone was swaying slightly in time with the hypnotic beat, but nothing else was happening yet.

Jordan was conscious of being the only non-native in the room. Feeling more than a little shy, she took a folding chair from a stack and set it up beside one of the village elders, an ancient man whom she knew only as Leroy. He nodded to her.

She was directly across from Silas. He smiled at her, and his eyes held hers for a heartbeat. Those clear green eyes were filled with warmth and welcome, and she suddenly felt more at ease.

Patwin was beside Silas, his neck and face still grotesquely swollen. Rose Marie and Christina and Peter flanked him, and they all nodded and smiled at her. Jordan recognized Mary John, sitting beside an elder.

Jordan had just confirmed the girl's pregnancy, but Mary had refused to name the father. Could it be Patwin?

The drummer changed the beat, and Leroy began singing. Soon everyone except Jordan was also singing. She hummed along, expecting Silas to be the one to lead the proceedings. She wondered when he was going to take control and call the meeting to order, or whatever the equivalent was here.

The song tapered off, and one of the elders, a woman called Linculla, got to her feet. She lit a taper of sweetgrass, blew it out and walked around the circle, using her hand to wave smoke at each person while murmuring what sounded like an incantation. When she reached her seat again she sat, and the drumming restarted, quieter now.

Still tense, Jordan waited for the format of the meeting to present itself, and for a pattern to emerge.

She felt a surge of relief when Peter Crow got to his feet. It was fitting that Patwin's father be in charge.

But Peter stood wordless for so long Jordan began to have an anxiety attack on his behalf. He must have forgotten his speech, she agonized, her stomach twisting into sympathetic knots.

"My son Patwin is in trouble," he finally said in a voice so soft Jordan had to lean forward to hear him. "I want him to know he is not alone in what he feels. When I was a boy," Peter went on in the same soft voice, "I was taken from my family and sent to residential school. It was a hard time, and I tried many times to run away. I was always punished, and I always ran again, because I longed to come home to my people."

Nods of understanding and murmurs of agreement came from the listeners. "A time came when I lost hope. I stole a boat late one night and went far out into the water where the waves were high and jumped in. But I was young and strong, and it was too damned hard to drown."

Everyone laughed quietly.

"Thank you for letting me speak."

There was a long silence, and without another word, Peter sat.

There was nothing but drumming for some time, and then the older man beside Peter got to his feet.

"I am Mary John's grandfather. I love my granddaughter and I want her to be happy, so I want to help Patwin. As a young man, I, too, was sent away to school. It was painful, and afterward I wandered far from the teachings of my childhood," Leroy said. "I drank and twice I went to jail for stealing. I was angry, and I wanted to make someone pay. Drinking took away some of the pain, but it made me do bad things. I beat my wife when I was drunk, and my son watched. When he grew up and I saw him doing the things I had done, I wanted to die for shame of what I had taught him. Instead, I asked for a healing, and I stopped drinking. If I can help Patwin, I would be glad."

He sat, and eventually, the young woman next to him stood. She'd been an addict and a prostitute, and she described her feelings of shame and hopelessness and the pressures young people were under wherever they went. "I know where you're coming from, Patwin," she said. "Because I've been there."

Jordan realized that the speakers were proceeding in order, clockwise from Peter Crow. Not everyone in the circle spoke when their turn came, but most did. They spoke from their hearts, and their wrenching honesty often had Jordan brushing away tears.

Then Leroy rose to tell about his grandson, who'd died from a drug overdose, and Jordan realized that if she chose to speak, it would be her turn next.

Her heart began to hammer, and she felt perspiration trickle down between her breasts. She wanted to talk of her breakdown, how Garry's addiction had hurt her.

She knew Helen would encourage her to stand and speak, to share her story.

When her turn came she drew in a deep breath and rubbed her sweating palms together. She started to get to her feet—but then shook her head and slid back into her chair. She just couldn't do it. The old habits of silence and secrecy were too strong.

The woman on her left stood, and Jordan felt relief, mixed with harsh disappointment and shame. Why wasn't she brave? Why couldn't she be open? These people were pouring out their hearts to help Patwin. She should have done the same.

She felt Silas's eyes on her, and knew that part of the reason she couldn't bare her soul here was because she didn't want him to feel sorry for her, to see her as a victim. She wanted intimacy, but wasn't ready to share her deepest, most shameful secrets with anyone.

So why did she feel she'd failed an important lesson?

CHAPTER SEVENTEEN

SILAS PERFORMED A CEREMONY after the meeting ended about an hour later. It was mostly in the Nuu-chah-nulth native tongue, so Jordan didn't understand it. What she did understand and what impressed her was the respect these people showed for one another.

Respect, compassion, honesty and caring. She could think of a lot of people back in Vancouver who would benefit from a healing circle.

She and Silas were quiet as they walked through the dark woods. Holding Jordan's hand, he shone the flashlight carefully so she could see the path. With each step, the tension between them grew. Jordan was hungry for him, and it seemed forever before they reached his cabin.

He opened the door and she followed him inside. She could see a faint light coming from his computer, but other than that it was dark.

"You don't lock your door." Jordan knew it was a stupid question—as far as she could tell, no one in the entire community locked anything.

"Locks are a symbol of fear. But—" he clicked the

latch down on the inside of the door "—tonight I don't want interruptions."

He drew her to him, and their mouths met with furious urgency.

"Let's try a bed this time," he whispered, and led her through the dark to the stairwell.

Up in his bedroom, the night sky shone down through the skylight above the bed. Silas lit a candle on the dresser, and without having to say a word, they began to remove their clothing.

Jordan, eager and a little nervous, fumbled with the button on her slacks.

"Here, let me." He was already naked, his bronze skin gleaming in the flickering candlelight. His fingers were fast and her slacks slipped to the floor. He sent her bikini panties after them.

Her pulse throbbed as she stepped out of them, and it was satisfying to note that his breathing was as irregular as her own. His eyes devoured her, and he whispered to her in his language, erotic-sounding, exciting phrases.

All the feelings that had overwhelmed her the first time they made love came rushing back. She wanted him with a mindless, consuming desperation. Their mouths met, the kiss deepened and it thrilled her to know that he was fully aroused. They tumbled to the bed, and the heat between them soared as skin caressed skin.

Impatiently, Jordan reached a hand down and tried to guide him into her, but Silas drew back and shook his head.

"No rush," he said. "We have all night."

With excruciating patience, he explored her body inch by inch with lips and tongue and fingers, making small throaty sounds of delight and passion. At first, Jordan tried to match him touch for touch, but soon her passion burned with such intensity, she simply gave herself up to him.

When at long last, he finally entered her, her release was immediate. And while her body contracted and throbbed, he reached his own climax.

Shuddering with pleasure, legs and arms limp, she looked up at the night sky through dazed half-open eyes. There were stars everywhere, and the moon had come up. Through the open window, she could hear a coyote yelping, another answering. From far away, an owl screeched. Jordan felt a deep and satisfying peace.

Silas didn't withdraw. He used his lips and tongue on her earlobes, her neck, the hollow at the base of her throat. He took her nipple into his mouth and teased it, and she felt herself tightening around him, drawing him deeper. Sweat made their bodies slick, and she licked his skin, thirsty for the taste of him, restless again with renewed desire.

When he was hard once more, he flipped them neatly over, so that Jordan was on top. He rested his palms lightly on her hips, looking up at her, into her eyes.

"Ride," he whispered.

Instead, she leaned forward and took one of his dark nipples gently between her teeth, nibbling, tasting. He let out his breath with a hiss. She trailed kisses down his ribs, and he murmured something urgent.

She moved just a little, and he caught the rhythm and gave it back to her.

The awareness of her sexual power made her laugh—it was new to her. She teased Silas deliberately, drunk with delight, and power gave way to the pleasure of pleasing him.

He went first this time, but she followed almost immediately. She collapsed on his chest panting, lost in wave after wave of powerful sensation.

He held her, still connected, and slowly, he turned her so they lay side by side, her leg over his thigh. As she dozed, she felt him begin to harden yet again.

Silas moved in a gentle, sleepy pattern, as slow and rhythmic as the tide. She drifted, caught between pleasure and sleep, feeling him grow large. Her orgasm came immediately.

Like a riptide, it consumed her. She heard herself cry out, harsh and wild, and he caught the sound with his mouth, groaning with his own massive release. Her body shuddered in long, shattering spasms, and tears poured from her eyes.

Silas licked them away. He held her and murmured lavish praise in her ear, and she had a sense of sanctuary, of safety and belonging, that went far beyond the physical. She'd examine those feelings later. Right now, her head was empty, her heart filled to capacity.

Contentment stole over her. Her body closely entwined with his, she slept.

SILAS LAY AWAKE, holding her. He could feel her heart beating, slow and steady. Her breath made small warm circles on his chest, and a strand of her hair tickled his cheek.

Her body was bone-slender, fragile in his arms, and he felt tender pride in protecting her, keeping her safe as she slept.

They'd traveled far together, farther even than he'd planned to take them. He'd felt her soul soaring, and his had joined it. Never before had he understood that two separate people could become more than the sum of their parts this way.

He stared up at the night sky, and the peace from lovemaking began to ebb. When he'd made his vision quest, he'd had a dream. He remembered it in vivid detail. He'd held a woman, just as he was holding Jordan now. But he'd been afraid in that dream, afraid of losing a part of himself if he gave too much. He'd dreamed he was drowning. The memory chilled him, and he felt as if he couldn't breathe.

Gently, he untangled himself from Jordan. He pushed the window wider. The night air was damp and cold, and he pulled the quilt up and tucked it around her shoulders. He was weary, on the verge of exhaustion, and yet filled with restlessness as well.

The healing circle, the ceremony he'd conducted, the lovemaking—everything had used his energy, and now he was running on empty. But he knew he wouldn't sleep, so silently, carefully, he pulled on pants and a light sweater, and made his way downstairs. He sat down in front of his computer to distract himself, but he could feel Sandrine's presence, and his heart sank.

Grandmother didn't let him get away with anything.

"What, Grandmother? What am I to do about this woman? There can't be a future for us, our worlds are too different."

"There is only one world, Grandson. All are cousins, all are children of First Mother."

Silas snorted. "Easy for you to say, you don't have to live here anymore."

"There is only one question, Wounded Bear Hawk. Is your heart moving toward harmony or disharmony? There is no third way."

He shut his eyes and groaned. "A simple yes or no would really help. Do this or do that. But no, it's always back to harmony. Harmony is really tough to master, Grandmother."

"It begins at the beginning, with your father. Make peace with him, Grandson. Until you do, harmony will elude you."

He opened his eyes. He knew what she meant, but he was no closer to taking her advice than he'd ever been. He was also no closer to knowing what to do about his feelings for the woman asleep upstairs in his bed.

JORDAN WOKE TO PALE dawn light spilling onto the bed from the skylight. The candle had either burned down or blown out sometime in the night.

Silas was sleeping beside her, his black silky hair

tumbled across the pillow, hawklike features at rest. His breathing was slow and even, and she lay for a few stolen moments, studying him.

He looked remote and regal in sleep, but there was also a sadness, absent when he was awake. Or maybe he just managed to hide it behind his enigmatic grin and that unnerving intensity.

The room was chilly, and he'd covered them up with the beautiful quilt. She buried her nose in it, drawing in the subtle male muskiness she associated with Silas, and another, more elusive fragrance, of wood smoke and the outdoors.

She slid out from under the quilt, careful not to wake Silas, grabbed her clothing and made her way down to the bathroom. She stepped into the shower, grateful that the water ran hot.

She smiled at his bar of green Irish Spring soap. His shampoo was generic, and she lathered her hair with it and rinsed.

Using the fresh towel on the bar, she dried off and dressed. And when she opened the bathroom door, the warmth of the woodstove and the smell of rich, freshly brewing coffee greeted her.

"Morning, pretty lady." He smiled at her. He was wearing low-slung jeans and an unbuttoned flannel shirt, sleeves rolled up to the elbow. He had moccasins on his feet, and his long, streaked hair swung free around his chiseled face. Lucky she wasn't in love with him. She'd spend her life just looking at him all the time. But lust, she was definitely in lust. There was an attraction between them stronger than any she'd ever experienced.

"Coffee's ready." He gestured to an old enamel pot on the stove lid. "You want some eggs for breakfast?"

Jordan couldn't help herself. She went over and hugged him. "No eggs, but coffee would be great. I didn't mean to wake you up, I was just going to sneak away."

He wrapped his arms around her tight, then released her. "You didn't wake me. The light did, same as every other morning. That skylight is a mixed blessing." He took a potholder from a hook, lifted the pot and poured coffee into two white earthenware mugs. He handed her one and gestured to the chairs at the table.

They sat. Jordan sipped and murmured her approval. "It's wonderful—the coffee—but the skylight, too. Like camping out, without the mosquitoes or bears." It felt good, being with him first thing in the morning like this, with the unspoken acknowledgment of their lovemaking reverberating like an echo between them. "So what do you have on the agenda for today?"

"The editor is on my case about an article that's overdue. And I want to spend some time with Patwin. There's also a meeting of the Tribal Council this afternoon." He stirred sugar into his coffee. "You?"

"I have the well-baby clinic this morning, then this afternoon the summer-school kids are having career day—they asked if I'd talk about the medical profession."

"Will I see you tonight?"

"Sure. By now, everyone knows I've slept over, so there's no point being discreet anymore, right?"

"Right." He smiled at her, holding her gaze. "I'll call you. Maybe we can go to Mabel's for dinner."

"I'd like that. Oh, before I forget, my cell number's different." She rhymed it off, and he repeated it.

"Why'd you change it?"

"Oh, I've been getting crank calls." She didn't look at him when she said it, and as usual, she felt a stab of guilt about being less than honest with him. But why muddy up a glorious morning with sordid details about Garry? She'd tell Silas about him, sooner or later. *Later.* She didn't want to spoil what was starting out as a perfect day.

BY NOON, SHE WAS FAMISHED. The well-baby clinic had been hectic but fun, and when the last mother left, Jordan hurried back to her apartment to grab a sandwich and freshen up for her trip to the school.

Singing under her breath, she slapped cheese on a thick slice of Michael's mother's homemade bread, added mayo and a second slab of bread, and was enjoying her first bite when there was a knock on her door.

Chewing, she opened it—and choked.

"Hey, Jordie, long time no see." Garry leered at her. "You're lookin' good, babe, but you oughta take something for that cough. Mind if I come in?"

CHAPTER EIGHTEEN

GARRY SIDLED PAST HER without waiting for an answer. He tossed an overnight bag onto a chair and surveyed the room.

"Well, isn't this cozy. Nice little hideaway you've got here, Jordie. A touch primitive, but what the hell, it's summer, right? You can pretend you're camping out."

Jordan couldn't get her breath. Hands shaking, heart pounding, she hurried to the sink and gulped down a glass of water. She turned to face him.

In the month since she'd last seen him, he'd grown shockingly thin. He'd been a good-looking man, with thick, curly blond hair and a trim body, but now the drug use was showing. His face was ravaged, his eyes sunken, hair lank and in need of a trim. There was a noticeable tremor in the hand that held the cigarette he was lighting. He looked exactly what he was—a junkie.

"Put that out. No smoking in my house." Her voice was reedy and thin, but her tone was defiant enough.

"Still got that ramrod up your ass, I see." He stubbed the cigarette out on her plate.

That made her mad, which was a good thing. The rush of adrenaline steadied her. "What are you doing here, Garry?"

"Now that's a dumb question for a smart doc, wouldn't you say? I come to see my wife, and she asks what I'm doing here." He was walking around the room, picking things up and setting them down again.

She didn't want him to touch anything of hers.

He shot her his little-boy-lost look, but now the effect was anything but charming. He looked slightly manic. "I just got out of a treatment center and want to get back together, Jordie. I still love you, in spite of everything you've done. This thing with that lady lawyer of yours, this separation agreement, now that's crazy. She's stonewalling reconciliation and billing you top dollar for nothing. We can sort things out ourselves."

Jordan felt violated by his presence and more than a little frightened. She tried to think clearly, figure out what to do. The RCMP constable was only in town three days a week. She tried to remember if this was one of those days. But even if he was, what could she tell him? Garry wasn't violent, at least not yet. And they were still legally married. How she wished now she'd gone ahead with the restraining order Marcy had suggested.

"At least the Indians here are friendly," he said, flopping down on the sofa, propping one ankle on the other knee, spreading his arms wide. Jordan noticed that he wore long sleeves. "The skipper on that water taxi was really interested when I explained that you were my wife. He didn't seem to even know you were married, babe. You trying to keep me your dirty little secret?"

So the entire village would know by now that Garry was here, and that he was her husband. Jordan's insides shriveled, and her thoughts flew to Silas. She should have told him everything about Garry, the drugs, the phone calls, the humiliation. Silas thought she was divorced. Why had she tried to hide the facts from him?

"Come sit down here beside me," Garry wheedled, patting the sofa. When she didn't move, he got to his feet and came toward her.

Jordan tried not to flinch when he put his hands on her shoulders, but when he yanked her close and tried to kiss her, bile rose in her throat and she shoved him away. It was all she could do to keep from wiping her mouth with the back of her hand. Putting the table between them, she leaned against the back of a chair. Her knees were trembling.

"Don't touch me again, Garry. Whatever was between us is over, you must realize that. The drugs destroyed my feelings for you. I *do not* love you anymore. All I want from you is a divorce."

"Aww, don't be like that." The bravado suddenly deserted him, and his voice lost its brazen cockiness. "Please, Jordan, I'm begging you. I came all this way to talk to you, it's important. Couldn't you spare me a few minutes?"

Something like panic flitted across his face, and reluctantly, Jordan felt a stab of pity for him. He was pathetic. He'd had such potential, he'd had every advantage, and he'd blown everything. She sank down on a chair.

"What is it, Garry?"

"I got fired." His face twisted into bitter lines. "I used most of my severance to pay debts, and to go to Edgewood."

It was one of the best treatment centers around. "How long were you there?"

"Three weeks."

Not nearly long enough, in her estimation. Minimal stay was usually five. He'd walked halfway through, just as he'd done with all the other programs she'd set up for him.

"Mom and Dad won't give me any money or let me stay with them," Garry whined. "I'm clean, but now there's nowhere to go. I used the last of my money on this trip. I need a loan, Jordan. Just until I get on my feet."

Before she could answer, Jordan heard a tap at the door and Christina walked in without waiting for a response, something she'd never done before.

She nodded in Garry's direction. In a breezy tone, she said, "Hey, Doc, you're gonna be late for that thing at the school." Her eyes flicked between the two, and Jordan knew that Christina was there in case she needed help. Obviously the word had gone out.

"Christina Crow, this is Garry Hughes, my—my, um, former husband."

"Hey, a real pleasure, Chris." Garry pulled himself

together and gave her a hideous facsimile of his once-charming grin. "If you've got things to do, Jordie, I'll just hang around here until you get back." He winked at Christina. "And go easy on that *former* bit, babe. Far as I know we're still husband and wife."

Jordan opened her mouth to protest and thought better of it. There was no point arguing with him over that. There were far more important issues at stake here.

Christina's presence bolstered both her courage and her resolve. "You're not staying here, Garry. And we have nothing to talk about, so it might be best if you catch the water taxi back to Tofino. It leaves in—" she glanced at the clock "—about two and a half hours."

"Jordan, *please*." It shocked her to see tears gather in Garry's eyes and trickle down his cheeks. He turned away, so Christina wouldn't see. The desperation in his voice was palpable. "Look, if it's that important to you, I'll sign the damned agreement—I've got it with me—in return for a loan."

It *was* that important to her. She gave in. "There's a coffee shop, go there and wait. I'll be about an hour and a half, I'll meet you there."

"Thanks. If I could just use your bathroom…?"

She couldn't very well refuse. She pointed, and he went down the hallway.

"You okay?" Christina's voice was low and concerned.

"Almost. I'll be better when he's gone."

"He's a junkie, right?"

"He says he's clean, but…I've been down that road too often with him."

Christina sighed and nodded. "Yeah, don't I know that story." She added, "You want me to get Silas?"

"No." Jordan drew in a shaky breath and got control of her voice. "No, absolutely not, but thanks. It'll be fine. Just—just keep a close eye on the drug cabinet in the clinic, okay? And tell my afternoon patients I'll be late. I'll get there as soon as I can."

"You sure you're okay with—?" Christina gestured at the hallway.

"Yeah. He's not physically dangerous."

"Just a train wreck in every other way, huh?"

"You've got it." Jordan gave her friend a rueful grin, and Christina left by the door that connected to the clinic. She left it ajar.

When she was gone, Jordan suddenly remembered that her medical bag was in her bedroom, across the hall from the bathroom. She walked over and glanced down the hall just as Garry opened the bathroom door.

"So, could you show me where that coffee shop is, Jordan?"

Eager to get him out of her space, she grabbed her handbag and carefully locked the door behind them. She pointed out where Mabel's diner was and hurried in the opposite direction to the school, praying that she'd be able to compose her thoughts enough to be able to give her presentation and then deal with the students' questions.

But all she could think of was Silas, and the sickness

in her gut made her dizzy. He'd know by now that Garry was here. He'd know Garry was a junkie. He'd know she'd been dishonest with him.

And she also knew that Silas valued honesty above everything else.

THE CAREER FAIR TOOK LONGER than she'd expected. The moment she was able to slip away, she called Marcy. She needed legal advice.

"I'm sorry, but she's in court all day," the secretary said.

Jordan left word for the lawyer to call when she was free, but for right now, she was on her own. Swallowing two antacid tablets, she headed over to Mabel's.

"There she is, my doctor wifey. Over here, Jordie."

Mabel's was crowded, but Garry's loud voice overpowered the quiet hum of conversation in the small diner. Every eye in the place turned toward her, and Jordan felt her skin grow hot. She avoided looking at anyone as she walked over to where he was sitting.

He got to his feet and ostentatiously held a chair for her. He put his hands on her shoulders and pretended to rub her neck. Skin crawling, she jerked away.

Garry looked different than he had a few short hours ago. His skin was flushed, his eyes unnaturally bright. When he sat down again, his hands moved restlessly, picking up and setting down the salt and pepper, the ketchup. He plucked a napkin from the holder and began shredding it. He was high. Jordan could hardly believe it. Where had he gotten drugs? Certainly, there were people in Ahousaht who dealt, but it wasn't the same as the city, where it was easy to score. A person had to know who to contact, and she couldn't see Garry managing it in the short time he'd been here.

He must have brought it with him, she decided wearily.

"Coffee, Doctor Jordan?" Grace filled a mug and set a menu in front of Jordan, refilling Garry's mug and giving him a wary, sidelong look.

"Just coffee, thanks, Grace." Jordan curled her fingers around the mug, shivering in spite of the afternoon heat. She glanced at the table nearest to her and met the concerned gaze of a burly logger, Rupert Joe. She'd treated him the week before for an infected eye.

"Hey, Doc," he rumbled. "How's it goin'?"

"Hi, Rupert." Jordan tried to smile, but she wasn't successful.

Garry reached under the table into his overnight bag and drew out dog-eared legal papers. With a flourish, he set them on the table. "So, here's your separation agreement, Jordie. Now, what's it worth to you?"

Well, that was direct enough. "How much do you want?"

"Fifty thousand should do it."

Jordan stared at him in disbelief and then she laughed. She couldn't help it. "I don't have anywhere near that amount."

"You have a pension plan, you can borrow against that. Besides, the banks will loan you any amount of money. You're a doctor."

"No, Garry." It was senseless to argue with him—
madness to agree to pay him money. She owed him
nothing. It had been a bad idea, meeting him here.
Marcy would find a way to get the agreement signed.
Jordan pushed her chair back and got to her feet.

"Thirty, then." He shook the papers at her. "Thirty
thousand—it must be worth thirty to get this thing
signed, right? You're getting off cheap. It'll probably
save you another trip to the psych ward. You don't want
to do that again, do you? Think of it as an investment
in your mental health, babe."

Even though everyone was pretending not to listen,
Jordan knew they couldn't help but overhear. Rupert
wasn't looking at Garry, but she could sense that the big
man was ready to come to her rescue if she needed him.

These were her patients, her friends, and Garry was
deliberately humiliating her in front of them. Shame
lodged like a sick ball in the pit of her stomach. Her legs
shaking, she walked to the counter and put ten dollars
down. When Grace hurried over to make change, Jordan shook her head and bolted for the door.

She made it outside before he caught up to her and
grabbed her arm.

CHAPTER NINETEEN

GARRY PULLED HER AROUND to face him. "Okay, bitch. Ten. Ten thou, I'm gone, you're a free woman."

She jerked her arm out of his grasp. "I'm free, anyway, Garry. I was free the moment I realized I wasn't responsible for you. If I have to fight you in court, I will." She took a shaky breath. "Unless you leave Ahousaht this afternoon, I'll call the RCMP and get a restraining order. And if you insist on following me now, or give me any hassle whatsoever, I'll wave to the loggers watching us through that window, and believe me, they'll see to it you don't ever follow me again."

He was still holding the separation agreement in one fist, and now he threw his bag to the ground and ripped the paper into shreds, tossing the pieces in her face.

The door of the café burst open and Rupert charged out. Like a human wall, he positioned himself between Jordan and Garry.

"You doing okay here, Doc?" He put a massive hand on her shoulder.

Jordan couldn't answer. She was trembling so hard she could barely stand, and Rupert must have felt it.

His voice was soft and lethal. "Maybe you oughta get on that boat, eh, mister? It's the last one out of here today."

"Gee, I'm too late," Garry sneered. "I seem to have just missed it."

Jordan turned and looked down at the wharf and her heart sank.

Charlie Tidian was already backing the water taxi out of the dock.

Rupert put his fingers to his mouth and gave a shrill, high-pitched whistle that made Jordan jump. A man on the wharf turned around, and Rupert motioned to him, waving at the boat.

That man, in turn, put his fingers to his mouth and emitted another earsplitting whistle, and Jordan saw Billy pop his head out on deck.

The man on the dock waved his arms, pointing at Rupert.

The boat made a slow U-turn and returned to the dock.

Rupert picked up Garry's pack in one massive paw and took hold of his upper arm with the other. "C'mon, mister. Looks like Charlie's waitin' for you, so get a move on." He hustled Garry down the incline and onto the wharf. Jordan saw him toss the pack on the boat and all but throw Garry over the rail.

Shaking, she watched as the ferry chugged into the inlet and headed around the point. Down on the wharf, Rupert waved an arm at her, and she lifted her hand and waved back.

For now at least, Garry was gone. She drew in one deep, shuddering breath, and then another. The shaking eased as she walked back to the medical center, forming a plan of action. She'd call Marcy and instruct the lawyer to go ahead with the restraining order. She'd tell her to make sure Garry knew it was in place.

And then she'd find Silas, apologize and tell him everything. But first, she had patients waiting for her.

By the time she reached her apartment, she was calmer than she'd been in several hours.

Glancing into her bedroom, she stopped short, shocked and outraged. She knew immediately where Garry had found the drugs. Her medical bag was on the bed, wide open, and it was obvious the contents had been ransacked. A quick assessment revealed he'd taken her supply of morphine, Ativan, Benadryl, Tylenol 3—and even Gravol.

Disposal syringes were missing, as was her triplicate prescription pad, which meant he'd be able to write himself orders for small amounts of morphine. He'd stolen a similar pad once before and knew exactly how to fill it out and counterfeit her signature.

She didn't hesitate. She found the number for the RCMP detachment in Tofino, identified herself, and in a few succinct sentences, told the constable exactly what had occurred and what was missing from her bag.

"Garry Hughes is on the water taxi arriving soon from Ahousaht," she explained. She described him and added, "We were married, but are now separated. If you need confirmation I can supply my lawyer's number.

He's an addict and a thief, and I'm prepared to press charges."

Her voice was steady and cool, and when she hung up, she felt nothing but satisfaction. Now if only she could stay this calm and clear when she talked to Silas.

SILAS WAS OUTSIDE THE CABIN chopping wood when Eli and Michael rode up on their bikes.

"Afternoon, gentlemen." He swung the axe up and brought it down with a satisfying thunk, and the stubborn block of alder finally split in half.

"You want some lemonade?" They came frequently to talk to him, and Silas always listened, never judging or lecturing them about the gossip they innocently relayed. He filed away snippets that often helped him understand more fully when someone came to him for help.

He brought out three glasses, the bottle of lemonade and a container of oatmeal cookies a grandmother had traded for his arthritis tonic and set it all on the chopping block.

The boys were thirsty, and he refilled their glasses twice. They were making inroads on the cookies when Michael announced, "Dr. Jordan's husband came to visit her today."

Eli nodded and swallowed. "Yeah, Uncle Silas. He's not nice like Dr. Jordan is. He swore at us, he called us little bastard half-breeds."

Silas was unprepared for the onslaught of emotion those simple statements caused, on all sorts of levels.

He waited a heartbeat, struggling to stay neutral. Casually, he said, "He obviously doesn't know that you're Nuu-chah-nulth warriors."

"Right." Eli crammed in another cookie and washed it down. His voice took on a confidential note. "And anyhow, he's a junkie, that's what Mom said."

"Yeah." Michael nodded vigorously. "Junkies do drugs, we aren't ever gonna do drugs, right, Eli? Cause they make you stupid, that's what our teacher says."

"She's right about that." Silas felt the muscles in his stomach tighten. "And who was Christina saying that to, about the man being a junkie?"

"To Doctor Jordan," Eli said. "We were under the window. When he swore at us, we followed him to Doctor Jordan's place and hid, because maybe he was going to hurt Doctor Jordan and we'd have to help, right? He was real mean to her, he kept saying they were still married and she should give him medicine because he was sick, and money to get divorced."

Silas felt sick. "That was thoughtful and brave of you, to watch out for her."

Eli beamed. "Yeah, but we didn't have to help her because Mom came then, she asked Doctor Jordan if she was okay, and if she should get you."

Silas swallowed. "And what did the doctor say?"

"She hollered no, no, not to get you, that she was okay," Michael reported. "And then she sent the man to Mabel's to wait for her so she could give him money."

"But he didn't go there, not right away," Eli said. "We followed him. He walked all around town and he talked to those two guys who live in Johnny Swann's old house. They were sitting out on the porch drinking beer."

Like attracts like, Silas thought. The men were bootleggers, and probably also dealt drugs, although he had no proof of that.

"They gave him money for something," Michael said.

Silas puzzled over that one. What would a junkie be selling? Wouldn't he more likely be buying?

Eli bobbed his head. "Yeah, and then he went to Mabel's and after a while Doctor Jordan went there too, and then they had a fight outside Mabel's, right, Michael? And he threw ripped-up paper in her face, and then Big Rupert Joe, you know Big Rupert Joe, eh, Uncle Silas? Billy's father? Well, he stood up for her and he got Charlie to turn the boat back and then he took the man's arm and made him run down to the wharf, and Rupert boosted him over the side like this." Eli stood up and demonstrated.

Jordan, why didn't you tell me? "So the man's gone?"

"Yeah, he's gone back to the mainland." The two sweaty boys nodded in unison. "And Doctor Jordan went back to her house and now she's at the clinic with Mom."

When the lemonade and cookies were gone, Eli and Michael thanked Silas and took off down the trail on their bikes.

He sat on the chopping block for a long time, not

hearing the staccato drumming of the scarlet woodpecker in the old tree or the monotonous rain warning
the birds were making. He was listening to Jordan's
voice inside his head. It wasn't difficult to recall every
single thing she'd ever said about her marriage, her
words were branded on his brain.

Garry, she'd said his name was Garry. That he'd
been in an accident. That he was a weak man. She'd
never once mentioned drugs, and she'd referred to him
as her ex-husband several times. Silas remembered that
clearly. She hadn't been divorced for long enough,
she'd said. It had indicated that she was free, just as he
was, and he'd felt relieved.

So she'd outright lied about that, if the little boys had
their story straight. And if Garry was a junkie, Christina
would recognize that right away. He'd wanted money,
did that mean that Jordan was supporting him?

She'd set herself apart from the rest of them at the
healing circle by not revealing her experience with de-
spair. And she'd lied to him.

The only condition he'd set was that they be honest
with each other.

Anger and a sense of betrayal churned in his gut,
along with regret and a fierce longing for something he
was afraid to name.

He'd begun to care for her far more deeply than he
wanted to admit, even to himself.

Half-breed, her husband had called Eli and Michael.
It was what his schoolmates had called Silas, in that fancy
private academy his father had forced him to attend.

Ironically, it was also what some of the kids here in Ahousaht had also called him, when he held himself apart during the long, painful summers he spent here as a boy. It was implicit in the words his father had thrown at him in that final, awful rage when Silas told Angus he was moving to Ahousaht.

"I've given you every advantage," Angus Keefer had said in that cold, quiet voice. "You could have a brilliant academic career, you could have all this—" Angus had swept an arm around his luxuriously appointed study "—and more. You have the brains, the education, the opportunity. But I can see that you don't have what it takes to overcome your heritage. You want to take the lazy route and go native, go ahead, Silas. Just remember that if you do, you're no longer my son."

Until now, Silas had truly believed he'd grown beyond the old feelings of exclusion and rejection. He'd believed himself capable of handling any emotional challenge with calm and rationality.

The pain in his gut said otherwise.

Grandmother, help me.

He waited, but this time Sandrine didn't respond.

He needed to get away, but he'd made a commitment to Patwin. He couldn't walk away and leave his brother. But he could take him along, if only Patwin would agree to come.

Silas went into the cabin and stuffed a bare few essentials into a pack, and then he closed the door behind himself and headed into town.

His mother's house smelled as it always did, of cooking and herbs and clean laundry. Rose Marie was out, and there was no answer when Silas called for Patwin, but he had a nagging sense that his brother was there. Silas knocked on Patwin's bedroom door, and when there was no answer, he opened it.

Patwin was sprawled across the bed. He tried to raise his head, but his neck was still too stiff. Instead, he gave Silas a loopy grin and said something, but his words were garbled and slurred.

Silas was across the room in two strides, fear a claw that squeezed at his heart. He took Patwin by the shoulders and dragged him to a sitting position. He sniffed Patwin's breath. Not alcohol, so that meant—

"What did you take?" He shook his brother hard, not caring that it would hurt his bruised throat. His voice rose. "You stupid idiot, what the hell did you take?"

Patwin laughed drunkenly, and swearing, Silas let him flop back on the bed.

Frantically, Silas searched the bedside table, the dresser drawers.

Nothing. He spotted Patwin's jacket, slung over a chair, and he stuck a hand in the pocket, pulling out packaged disposable syringes and two small vials of morphine.

Rage filled Silas as he put together what Michael and Eli had said about the transaction at Johnny Swann's. Garry hadn't been buying, he'd been selling. And what he'd sold had ended up in Patwin's veins.

CHAPTER TWENTY

THE MORPHINE MUST HAVE COME from Jordan. Had she given it to her husband as a bribe, to get him to leave?

However it had gone down, the end result was that Patwin had gotten hold of it. Silas took the vials into the bathroom, broke them open and flushed them. He broke the syringes into pieces and buried them in the garbage. He went back into Patwin's room and threw a few things into a backpack he found in the closet. Wrestling his brother into his jacket, he hauled him to his feet.

"You and I are going for a long walk," he said through gritted teeth. He looped one of Patwin's arms around his shoulders, stopping on his way out long enough to scribble a note for his mother: *Gone into the bush with Patwin. Be back when we get back.*

SHIVERING IN THE SUDDEN CHILL of the setting sun, Jordan hurried along the path to Silas's cabin. The afternoon had been so busy she hadn't realized the weather was changing. The evening sky was ominously overcast, and the stiff breeze off the ocean was colder than usual.

After the call to the RCMP, she hadn't had time to think about anything except work. There'd been a baby with severe croup, an old, diabetic man with a seriously infected leg, an entire family with gastroenteritis, which Jordan suspected was from tainted meat, and then, worst of all, an eleven-year-old girl with a vaginal infection. Jordan suspected she was sexually abused. When Christina had called in the social worker, the girl was taken into custody, pending an investigation.

Now she was weary, and if it hadn't been for Christina, she'd also have been famished. The nurse had made her sit down and eat an egg sandwich.

Jordan hurried through the trees, trying to figure out what to say to Silas, how to explain what had occurred. The RCMP had called her back to say that Garry was in custody in Tofino. A search of his bag had produced her prescription pads and some of the drugs she was missing. He'd appear before a magistrate tomorrow morning.

The sound of bike tires behind her made her turn, and when Eli and Michael reached her, she smiled at them.

"Hi, Doctor Jordan." They pulled up on either side of her, pedaling so slow she marveled at their ability to balance the bikes.

"Hey, boys. Where are you off to?" Crazy question. As far as she knew the path led to only one destination.

"To Silas's house," Eli said. "He asked us to keep an eye on his place for him, so we're going to make sure the windows are all shut because there's a storm coming in."

Jordan's heart sank and she slowed and then stopped. "Where's Silas gone?"

Michael dismounted to stand beside her. "Him and Patwin went into the bush. Patwin was real sleepy, but Silas made him walk, anyway."

Jordan frowned. That didn't make sense. "When did they go?" Surely Silas would have said something this morning, if he'd been planning a trip.

Michael said, "A couple hours ago, right, Eli."

"Yeah. A couple hours now."

That could mean anything, of course, since the kids had no sense of time, which made her next question idiotic. But she asked it, anyway. "Did he say when they'd be back?"

"Nope." Eli shook his head. "They took sleeping bags, though. So maybe a couple days. Maybe even a week, eh, Michael?"

"Yeah, prob'ly a week. My dad stays a week when he goes into the bush."

"Okay." So anywhere from a day to a month. Puzzled, she turned around and started to head back on the path, her heart heavy and her feet dragging. "I was going to see Silas, but if he's not there I'll head home. Thanks, guys."

"You want us to ride back to town with you?" Michael said. "We can still get to Silas's after, it won't be dark for a while."

"No, no. I'm fine on my own, I'm not scared." Not of wild animals, not tonight.

"Yeah, that bad man who scared you is gone, right, Doctor Jordan?"

She wasn't paying attention. She was thinking of Silas, and why he'd left her without a word. "What bad—oh, Garry. Yes, he's gone." She kept forgetting that not much went on without these two knowing about it.

"Yeah, we saw Billy's father running with him down to catch the boat." They glanced at each other and snickered. "Billy's father's really strong, eh? He boosted him on board good, didn't he, Doctor Jordan?"

"He sure did."

They exchanged telling glances. "That man, he's your husband, right, Doctor Jordan?"

"Yeah. But not for long."

"And he's a junkie, right?"

Jordan stopped walking and faced them. She was careful to keep her tone curious and conversational. "Now where did you hear that?"

"Eli's mom said it. When she was talking to you, right, Eli?"

"But how did you overhear what Christina said? We were inside my house."

They looked at each other and then Eli said, "We hid outside your house, because that man called us half-breeds and we didn't like him and we didn't want him to hurt you."

Jordan was beginning to suspect what might have happened with Silas, and it made her feel sick to her stomach. "That was thoughtful of you. Did you guys happen to tell Silas what Garry and I were saying?"

"Yeah. We told him your husband was a junkie, and

he wanted money and stuff from you. We told him you were scared, but then Eli's mom came and that guy left."

"Um-hm." If they were listening at her window, Silas knew everything. He knew about Garry and the drugs. And that she'd been less than honest with him. But why wouldn't he give her a chance to explain?

She'd planned to tell him that she'd skipped the sordid details of her life because she wanted him only to know the best parts of her. She'd wanted him to see her for herself, not in the shadow of Garry and drugs and bad decisions. And she'd been afraid.

She'd learned early in life to smile and be agreeable even when she was miserable, because she was afraid that if anybody knew her real feelings, they wouldn't like her. And, as a child, that meant she'd be moved to another foster home. Helen had helped her to identify and release some of what she was feeling, but old habits died hard. She'd been less than open with Silas.

Right now Jordan felt like beating the ground with her fists. Instead, she managed a smile and a jaunty wave to the two culprits who'd just ruined her love life. It wasn't their fault.

"Bye, guys. See you later."

"Bye, Doctor Jordan." They sped off, and Jordan dragged herself back to her apartment.

Too tired and sick at heart to eat, when she went to bed she couldn't sleep. Around eleven, she swallowed a sleeping pill, and when her cell rang at midnight, she could barely drag herself out of her drugged sleep.

At first, she assumed it must be Garry. But she'd had the number changed, and the only people she'd given it to were Silas, her lawyer, Helen—and her brother. Eagerly she punched the talk button, and his familiar, dear voice spilled across the miles and into her heart.

"Hey, squirt, I bet I woke you up, sorry about that. I thought I'd just let it ring when your answering service didn't kick in."

She'd forgotten to activate it, and now she was glad she hadn't. Thank God she'd left her new number on his machine.

"You can wake me up any old time you like." Jordan sat up and shoved both pillows behind her. "How are you, Toby?" Shivering, she wrapped the quilt around her shoulders. She could hear rain beating down on the roof, and the air from the open window was damp and chilly.

"A little drunk at the moment, I'm celebrating because I finally finished that damned yacht. Got paid, too, so I blew some on a bottle of really good wine. Wish you were here to share it with me, kid."

"God, how I wish I was." Exhausted and empty and terribly lonely, her eyes filled with tears. She did her best to keep her voice steady. "So what are you going to do now?"

"Well, that's why I'm calling. I thought, if it wouldn't disrupt your life too much, I might mosey on over there and visit you for a while."

"Oh, Toby, yes, please! I'd love it if you came and stayed with me. When?"

"I'll fly to Vancouver tomorrow, and then see if I can catch a flight over to Tofino. How do I get from there to Flores Island?"

"There's a water taxi, but it only runs a couple times a day. The fastest way is the floatplane, but it's more expensive."

"Money's no object. And now that I'm filthy rich, what can I bring you from the big city?"

That was easy. "Häagen-Dazs, please. Almond-pecan. A huge tub of it—I can't get it here." And she'd never needed it more than she had tonight.

"Done. See you tomorrow, squirt. With ice cream in hand."

She hung up, feeling a little easier just knowing her brother was coming.

She worried over sleeping arrangements. The rump-sprung sofa in the living room wasn't inviting. Maybe Toby could use one of the treatment rooms while he was here. She'd check with Christina in the morning.

Then, inevitably, painfully, her thoughts turned to Silas. Where was he sleeping tonight? The rain was hammering on the roof, steady and unrelenting. It couldn't be very comfortable in a tent on a night like this.

Maybe he'd come back tomorrow, and she could talk to him. Even if he didn't understand, even if he didn't want to go on with their relationship—even if he was furious with her—at least she'd have the satisfaction of explaining herself.

Why was it so important to her? She hadn't really

known him that long. Yes, the sex was amazing, he made her feel as if she'd never really known passion before. But that was only one part of the equation. There was a maturity, a depth of character in Silas she hadn't found in other men. He was funny, playful and quirky. Kind, he was incredibly kind. Thoughtful. Puzzling— there were aspects to his healing practice she didn't begin to understand. But she loved being with him, she loved talking to him, she loved— Stillness came over her. *My God.*

Could she have fallen in love with Silas Keefer? How did a person really know if they were in love? She'd believed she loved Garry, and look where that went.

This feeling for Silas was different, though. Bigger, more profound. Frightening, as well, as if something inside her were breaking open, some deep, scarred place she hadn't even known was there.

If she was in love with Silas, she was going to have to admit it to him. Regardless of the consequences. She was still thinking about what those might be when she finally fell asleep again, lulled by the steady patter of rain on the roof.

THE BUSH WAS WET, and Silas had been listening to Patwin grouse about it for hours now.

"If this is what it means to be an Indian, I'm giving up my status," the younger man said in his new hoarse voice. "Rain's dripping down my neck, my sleeping bag's damp and every stitch of my clothes are soaked.

This stupid fire is more smoke than flame, and you didn't even bring a tent, never mind whiskey to treat hypothermia. Lucky you remembered matches, or we'd have been really screwed. Didn't you even check the weather channel before we started out? What kind of Nuu-chah-nulth warrior are you, anyhow, big brother?"

The drugs seemed to be gone from Patwin's system. Silas had half dragged him along at first, but it wasn't long before Patwin could walk on his own. When he'd seemed rational, if a bit hyper, Silas asked him about the morphine.

"Oh, shit, I'm sorry, Silas. One of the guys dropped over and sold it to me. My neck hurt so bad I really needed it."

"Johnny Swann. Did he say where he got it?"

"No idea."

"Why did you take it, Patwin? After everybody at the healing ceremony told you they'd do anything to help, you turn around and take morphine?"

"I'm sorry, Silas. I told you, my throat hurt like fire, I just wanted the pain gone. And the doc gave me morphine anyhow, I figured a little more wouldn't hurt."

Silas was too angry and sick at heart to pursue the matter at that moment, so they just kept walking.

Patwin finally asked, "Where the hell we going, anyways?"

"To the old fishing camp."

"I don't wanna go fishing. I hate fishing. Dad used to take me out on fishing trips, I always hated it."

"At least Peter taught you a little about living in the

bush," Silas said. "The only survival training I got was in making panty raids on the girl's dorm without getting caught."

"Lucky you." Patwin wasn't interested. "Why the hell didn't you bring rain slickers, Silas?"

"Too heavy to pack." He hadn't thought of it. He'd been thinking of Jordan instead. "The garbage bags were a good idea."

They wore black plastic bags like tunics in an attempt to keep at least a little dry in the downpour, and they'd made a makeshift shelter out of branches. But it wasn't doing much good, not the way the rain was pelting down.

"Can we go home in the morning?" Patwin whined. "*Please?* I promise, if I live through this I'll never try to off myself again. And I won't do drugs anymore, you've got my word on it." Patwin shivered, yawned and took a sip from a tin cup, and then spat the mouthful out. "Shit. That's the worst coffee I've ever tasted, and the detention center had some pretty bad sludge."

"You mean that? About not doing suicide or drugs again?"

Patwin didn't answer for a moment, but then he nodded. "Yeah, I do mean it, so you can tell Dad and the rest of the family to call off the twenty-four-hour watch, because it's making me nuts. I wake up at three in the morning and Mom's sitting beside my bed staring at me, for cripes' sake. It's freaking me out." He was quiet for a while, and then in a diffcrent tone he said, "I talked with Mary yesterday. I told her I'd do my best for the baby, whether or not we end up together. It's not the kid's fault we aren't ready for it."

Silas nodded. "Good. How did Mary feel about that?"

"I dunno. She didn't say much. She's still got this cockeyed idea that the baby will help her batty mother get over her brother dying. She says you helped her, though."

Silas shifted uncomfortably, trying to find a spot where the rain wouldn't drop down his neck. He wished it would stop raining. He wished that Patwin would go to sleep so he could have the remainder of the night in peace. Wouldn't you think that with a sore throat the kid would let up on his vocal cords? But no.

Silas had struggled all afternoon and evening to stay even-tempered through the barrage of complaints and comments, but it was a strain. He had an overwhelming urge to snap at Patwin, to tell him for God's sake to shut up for a while so he could think.

Funny he'd never noticed how much Patwin talked before. Was it because no one really listened to him? He'd always been the baby of the family, spoiled and pampered but not really taken seriously.

"Want some jerky?" Patwin dug in the food pack and pulled out a strip. "The stuff tastes like shit, you've gotta be really hard up to chew on it. I dunno why you didn't bring some real food, chips and cheesies and maybe chocolate bars—or peanuts."

Silas sighed. They'd been over that several times already. He'd grabbed whatever was at hand because all he'd wanted to do was get far away from the village. Well, they'd done that, all right. If they hadn't gone so far, he'd have headed back when the heavy rain started. He wasn't enjoying being wet, either.

Silas stuck another piece of wood on the fire. It didn't burn any better than the others had, and he coughed as the thick smoke drifted his way.

"So you got something good going with the doc, Silas? I heard Mom say you two were an item."

"The old Ahousaht radar," Silas growled. As if he needed any reminder that it was alive and well. "We're friends." *Or we were.* He got that peculiar sinking feeling in his gut every time he thought of Jordan—and her husband. And what the kids had said about him being a junkie. And all the things she hadn't told him.

"How come you never got married or had any kids, Silas?"

"I don't really know. I'm a loner, I suppose." It was a question he'd asked himself plenty of times.

"What happened with that nurse, that Melinda Paul? You were pretty tight with her, weren't you? How come you didn't marry her?"

Patwin was probably trying to work out his own relationship with Mary, but this personal probing was maddening.

"I cared about Melinda, but marriage wasn't in the cards. Her family was from Edmonton, and that's where she wanted to live. Geographical differences."

It was a simplistic explanation. Melinda would probably have stayed in Ahousaht if he'd agreed to get married the way she wanted. He just couldn't do it.

"Guess you didn't love her, eh?"

Silas started to say that he *had* loved Melinda, but stopped. This love thing had different levels, just like healing.

"How about Doc Jordan? You in love with her?"

"No." Silas closed his eyes, wondering why the question made his chest hurt. It was over with Jordan, but he wasn't about to tell Patwin that.

He rubbed a hand across his heart and the plastic bag crackled.

"You think it's better for a guy to have lots of women, or stick to just one like Dad did with Mom?"

Silas knew that Rose Marie had been Peter's first and only love, because his stepfather had told him so one afternoon when they were roofing Silas's cabin. He'd loved Rose Marie before she'd married Angus Keefer and he'd waited for her. He had still been there waiting for her when she'd come back, sick and desolate, after her marriage had ended. Peter had brought her a little gift every day—flowers, bird feathers, unusual stones—encouraging her in every way he could devise to get well again.

"One woman," Silas said at last. "Grandmother used to call it finding the other half of yourself. But nowadays it doesn't happen too often."

"How do you really know when you're in love that way?"

"You're asking me? I don't know." But Silas thought

of making love to Jordan, laughing with her at the hot springs, carrying her home when she'd hurt herself.

Patwin said in a plaintive tone, "I wish sometimes that we could just live like they did in the old days, before television and big stores and motorboats and all that. It was easier then, I think."

"It's never been easy. Sandrine's stories prove that."

"Remember the one she used to tell about the gray wolf pups that came to our island?"

"Making friends with First Woman, yes."

Patwin sounded a little embarrassed. "Tell me the story of how they became her children, okay, Silas?"

"In the beginning, there was a male and female gray wolf. One spring, after a long, cold winter—"

Silas's voice took on the rhythmic cadence of the storyteller. Before long, he could hear Patwin's breathing grow even and slow. Soon, the younger man was asleep, curled inside his sleeping bag.

With great gratitude, Silas let his voice trail off into silence. There weren't many hours of darkness left, and he needed this quiet to try to make order out of his thoughts. He had to figure out why he felt so angry and betrayed by Jordan, and was still so drawn to her.

CHAPTER TWENTY-ONE

JUST BEFORE 7:00 a.m. the following morning, Elsie Hays, an elderly diabetic, collapsed while mixing up a batch of bread. Her daughter-in-law came running to get Jordan, who'd just stepped out of the shower.

Throwing on sweats and racing through the driving rain to Elsie's house, Jordan found her patient unconscious; face, hair, arms and chest covered in sticky white dough. Taking a blood glucose test, Jordan confirmed that Elsie was in a diabetic coma and used an IV injection of glucose to revive her, getting sticky dough all over herself in the process.

She then spent a frustrating hour trying to convince Elsie that she had to pay more attention to her disease and use a Glucometer regularly to check her blood sugar.

"I can't be bothered with all that hocus-pocus," Elsie snorted. "I got work to do, that whole batch of bread is ruined now. And if I'm gonna die, I'll die making bread, the hell with it."

Frustrated, Jordan trudged back to the clinic and found four young men anxiously waiting for her.

Swollen, dirty and badly bruised, they were all in high spirits, laughing and joking about the fight they'd had the night before.

Jordan treated them for cuts, abrasions, broken ribs, one broken nose and a fractured jaw, and they explained that they'd gotten drunk and started fighting over the outcome of a televised football game. They'd fought themselves to a standstill, collapsed on the floor to sleep it off and awakened this morning barely able to move.

"We have to get to work this morning in Tofino— we're building a house," one of them told her cheerfully.

Wondering how anyone could work with the injuries they had, she patched them up and sent them on their way in time to catch the water taxi.

They were no sooner out the door than a frantic mother arrived with a three-year-old who'd just swallowed a bottle of baby aspirin. Fortunately, the obliging little girl was willing to also swallow a dose of syrup of ipecac, and the explosive vomiting that followed accounted for all the pills. It also meant that both Christina, who'd just come to work, and Jordan, who'd already changed clothes once that morning, had to change again. The treatment room reeked of vomit.

"Mom just called, Silas and Patwin got home a while ago," Christina announced as she and Jordan snatched a cup of tea and a sandwich for lunch.

"Mom says they look like drowned rats," Christina went on. "And Patwin says he'll never go into the bush again, with Silas or anyone else. Apparently Patwin used up all the hot water showering, ate four eggs and half a pound of bacon, and then went to bed. Silas headed home, Mom said, as cranky as a bear after hibernation."

Jordan had hoped to take an hour off that afternoon and track Silas down, but now she revised that plan. Better to wait until he was rested and more receptive to what she had to say.

Christina munched on ham and cheese. "What time do you figure your brother might get here?"

It was good to have something to look forward to besides explaining herself to Silas. "Late afternoon, I think. He's got to make connections from Vancouver."

"Well, it would be nice if things slowed down a little before he got here. What a crazy morning."

But the afternoon wasn't much better. Jordan treated twin screaming babies with earaches, a young woman with a broken toe and a stoic logger who'd severed his finger and brought it in with him to be reattached. Through it all, Jordan kept expecting Toby to walk through the clinic door. When she finally looked at her watch, she was stunned to see that it was after five.

"That's it, there's no one else waiting. I'm going home," Christina said with a relieved sigh. "You gonna go down to the wharf and wait for the floatplane?"

"I think I might. Why don't you drop over later this evening and meet Toby? He's cute, single and he told me he's got some money."

Christina grinned and her lovely dark eyes sparkled. "What more could a girl want? I'll wear my best jeans."

Jordan washed up and pulled on a hooded slicker. Outside, it was still raining, but it had slowed down. The air smelled fresh, and because it was supper time, there was no one out except her. She ambled down to the dock where the floatplane would land, and leaned against the piling, trying to formulate what to say to Silas when the opportunity arrived.

All she could do was apologize and tell him the truth.

Within ten minutes, she heard the plane approaching. Her heart started to hammer with anticipation when it landed and taxied to the dock. The door opened, and for a moment she didn't recognize the emaciated man who stepped out.

"Toby?" She couldn't control the shock in her voice. Recovering quickly, she ran toward him. "Toby, what's happened? What's wrong with you?"

"Hey, squirt, good to see you, too." He was limping as he took the last two steps to her and grabbed her in his arms, and she could sense that he was in pain. The bones in his narrow face, a masculine version of her own, stood out in sharp relief. His eyes were sunken, with deep hollows carved beneath them, and he looked years older than thirty-four.

"Tore a muscle in my leg, you know what that's like. But I brought the ice cream you wanted; it's in that insulated box," he said with a grin.

Only his smile had remained the same.

Jordan's gut twisted with fear, and she bit back the questions on the tip of her tongue.

"You grab that box, and I'll bring my bag, okay?"

Jordan took the box, shooting a horrified sidelong glance at Toby. She was stunned by his appearance. "We have to walk a ways, up the hill and along there." She pointed and hesitated. "Will you be able—?"

"Sure, I'll take it slow. Besides, I travel light." He shouldered his bag and looked around. "So this is where you're hiding out from the world, huh? Looks wild and wonderful, lots of boats, surrounded by ocean… Just my kind of place."

Jordan understood. He didn't want her asking questions. So she bit them back for now, adjusted her stride to his painfully slow one and chatted about the village as they slowly made their way to her apartment. And every step of the way, her apprehension grew.

She opened her door and welcoming waves of heat met them. Someone had come by and lit the stove. They'd also delivered homemade pizza. It smelled delicious.

"You've got a pizza place here?" Toby dropped his bag and went over to the counter. His voice took on a reverent tone. "Great Scott, they also deliver homemade apple pie?"

Tears came to Jordan's eyes. Nobody but Superman and Toby would ever say *Great Scott*. It brought back childhood memories. And she'd bet it was Rose Marie who'd brought the food and lit the stove, knowing that her brother was coming and that Jordan wouldn't have had time to cook.

"No pizza delivery, but I have good, generous friends

who are also fantastic cooks," she explained, forcing cheer into her voice. "Take off your jacket, sit down at the table and we'll eat."

"I brought wine." He dug in his bag and produced a bottle of white and another of red. "The guy in the liquor store said these were excellent little vintages with a delightful bouquet, not that I'd know one kind of plonk from another."

"Me, neither, I don't even have any wineglasses. These will have to do." She produced two mismatched juice glasses, and he made a ceremony out of opening a bottle and pouring.

The pizza was ambrosia, loaded with cheese and roasted vegetables. In spite of her concern about him, Jordan was hungry, and she wolfed down several slices, noting that Toby kept up with her. At least he still had something resembling an appetite.

He kept up a steady stream of conversation, describing the small yacht he'd just finished, making her smile with wicked descriptions of the nasty man who'd commissioned it.

She got up to put coffee on and cut two healthy slices of pie.

"We'll have some of my ice cream with it," she declared, opening the insulated container. "And then I'll have to put it in the big fridge in the medical center, because it won't fit in mine."

It took self-restraint, but she managed to wait until the pie was eaten before she asked. She'd refilled their coffee cups and sat facing him across the round table.

He was recounting some sailing story when Jordan reached across and touched his arm.

"Enough already with the diversions. Toby, level with me. What the *hell* is wrong with you?"

He gave her a wry smile. "Spoken like a medical professional. Guess it was crazy of me to think you might not notice."

"Not *notice*? How could I not notice?" Her voice rose, edged with panic. "You're in pain, you're limping, you've lost about thirty pounds. Oh, Toby, why didn't you tell me you were this sick?"

He wouldn't look at her. "Didn't want to worry you, I guess." He gave a hopeless shrug. "And once I got diagnosed, there was nothing to be done, anyway."

Terror gripped her. "What do you mean? There's always something. Who did you see, I'll get you a referral—" She stopped abruptly to take a deep breath. "Okay, Tobe. Start at the beginning and don't leave anything out."

"It started over a year ago," he said with resigned sigh. "Joints aching, tired all the time, no appetite."

Jordan remembered passing comments he'd made, but she'd never suspected anything serious.

"I went to the doctor, and he said I had a flu that was going around. But then I started losing sensation in my hands, and the pain got so bad I finally went back. This time he ran some tests, and sent me to a specialist who ran more tests. I've had so many needles stuck in me it's a wonder I'm not leaking." He tried for a grin but missed.

"And? What were the results?"

"Side effects from neurotoxins in the chemicals I use for boatbuilding." His tone was ultracasual. "The kind of boats I build, you have to use fiberglass and other compounds. I just wasn't ever very careful. They've done some damage to my central nervous system."

Neurotoxins. Cold horror started in Jordan's belly and moved upward to her heart. *Central nervous system damage.* There was no known antidote for that condition. "Were the blood tests conclusive?"

"Apparently. I saw several specialists, and they all agreed. They suggested a good balanced diet and heavy doses of B vitamins, and told me to quit my day job. One came right out and said that what I had wasn't curable at this time. And when I forced it out of him, he didn't hold out much hope that I'd make old bones."

"We'll see about that. I'll run my own tests in the morning. I know the lab guys at St. Joe's, they'll work them up right away as a favor." Jordan thought that the dinner she'd just eaten was going to come back up. It was inconceivable that her brother was terminally ill.

"More needles?" Toby groaned and shook his head. "I'd rather not, I doubt I've got enough blood left as it is. You guys and Dracula have a lot in common, know that? Besides, they were pretty certain that's what the problem was, why go through it all again?"

"Because I'm stubborn and I never rely on any diagnosis but my own." That wasn't entirely true, but she wasn't about to accept what amounted to a death sentence, not when it came to her brother.

"I dunno, Jordan—"

Hearing a knock at the door, Jordan opened it to let Christina in.

"It's still pouring out there," she said, shucking off her jacket and shaking rain from her thick mop of black hair. "Hey, you are cute," she said with a killer smile, extending her hand to Toby. "Can't always trust sisters, they tend to exaggerate. I'm Christina Crow, Jordan's right-hand nurse."

"And best friend," Jordan added, realizing after she'd said it that it was true. Christina had become closer to her than any woman ever had. "Meet my big brother, Toby Burke." It took effort to sound lighthearted. It took effort to keep from throwing herself on the floor and screaming at the injustice of life.

With some difficulty, Toby got to his feet and shook Christina's hand. "Great to meet you. Nice to know someone's taking care of my baby sister."

Christina laughed. "You've got that ass-backwards. She's the one taking care of us."

Jordan knew that Christina must recognize the signs of serious illness in her brother, but the other woman was far too professional to show it.

"Jordan says you're a master boatbuilder. When my kid brother Patwin finds that out, he's gonna be dogging your heels and driving you nuts asking questions."

"There's nothing I love more than talking about myself and what I do," Toby said with a grin. "Doesn't everybody?"

Jordan poured wine for Christina, who sipped it and

whistled in appreciation. "Wow. That's Opus One, a Robert Mondavi Bordeaux, right?"

Toby tilted the bottle and read the label. He whistled. "How the heck did you know that?"

Christina smirked, pleased with herself. "When I was in university, a group of us decided to become wine snobs. I did my homework."

"Well, I'm impressed," Jordan said.

"So am I," echoed Toby, but from the bemused expression on his face as he looked at Christina, Jordan thought his reasons were vastly different than hers. When she asked if it was all right if Toby used one of the examining rooms to sleep in, Christina jumped to make up the bed for him while Jordan put on another pot of coffee.

The three of them talked past midnight. Hauling photos out of his pack, Toby showed them the boats he'd built, some of them in exotic locations like Hawaii and Thailand.

Jordan looked at the sleek, shiny yachts and wanted to rip the pictures up. These rich-man toys were the reason her brother was sick.

Toby held up a single grainy black-and-white snapshot mixed in the bunch, of Toby and Jordan at about four and two, holding their mother's hands in front of an old Ford.

"Dad's first car," he said. The hand holding the photo was trembling, but Jordan tried not to notice. She studied the photo.

"God, Mom was so beautiful, I didn't know you had

this. Can I have a copy of it? I only have two pictures of Mom." And one was her parents' wedding photo, which was pretty much destroyed. When Jordan was a teen, she'd used nail scissors and carefully eradicated her father from the picture.

"You look exactly like her," Christina said, peering over Jordan's shoulder. "Same gorgeous bones, aristocratic nose, sexy mouth."

"We've both got Dad's blue eyes, though," Toby said. "Mom's were hazel, if I remember right."

"I know your mother died really young," Christina said. "What about your dad?"

There was an awkward silence.

"Dad's still alive," Toby finally said. "He's not doing too well, though. He's in a care facility in Vancouver."

"Sorry, I just assumed—" Christina glanced at Jordan's shuttered expression. She got up and grabbed her jacket from the peg by the door.

"It's time I headed home, got to get to work in the morning. My boss is a stickler for being on time."

"The old bag will probably be late herself," Jordan said. The last thing she wanted to think about tonight was Mike Burke.

After Christina left, Jordan opened the connecting door to the clinic and showed Toby where he'd be sleeping.

"Unless we have a major emergency, we won't be using the room," she assured him. "So sleep as late as you like, we'll try to keep the noise level to a minimum."

"I can't seem to manage more than three or four hours at a stretch these nights, so don't worry about me." Toby wrapped his arms around her, pressing his lips to her hair. "Thanks, squirt. I feel at home already."

Loving the feel of his arms around her, Jordan hugged him back hard. His ribs made her feel as though she were hugging a skeleton. Appalled, the fear she'd tried to subdue came rushing to the surface.

"How long can you stay, Toby?" She hadn't dared ask until now.

"No set time limit," he said with a shuddering sigh. "I'm afraid I don't feel up to working at the moment, and even if I did, I'd have to find another kind of job. My days as a boatbuilder are over. But the good news is I've invested my money, so I can afford to retire young."

He'd kept his voice steady, but Jordan could sense the desperation and sadness that underlined the words. "I can't think of a better gift than having you around for a very long while. You need time to just relax and heal, Toby."

"I dunno, squirt." He drew back, not meeting her eyes. "Maybe I'm not going to get over this." He gave a ghost of a laugh. "You know, I'm glad I didn't get married or have kids. It's easier to die when nobody's depending on you."

His words tore Jordan apart. "Don't you dare talk about dying." Her voice was fierce and furious. "I'll murder you myself if I hear you say anything like that again."

"Okay, Doc." He grinned and bumped her chin gently with his fist. "See you in the morning."

Jordan went back to her own bedroom, certain she wouldn't sleep. For an hour, she went over everything she knew about neurotoxic poisoning, which wasn't very much. She'd only seen two cases at St. Joe's. Both men had been admitted, and later died. But Toby would survive. He *had* to survive. She'd find a way, medical science *must* have developed something to treat the condition by now.

Toby's going to get over this. He's going to be fine. She repeated it over and over in a sort of mantra until at last, worn out, she fell asleep.

SHE OVERSLEPT THE NEXT morning. When she finally stumbled into the kitchen, Toby had the woodstove going and a pot of coffee almost ready. There were eggs in the black iron frying pan, and bread sliced for toast.

"I lived in a shack in Mexico once and learned how to cook on stoves like this," he announced proudly, pouring Jordan a mug of coffee. "How do you want your eggs?"

She thought of the blood tests she wanted to take. "Have you had coffee yet? Or any food?"

"Not yet."

"Good. Come into the clinic with me, and I'll draw blood for those tests." Most doctors weren't good at that particular procedure, but she'd improved her technique with the help of a tech at St. Joe's. He'd been an addict himself, and he was an expert.

"Ah, Jordan, I wish you'd just skip this. We already know what it is." Muttering under his breath, he followed her, averting his eyes as she expertly poked him and filled vials with his dark blood.

"Done," she announced after a few moments.

"Don't drink it all at once," he growled as she carefully labeled the vials and then took him back to her apartment.

"Did you sleep at all, Toby?" There were dark shadows under his eyes, and in the morning light he looked gray and fragile.

"As much as I ever do. I got up around five when it stopped raining. Two little guys, Michael and Eli, came by just after six. Neat kids. They brought some kindling for the stove and that loaf of fresh bread, and they offered to give me a guided tour of the village."

"Eli is Christina's son."

Jordan saw the expression on his face change and added, "She's a single mom. She and Eli live with her mom and dad."

"She's doing a great job, he's a nice kid."

Jordan swallowed the coffee he'd poured and sighed with pleasure. "They're both great kids. They bring me kindling to light this monster of a stove. I buy fresh bread from Michael's mother, and they run errands whenever I need them." She thought of them outside the window, making sure Garry wasn't going to turn violent, and had to swallow hard. "They're sweet and thoughtful, and what they don't know isn't worth knowing. They have ears like small elephants."

"Apparently. They asked me if I knew the bad man called Garry who was here the other day visiting you. They said he was a junkie. Is that true, Jordan?"

"Yes, it is. He turned up without any warning." She should have known that absolutely nothing stayed secret around here. *And haven't I learned that secrets are dangerous?*

"He won't be back," she added. "He's in a jail cell in Tofino. He ransacked my medical bag and stole drugs and prescription pads. I had him arrested when he got off the water taxi."

"Too bad I didn't get here a little sooner." Toby clenched his teeth, his voice cold.

Jordan looked at her frail brother and was endlessly grateful he hadn't been there. Toby's spirit might be that of a mountain lion, but he wasn't strong physically.

"You didn't tell me about the drugs, squirt."

"No. I—I didn't tell anyone for a long time. I was ashamed. I guess I felt that in some way it was my fault. It started with that accident he had."

She outlined the sequence of events, holding nothing back, not even the breakdown she'd had, or her short stay on the psych ward. Talking about it was cathartic, and she wondered again why she hadn't been just as honest with Silas.

"I kept thinking he'd get over it. I guess doctors are the worst at facing up to sickness when it's someone they love."

Oh, God. Toby.

For a moment she could hardly get her breath.

Toby took her hand. "Are you legally free of him now?"

"Not quite. He's been stonewalling, but this latest prank will give my lawyer leverage. I can't wait for the divorce to go through. I made such a bad mistake, marrying him." She expected Toby to agree.

Instead, he shook his head. "I think whatever happens, happens for a reason," he said slowly. "When I look back on everything, I can see how much I learned from it, even the time I spent in jail. It was all an opportunity."

Aghast, she stared at him. "You can't really believe that. What about your health, Toby? How can this possibly be an opportunity?"

He shrugged. "Maybe it's time for me to make a change. I had this girlfriend in Mexico, she made me think about a lot of stuff like that."

"How come you broke up with her?"

"I have this problem with commitment. At least, that's what she claimed when she walked out." He poured more coffee. "You think you'll ever get married again, Jordan?"

"Not likely." But for some reason, Silas popped into her head, which was ridiculous. "There's a theory that people attract what's familiar to them, and for me that's obviously guys with substance abuse problems, like Garry."

"Because of Dad." Toby stirred sugar into his cup.

"Because of Dad."

"Well, he doesn't drink at all anymore, hasn't for

quite a while." Toby's voice became urgent. "Take a couple days off and come with me to Vancouver, Jordan. I talked to the doctor at the nursing home, he says Dad's liver is shot and his kidneys are failing. It might be the last time we get to see him."

She didn't even have to think about it. "I've got nothing to say to him. He *abandoned* us, Toby. You're a better person than I am, forgiving him for that."

"It's easier than holding on to bad feelings, squirt. I just don't have the energy."

She didn't want to hear any more about Mike. "Are you going to make me those eggs you promised? Because you won't like the way they turn out when I fry them. Christina's mom has been trying her best to teach me how to cook but it looks like a lost cause."

"Christina's a babe." He broke eggs into the pan and added salt and pepper. "Can she cook?"

"Absolutely. Everybody around here can. Except me."

"I think I'll ask her to marry me."

"I'll tell her you said that."

"Maybe hold off a day or so, I don't want to seem too eager."

Relieved that she'd gotten him away from talking about Mike, Jordan popped bread into the toaster.

He set her plate of eggs on the table, and Jordan noticed that he had to use both hands to keep from dropping it. Sitting across from her, his hand shook violently as he tried to get eggs into his mouth. He finally set the fork down and with some difficulty, got to his feet. "I think I'll find my guides and do the tourist thing. See you later, Jordan." He grabbed his jacket and fumbled his way into it.

Watching him limp out the door, Jordan lost her appetite. She scraped the remains of their food into the garbage.

The blood she'd drawn that morning would determine whether or not she needed to worry. Until the results came back, she'd try her best to put her fears on hold.

CHAPTER TWENTY-TWO

"So there's no real treatment that you know about?" Christina was putting the vials of Toby's blood into special protective containers and then sealing them into a Purolator express envelope. Louie would take them to the dispatch office in Tofino, and they'd be in the lab at St. Joe's by that afternoon.

"No. All I'm hoping is that the diagnosis the other doctors made left some room for doubt." Jordan had been struggling to stay optimistic, but it was difficult.

"When will you get the results?"

"Maybe tomorrow. The head tech, Beryl Frazier, is a friend of mine—she'll work them up fast. I gave her my cell number and asked her to call the moment she knows."

"I really hope those other guys were wrong. I like your brother a lot."

"God, so do I," Jordan sighed. "On both counts."

Christina waited a beat and then said, "Speaking of brothers, what's up with you and Silas? Things seemed to be going like hotcakes. But when he came by the house this morning to talk to Patwin and I told him Toby was visiting, Silas got his wooden-totem-pole look. He'll never tell me, so what's up?"

The old Jordan might not have told, either. The new, revised edition stopped the chart work and took a deep breath.

"As far as I can tell, he'd avoiding me like I've got the Ebola virus. And this is what I did to earn it," she said, and told Christina in detail, not sparing herself. "He hasn't spoken to me since Garry was here, when Eli and Michael spilled the beans."

"Damn that kid of mine. I should have sent him to summer camp rather than let him run wild around here with Michael."

"Don't shoot the messenger. It was my fault, not theirs."

"Silas is obviously being a bonehead about this," Christina said. "So you didn't tell him the entire truth the moment you two met, and you were a little generous with the facts about your divorce. Nobody's perfect, not even my sainted bro."

"Yes—that environmental thing with the toilet."

"Yeah, that scares the hell out of me, too," Christina agreed. "No water, his toilet freaks me out, how can that possibly work? But seriously. In my opinion, the guy has major issues with abandonment, which makes him one of those modern breed of guys who can't seem to commit. Notice how well I picked up on the jargon in that course I took on psych nursing?"

"I'm more impressed with the wine thing." Jordan thought over what Christina had just said. "So let me get this straight, you don't think it's my lying to him that's at the root of this awful silence?"

Christina shook her head. "Nope. Think about it. Silas was only a baby when Mom left him. How was he to know she loved him and wanted him? It took her years to get that asshole of a Keefer to agree to visiting rights. By then, Silas must have felt she didn't care. And then when he did start coming here, we gave him a rough time because he was so different. And Keefer never remarried, so there was no home life there, for sure. He lived in some mausoleum with only hired help for company, and get this, his dad packed Silas off to boarding school when he was five, even though Keefer was living only a couple of miles away from the place. Then when Silas decided to come and live here, Keefer excommunicated him. Abandonment in spades, honey."

"And you know this—how?"

Christina gave her a baffled look. "Silas told Sandrine, Sandrine told Mom, and Mom told me, of course."

"Of course," Jordan said in a weak voice. The Canadian military could benefit from studying communication systems in Ahousaht. "I really have to talk to him. The longer I put it off, the harder it gets."

"So go right now. You're clear for a couple hours."

Jordan hesitated. "I wanted to get these charts—"

"Go. They'll wait. Stop procrastinating."

Jordan went. The woods were wet and heavy with the recent rain. She hadn't thought to bring an umbrella or a hat, and water dripped onto her hair and trickled under her collar. But the air was warm, so the atmosphere felt almost tropical.

As she walked along the now familiar trail, she thought about Christina's abandonment observations. They'd made her feel uncomfortable, because they applied to her and Toby just as much as Silas. They'd each chosen different ways of dealing with the fear, but it was a common thread, all right. Trust Christina to pinpoint it.

When she reached the cabin and Silas answered her hesitant knock, she realized by the closed expression on his face that this was going to be even more difficult than she'd anticipated. Her heart sank.

"Hello, Jordan. Come in." He stood aside as she slipped past him. He didn't ask her to sit, so she turned to face him.

She'd planned a dozen different openers. Taking a deep breath, she scrapped them all for the most direct approach.

"Silas, you know about Garry coming here to see me."

"Michael and Eli filled me in."

"Well. I should have told you more about him, I'm really sorry I didn't. I should have been up-front about the fact that he's an addict and that we haven't been separated very long. We're not divorced, but I'm working on it. Or rather, my lawyer is."

His eyes pinned her, cold and green. "Why didn't you tell me?"

"I—I was ashamed." Her heart was thundering and her palms were wet. It was hard to admit how she felt.

"I didn't want you to know how dumb I'd been. See, I—I supplied Garry for a while with morphine. I feel really stupid about having done it. I believed him when he said he was still in pain." She described the horrible night when Garry had overdosed and shown up in the E.R. "That's when I had a breakdown and checked myself into the psych ward. A psychiatrist helped me face up to the fact that I couldn't do anything for him and that I didn't love him. But I should have smartened up a lot faster than I did, and I feel like an idiot about that."

Instead of disagreeing, Silas nodded, which Jordan didn't think was a good sign at all. And then it got worse. In a voice cold enough to freeze her heart, he said, "So you gave him morphine again when he came here?"

Jordan felt as if he'd struck her. "*No.* I did not, absolutely not." She took a breath to explain what had happened, but he beat her to it.

"Then where did he get the vials he sold to Johnny Swann?"

"Johnny Swann?" She couldn't stand up anymore. She sank onto the sofa. "I didn't know about that. Garry stole all the drugs out of my medical bag before he left. I didn't know he'd sold any, but it makes sense. When the RCMP picked him up in Tofino, some of the morphine was missing. I just assumed he'd used it himself."

Silas shook his head. "No. Your *husband* sold it to Swann who then sold it to Patwin. And he used it." He told her about finding Patwin high, and finding the morphine and syringes. "No one knows about it, and Patwin doesn't want anyone to know. I gave him my word."

"I won't tell anyone." Shock made her feel sick. "Oh, Silas. I'm so sorry, I didn't know. Is he—is Patwin okay?" This went much deeper than she'd thought. He must have felt totally betrayed by her.

"He's okay. I walked him until the stuff wore off. He says he's ashamed and won't do it again. Which, of course, he's said plenty of times before."

There was cynicism in his voice she hadn't heard before.

"And—and you blame me for what Garry did. You actually thought I'd given him the morphine. Why didn't you come and talk to me about it? Or were you planning to just avoid me for the rest of the year?"

Silas shook his head. "I don't blame you for what anyone else did. And I'm not avoiding you. I just need some time to think, Jordan."

"That sounds like don't call me, I'll call you." She was getting really mad at him now. It helped her not to feel hurt. "So what happened with us was the equivalent of a one-night stand, and now you'd rather pretend it didn't happen at all."

"What we had was good, Jordan, I'm not denying that. But it was pretty much based on fantasy, wouldn't you say?"

"No, I wouldn't say that. Sure, I made a serious mistake not telling you about Garry, but I've apologized for it. Didn't you tell me that communication is the basis for your healing practice?"

"Yes, but you're not my patient."

"So what am I, then?" She lost her temper. "Just

somebody who was convenient and willing when you needed a roll in the hay?" And wasn't that pretty much how she'd viewed it, as well? She knew she was being unreasonable. She knew she wasn't helping things by pushing him, but she couldn't stop herself. He was dumping her, and it hurt. She wanted to hurt him back. She wanted to dump him first.

"Jordan, you know that's not true. You're jumping to conclusions. Let's just give ourselves a little time."

"There's no point, because this is *so* over." She turned and headed for the door, even more furious—and hurt—because he didn't make a move to stop her. "Goodbye, Silas. It's lucky we didn't let this go any further, at least neither of us had much invested." She stormed out, slamming the door behind her, not caring that it was a childish thing to do.

Helen had told her that she needed to get in touch with her emotions, figure out how she felt about things rather than what she thought.

Well, Jordan fumed as she stomped along the path back to the village, she'd sure as hell mastered that little exercise. She was a sad, sorry bundle of feelings at the moment, with not a rational thought in her head.

She was sick with worry about Toby, heartsore and furious over Silas, disgusted with Garry.

Men. The world would be a simpler place if there were only women in it.

FOR THE REST OF THAT DAY, anger buoyed her up. The clinic was busy, and then Toby invited Christina and

Jordan out for dinner to Mabel's, which meant there was no privacy to talk to Christina about the disastrous meeting with Silas.

Jordan managed to hold her center until the call about Toby's blood tests came early the following morning.

When the phone rang, she was alone in the clinic, again working on charts, and as Beryl read out the results to her, Jordan had to struggle to maintain control. The blood work was a veritable death sentence.

The levels of toxins in Toby's system were even worse than she'd feared.

Shaking, Jordan managed to thank Beryl and hang up the phone. She was grateful that Toby had gone out fishing with Michael's father early that morning. She'd be able to pull herself together by the time he got back, she told herself, and they could talk about treatment.

Treatment? Jordan smashed both fists down on the table. Who was she kidding? There wasn't any treatment. The only alternative therapy she'd heard of was chelation therapy, an IV procedure that claimed to improve circulation and remove harmful toxins from the blood. Jordan hadn't found any conclusive scientific studies that proved it worked on neurotoxic poisoning.

Which left diet and B vitamins, a pitiful arsenal that might prolong her brother's life by a few weeks or months, but she couldn't make herself believe they'd affect the inevitable outcome.

The clinic door opened and Christina came breezing in. She set a small bag on the desk. "This is rose-hip tea, concentrated vitamin C, for strengthening the immune system. I thought it might be good for Toby. Brew it up and add honey, it's pretty bitter without it."

Jordan was staring at the charts like a zombie. Toby was her only family. If she lost him, she didn't know how she could survive.

"Hey, earth to Jordan. What's up?"

Jordan looked up at her friend. In a shaky voice, she said, "They just phoned me about Toby's blood tests." She cleared her throat and gave Christina a fast, concise rundown.

The other woman pulled a chair over and sat down hard. "Shit. That's some bad news, eh?"

"Really bad."

"You know, I've been thinking about it, and maybe Silas could help."

Jordan felt Silas wouldn't help her across the road at the moment, but she didn't say so. She raised an eyebrow and waited.

"Mom had a rare blood disease before I was born— TTP. Sandrine cured her."

Jordan nodded. "He told me about that. He said it convinced him he should study native healing."

"Yeah, well, if Sandrine knew how to heal Mom, and Silas learned from her, maybe there's a chance he can help Toby."

Jordan thought about it. "I'd try anything, and I'm pretty sure Toby would, too. The problem is, Silas and I aren't speaking at the moment."

"He's so damned stubborn," Christina groaned. "But he'll get over it. Just give him time."

"No." Jordan shook her head. "We had a couple dates, but that's as far as it goes."

Christina frowned. "I thought you two were good together. I'm sorry it didn't work out."

"Me, too. Do you think he'll refuse to treat Toby? He's pretty mad at me."

"Silas is a healer. Being mad at you won't matter. When it comes to healing, there's no personal baggage involved. And anyway, you don't have to even talk to him about it. Toby has to go to Silas himself and ask for healing."

"Toby has to do it himself?" Jordan had envisioned begging on bended knee.

"Yeah, that's the way it works," Christina explained. "The sick person has to make the decision to ask for help. Motivation, the shrinks would call it."

"I'll talk to Toby. He's pretty stubborn, too, but you never know. He might just go for it. He doesn't have a lot of options."

"Yeah, well, if he does, there's a sort of ceremony involved. He has to formally ask Silas for a healing and give him something in return. At the initial meeting, it's usually tobacco—not the commercial kind—a raw, wild version that's reserved for ceremonial use. If Toby decides to go for it, let me know and I'll take him to see Auntie Lena. She can supply him with the tobacco."

Tobacco? Jordan tried not to react. To a medical doctor, it sounded like so much hocus-pocus, and she was afraid Toby would feel the same way. But on the other hand, there was Rose Marie, alive and well, a

powerful testimony to the effectiveness of native healing. Jordan had to admit that Silas had some indefin-
able quality about him that could inspire great trust and
confidence. Passion—he had passion. God, did he have
passion.

"I'll talk to Toby." She felt a tiny seed of hope sprout,
and her dread eased just the slightest amount.

CHAPTER TWENTY-THREE

THAT AFTERNOON, Toby came home from the fishing trip so tired he could barely make it from the wharf up to the medical center. He collapsed on the sofa and Jordan tucked a blanket around him. He was still deeply asleep when she finished up for the afternoon.

She looked at him lying there, gray and trembling even in sleep, and the fear she'd been keeping under control broke free, a wild and terrifying thing that gripped her abdomen and pummeled her heart. She couldn't lose him, she just couldn't. She'd do anything, endorse any far-fetched treatment if it would add even a day to her brother's life.

She showered and then, anxious not to wake Toby, sat quietly with an unread medical journal in her lap until he groaned and sat up, rubbing his hands over his thighs, grimacing with pain.

When he noticed her, his expression changed as he hid the pain, and he gave her a smile so sweet she felt tears burning behind her eyes.

"Hey, squirt. How long have you been sitting there perving on me?"

"No time at all," she lied, getting up to put the kettle on. She made up cups of the rose-hip tea Christina had brought, lacing it with honey.

Toby tasted it. "This isn't exactly Seagram's, but it's not bad. Is it some kind of tonic?"

"Christina brought it for you. It's high in vitamin C."

"And it's going to fix me right up, eh?"

"Not exactly. It might help, though. Vitamin C is a powerful antioxidant. A guy named Norman Cousins cured himself of cancer just by taking mega doses of vitamin C."

Now was the time. Jordan drew in a breath. "I got those blood results back today. And the other doctors were right."

His shoulders slumped. "I didn't think they'd have made a mistake. I know there's no real treatment, Jordan."

"A good diet, doses of vitamin B—"

"They told me that. And when I nailed them for a prognosis, they gave me the straight goods. They said a couple years, maybe five."

"There's something you could try." Jordan told him all about Rose Marie. "At that time, conventional medicine had no treatment for what she had. She came here unable to even walk, and her grandmother Sandrine cured her. She's dead now, but Christina's brother, Silas Keefer, learned to be a healer from Sandrine."

Toby gave her a mischievous grin. "That's your boyfriend, right?"

"Who told you that?" As if she didn't know.

"None other than the gossip rats, Eli and Michael."

"They're a little behind on the news. We had a thing going for about two minutes, but it's over. He dumped me."

"Want me to beat him up for you?"

"I want you to ask him to help you get better."

He shook his head. "When I found out about this, I decided I wasn't going to fall into the trap of running from one so-called healer to another. You can waste what life you have left doing that, Jordan."

She wanted to scream at him. Instead she said in a rational voice, "It wouldn't hurt to try this one thing. You're here, it's not as if you have to travel to see him. Think about it, okay?"

"Okay, I'll think about it." He was humoring her. Jordan was about to push him on it when his cell phone rang.

Toby answered, and while he talked, Jordan put kindling in the stove and lit a match to it, trying to figure out what to make them for dinner. She could probably manage macaroni and cheese from a package.

"Jordan." The tone of his voice told her something was wrong. She turned, and he put his arms around her, holding her close against his trembling body.

"That was the nursing home. Dad died an hour ago, there wasn't any warning. He just laid down after lunch and died in his sleep."

She didn't feel anything, Jordan told herself. After all, she'd thought about this, about what she'd do when it happened. She'd decided a long time ago not to go to her father's funeral—what was the point, when she hadn't seen him in years, and had no feeling for him?

"They want to know what arrangements to make."

She could hear the strain in Toby's voice, feel the tension vibrating through his frail, thin frame. She knew what he was going to ask, and she knew what she was going to have to do, because she couldn't let him go through this alone.

"Will you come to Vancouver with me, Jordan?"

"Of course." It made her angry, because Mike was winning this one after all. But she had to go for Toby's sake.

THEY ARRIVED IN VANCOUVER the following afternoon and rented a car for the drive into the city. The Lower Mainland was having a hot and surprisingly dry summer. There were watering restrictions, and even the manicured lawn at the rest home was brown instead of green. It made Jordan nostalgic for the wild green island she now called home.

The staff knew Toby, and they greeted him with soft murmurs of sympathy. One of the older nurses hugged him, and there were tears in her eyes. "I'm so sorry about your dad, he was a great favorite here."

Toby said, "Thanks, Lucy. This is my sister, Jordan."

"Of course it is." The portly woman took Jordan's hand in both of hers and patted it. "Hello, dear. I recognize you from the pictures in Mike's room."

Jordan gaped at her. *Pictures? What pictures?*

Lucy didn't seem to notice Jordan's reaction.

"I'll take you down there," she said. "We locked the door—you just never know around here. Everything's just the way he left it. I put some cartons in there for you, but if you need more, just holler." She led the way down a hallway lined with old people in wheelchairs.

The room was small, with a double window along one wall, wide open to the afternoon air, but there was still an odor of strong disinfectant. The narrow bed was neatly made, with a blue comforter folded at the bottom. On the dresser was a model of a sailboat and above it a corkboard covered with snapshots.

Her parents' wedding photo was at the top, the original of Jordan's—the one she'd cut up. Next to it was one of her mother smiling but harried. She was holding a fat, crying baby—Jordan—on one hip. Her free hand clasped that of a little boy in a sailor suit who was squinting into the camera and obviously struggling to escape.

Next to it was another black-and-white shot of their mother, more professional, probably taken by a street photographer. Tall and slender, she was striding along, wearing a fashionable tweed coat, a perky little hat and heels, and she was smiling in a dreamy sort of way. Jordan could see her own face in this picture. She touched the photo with her fingertips.

"That was just before Mom and Dad were married," Toby said. He was standing at her elbow. "Dad told me she quit training to be a nurse to marry him."

"Big mistake." Jordan snorted, staring at the photo

and wondering when that young woman first realized
she'd taken a wrong turn.

"Dad loved her," Toby said, contradicting Jordan.
"He didn't really start drinking until after she died."

Jordan barely heard him. Incredibly enough, she was
looking at a row of photos of herself, her graduation
from high school—why had she never noticed that the
hem on the white organdy gown was uneven? And there
was that snap of her and Toby during her first year at
med school. He'd appeared unannounced at her dorm
and taken her to a Chinese café for lunch. The waiter
had taken their picture.

"You must have given these to Mike," she said. There
she was, graduating from university, looking solemn.
In the next, she was receiving her medical degree. Jordan was becoming increasingly uncomfortable, realizing that Mike had had these pictures of her.

"I had copies made for him." Toby touched a photo
of himself, shoulders hunched, face set in grim lines.
"This was when I got out of jail. I was mad at the world
in those days."

"You had reason to be." But now Jordan was staring
at her own wedding photo. She and Garry had been married at the registry office, but his parents had arranged
a small reception in their home. The Hughes had hired
a photographer. Jordan wore a simple white sheath dress
and jacket. She was sitting on the arm of a sofa, smiling up at Garry with much the same dreamy, hopeful
expression her mother wore in her own wedding photo.

One of the few photos of Mike showed him stand-

ing in front of a cake, smiling. His face was lined and
haggard, and he had several missing teeth.

"That was two years ago. It was his five-year cake
at AA," Toby explained. "He was really proud of getting sober."

Jordan looked at the picture and saw a stranger. She
doubted she'd have recognized her father had he been
brought into the E.R.

"We'd better get started." Toby opened a drawer
and began packing pajamas and the few worn shirts
into a carton. Jordan began to unpin the photos and
slide them into an envelope. It was like filing away
their family history once and for all, and a terrible sadness filled her.

For the rest of that day, the photos flickered across
her mind like a slide show. She and Toby spoke with
the funeral director, arranged for a simple service the
following day, and finally checked into a comfortable
downtown hotel.

"I'm bagged, I'm going to order something from
room service," Toby said apologetically when she asked
if he wanted to meet for dinner. "And I still have to call
some of Dad's buddies and let them know about the funeral. Then I'm going to bed."

With the empty evening ahead of her, Jordan thought
of calling friends from St. Joe's but decided against it.
Instead, she ordered chicken salad from room service,
had a long, hot bath and curled up in bed with a magazine she'd bought at the airport, determined to ignore
the brown envelope she'd shoved into her carryall.

After fifteen minutes, she swore at herself and re-
trieved it.

"Damn you, Mike Burke." She dumped the photos
onto the bed. "Don't think you can get around me this
easily, just by tacking up a few sorry pictures. It doesn't
make up for a thing," she whispered in a fierce, shaky
voice, picking up one shot after another, studying it,
laying it down, only to pick up the next.

Before long, her heart was beating hard and her
hands were trembling. She had the irrational feeling
that there was a key hidden here that would unlock
something she needed to know, not only about Mike but
about herself.

She studied her father's young face in the wedding
photo and reluctantly admitted that although she'd always sworn she looked like her mother, she had his
stubborn jawline. What else had she inherited from this
man who'd died a veritable stranger to her? Who, her
brother had said desperately wanted her forgiveness,
but had never been able to say it to her.

She saw so clearly the damage done to her father's life
by his not being able to address and then act on his deepest emotions. And as she looked at the photographs, Jordan recognized that she'd done exactly the same thing.

With Mike, with Garry…and now with Silas.

She glanced at the clock. It was almost midnight.
Silas would be sleeping.

Well, too damned bad. Getting dragged out of sleep
by a woman who wants to say she loves you isn't the
worst thing that can happen to a man. It was far worse

to die without ever having spoken your truth. She pulled
out her cell phone and dialed Silas's number.

HE SAT ON HIS FRONT STEPS in the darkness, swatting
mosquitoes and thinking over the things Christina had
said. She'd left some time ago, but the sound of her
voice reverberated in his head.

She'd come to tell him Jordan's father had just died,
and that she and her brother Toby had gone to Vancouver to arrange the funeral. Christina had also said that
Toby was seriously ill.

"She doesn't have any other family but this one
brother," Christina had told him. "And because she's
never had anyone but him to care about her, I think it's
hard for her to trust anyone. If you have feelings for her,
cut her a break, why don't you?"

Silas looked up at the night sky. After Jordan's visit
and the harsh words they'd exchanged, he'd tried hard
to put her out of his mind. It hadn't worked.

How dare she casually dismiss what they'd had between them? After his anger faded, he'd told himself he
felt only relief. He didn't want an emotional relationship, he was a loner, better off by himself.

But tonight when Christina said Jordan's father had
died, all he'd wanted to do was hold her in his arms.

Jordan had told him she had no feelings for her father, but he knew that wasn't true. He'd tried to pretend
he had no feelings for Angus, either.

The door to his cabin was open, and he heard the
phone ring. Getting up, he went to answer it.

"Silas here."

"It's Jordan."

He felt as if his lungs had stopped working. He heard her quick intake of breath, and in that instant he could see her clearly: her blue eyes, the fine narrow bones of her face, long nose, bow-shaped lips... His heart turned over. She was the woman in his dreams, the other half of himself. Her image had been imprinted on his heart and soul before he was born, but he'd been afraid to recognize her—until now.

"I called to tell you that I'm in love with you," she said in an aggressive, angry tone. "I don't care whether that embarrasses you or not, I don't even care what you say back. I just wanted you to know. I promised myself I'd be honest with you, and that's exactly what I'm doing."

And before he could get his breath back, she hung up.

CHAPTER TWENTY-FOUR

STUNNED, SILAS SAT for several moments. Then he sprang to his feet and danced, giving a wild, whooping cry that set all the dogs in the village barking. Thanking the spirits of modern technology, he tapped out her cell number, praying she hadn't changed it yet again.

It rang, and after a few tense moments, she answered. Her voice was hesitant this time. She knew it was him.

He didn't waste words either. "When is your father's funeral?"

"Tomorrow afternoon."

"If you tell me where and when, I'll be there."

She hesitated, but then she told him.

THE FUNERAL WAS AT TWO. Silas arrived at the Vancouver airport at eleven, and on an impulse he took a cab to his father's house on the city's west side.

The old, rambling stucco house looked a little more run-down than he remembered. There was moss growing on the roof, and the lawn was dry and patchy, but the roses were blooming. It took courage to walk up the driveway and ring the doorbell.

A tiny Asian woman opened the door.

"I'm Silas Keefer. I'm here to see my father." And he hoped his nervousness didn't show.

Her perfectly arched eyebrows shot up, but all she said was, "He's having his lunch on the sunporch."

"I know the way." Silas walked down the hall, through the den, across the kitchen. He stepped out onto the sunporch.

Angus was sitting facing the garden. He was alone at a round, glass-topped table, newspaper spread out, eating a sandwich. Silas was shocked at how old he looked, older even than his seventy years. His hair was mostly white now, with only a few flecks of brown over his ears. In spite of the warm summer day, he was wearing a blue sweater, and his shoulders were slumped. His tall frame was much heavier than Silas remembered.

"Hello, Dad."

Angus's head whipped around, and he stared at Silas over the top of half-moon reading glasses. His face was deeply wrinkled, but his authoritative baritone voice was still the same.

"Silas." There was no welcome in the word, only shock. Angus didn't get up. "Where the hell did you drop from?"

"Ahousaht." The single word was like a gauntlet thrown down between them.

Angus scowled. "And what are you doing here?"

"Visiting you. Can I sit down?"

"Of course, sit." Angus waved a hand at a chair. In

a gruff tone, he said, "You want some lunch?" Without waiting for an answer, Angus bellowed, "Kim, make another sandwich." He swept the newspapers aside and then studied Silas, his green eyes narrowed. "I see you've gone native. Still no barbers in Ahousaht?"

Silas refused to be baited. "It saves on haircuts. How are you, Dad?"

"So-so. Have to have another operation on my hip. I broke it a few months back, it didn't heal the way it should have."

Silas hadn't noticed the heavy cane beside Angus's chair.

"Sorry to hear that. You're retired now, of course?"

"Two years ago. I still guest lecture at the university occasionally."

Kim set a sandwich in front of Silas. "Hope you like roast beef. You want some tea?" She poured Silas a mug of the strong Irish Breakfast Angus had always preferred, and left them alone again.

Angus waited while Silas took a bite of his sandwich. "So I assume you're here because you need money, right?"

Silas swallowed the food with difficulty, struggling with the anger and outrage that flared in him. His first, powerful impulse was to get up and walk out. Before he could do it, however, he seemed to hear an echo of Sandrine's voice in his head, urging him to take the peaceful path. Like all of Sandrine's teachings, it wasn't easy.

"I don't need anything, Dad," he was finally able to

say. "I came because we haven't spoken in a long time, and I thought it's time we did."

Angus eyed him suspiciously. "And what brought about this change of heart? You thinking of coming back to the university?" There was the slightest note of hopefulness in his voice.

"No. I'm happy where I am, doing what I do."

Angus sneered, "And what exactly is that?"

Silas could have truthfully said he was a writer. He knew it would be more acceptable to Angus, but gaining his father's acceptance wasn't necessary. What he wanted instead was harmony.

"I'm a healer, Dad." And in stating it, Silas thought about the real meaning of the word, to make whole, to restore well-being. If only he could do that with his father.

"Bunch of mumbo jumbo," Angus scoffed. "Never get anywhere in the world that way."

"Depends on where a person wants to go." Silas took another bite of sandwich and chewed slowly. It gave him time to think. When he'd swallowed, he knew exactly the direction he wanted for his life. "I'm hoping to get married soon, and have kids." It took all his courage to put it into words. He and Jordan hadn't discussed any of this. He was relying heavily on trust and intuition here. "I hope that you'll come to my wedding and, if I'm lucky enough to have them, be a grandfather to my children. The thing that seems to matter most to me these days is family."

"She from Ahousaht?"

"Yes, she is." And she was, at least for the next year.

Silas knew Angus was asking whether the woman was First Nations. Let him think so. It was wicked to tease the old man, but he richly deserved it. It was never going to be easy with Angus. Silas waited for the lecture he was certain was coming.

"Coming to Ahousaht would depend on whether I'm mobile enough. Unless you wanted to get married here."

Speechless, Silas stared at Angus. When he got his voice back, he said, "The woman makes that decision, but I'll ask her."

"Bring her here to meet me," Angus ordered. "I'll ask her myself." Then he said, "How's your mother doing, anyway?"

And for the next hour, until he had to leave for the funeral, Silas had an almost-enjoyable conversation with his father.

THE FUNERAL WAS HELD in a small room at the chapel. There were a dozen people present, three of them nurses from the rest home.

Jordan held tight to Toby's arm with one hand, and Silas with the other. His strong fingers interlaced with hers; his tall, powerful presence giving her strength and comfort. She didn't cry, but she hadn't expected to feel such a deep, gut-wrenching sadness and regret. She also felt a kind of peace that came from knowing that in spite of everything, her father had cared.

The chaplain read from the Bible, and then gave a

short, kind summary of Mike's life. Jordan listened closely as several strangers got up and spoke about her father. The man they described was kind, generous and had a sense of humor. But to Jordan, he was still a stranger, and that was the saddest thing of all.

"Mike helped me get sober," one of the men said. "He was my sponsor, and he used to tell me if he could do it, anybody could."

When the service ended, a wizened little woman came up to Jordan and Toby and shook their hands. "Mike and I were good friends over the years," she said, wiping away tears with a tissue. "He helped me through a rough time in my life. I wanted you to know he talked about you two all the time, he was really proud of you."

Even the day before, Jordan's response would have been skeptical and sarcastic. Now, she held the woman's hand, said thank you and meant it.

Afterward, Silas took Jordan and Toby to a restaurant. She sat quietly, picking at her food, watching and listening as the two men she loved got to know each other. As far as she could tell, they even liked each other.

Her heart ached for Toby. His navy suit hung on his emaciated body, and his skin was gray from exhaustion. Nothing could disguise the fact that he was very ill.

The contrast between Toby and Silas was startling, and she kept stealing glances at Silas. She hadn't seen him dressed up before, and it almost hurt to look at him, he was so handsome. His exotic black hair with its white streak was held back neatly at the nape of his neck, charcoal suit perfectly tailored to his long, lean body, white dress shirt immaculate. He caught her looking and smiled at her, green eyes eerily transparent in the softly lit restaurant.

He'd met them outside the funeral chapel, and there hadn't been any opportunity for private conversation. The memory of the phone call she'd made to him was now uppermost in her mind, and she alternated between acute embarrassment and defiant pride at what she'd told him.

So now he knew she loved him. But when he'd called her back, he hadn't said a single thing about how he felt. The fact that he'd come to Mike's funeral was encouraging, but maybe he was just being kind.

"I'm going back to the hotel for some shut-eye," Toby said. "Why don't you two drop me off so you can take the car and do some sightseeing?"

"Thanks, we'll do that," Silas said, turning to her. "As long as Jordan drives. I haven't been behind the wheel of a car since I moved back to Ahousaht. Is that okay with you, Jordan?"

"Sure." She knew she didn't sound enthusiastic. This meant she'd have to really talk to Silas, and now Jordan wasn't at all sure that's what she wanted to do. Maybe too much truth wasn't a good thing, after all.

She drove to the hotel and Toby got out. Pulling the car back into the late-day traffic, Jordan asked, "Where do you want to go?" Her nervousness was escalating into something like full-blown panic.

"A place where there's trees, where we can go for a walk."

That was easy. She aimed the car west along 16th Avenue, toward Pacific Spirit Park, glad that he didn't say anything until she'd found a shaded spot to park and turned off the motor.

"This is a good place." He took off his suit jacket and flung it and his tie into the back seat. "I used to wander in these trees a lot," he said as he got out and held the door for her. "The school I went to is only a few blocks away."

He led the way into the old-growth forest, and the incongruity of him in his white shirt and suit pants and her in a short black dress and heels would have made Jordan smile, if she wasn't so tense.

Almost immediately, the traffic noise died and the bustle of the city seemed far away. Sunlight splintered down among huge old cedars and pines, and gigantic ferns bordered the well-worn pathway. They walked in silence, and the nervous anticipation Jordan felt slowly drained away when Silas took her hand in his. Just being with him gave her such happiness.

"I'm sorry about your father, Jordan. I hope he has a good passage into the spirit world."

"I hope so, too." It seemed natural and easy now to tell Silas about the photos. "I keep thinking that it would have made such a difference if he'd called me, told me how he felt."

"Sandrine used to say that at any given time, people are doing the very best they know how. If they make mistakes, it's because they don't know any better at that moment." He took a few more steps and then stopped. "Talking about mistakes, I saw my father today."

"How did that go?" He hadn't seen his father in years. Christina said their last conversation had been painful for Silas. "Was it really bad?"

To her amazement, he laughed. "He wants to meet you."

"*Me?* Why did you tell him about me?"

"Because you're the woman I want to marry. I told him I hoped he'd be a good grandfather to our children."

Stunned, Jordan snatched her hand out of his. She squinted up at him, unable to take all this in. "You told your father before you even talked this over with me?"

"That's the mistake I was talking about." His green eyes were dancing, teasing her. "Sorry about that. He also thinks you're First Nations. And he's going to try to bully you into having the wedding on his dried-up lawn."

The implications were slowly dawning on her, and she wanted to thump him one. "Now you're telling me you out-and-out lied to your father."

"I didn't lie to him. He just made assumptions."

"Yes, well you and your father have a lot in common in that regard."

"Jordan." He took both her hands, holding them firmly, forcing her to face him, to look at him. There was no more teasing in his voice or in his eyes.

"I know you love me—you told me so. And I love you, so isn't marriage a logical next step?" His smile wasn't quite as confident as his words. "I'll make you happy, I promise you that."

Just being with him makes me happy. She wanted so much to say yes. But— "We can't get married, Silas. For one thing, I'm not divorced yet." Although she'd spoken to Marcy that morning, and the process was well under way. "But there are other, more important issues. I can't stay in Ahousaht permanently. I love it there— I love the people—but I know myself well enough to know that after a year I'll probably want to come back to the city. Back to the E.R."

He nodded. "So we'll come back. I called a friend today, a prof in the medical department at the university. He says there's a real need for native healers at the Alternative Medical Clinic. And there's an indigenous studies course I could teach if I chose."

"You wouldn't be happy away from Ahousaht."

"I used to think that. Now, I know I won't be happy anywhere without you. We could compromise, spend the winter in Vancouver, the summer in Ahousaht."

She couldn't believe the concessions he was willing to make for her. *For them.* She loved him more than she'd ever loved anyone. It tore her apart to refuse him.

"I can't marry you, Silas. Not now, not for the foreseeable future."

Disappointment flashed in his eyes. "Okay. I'll just stick around and ask again another time, then. But why are you so dead set against it?"

"Because of my brother. You saw Toby, he's terribly ill. He doesn't have anyone but me, and I want to take care of him." She was afraid of what might happen to her if she lost Toby. Maybe she'd have nothing left of herself to give, to Silas or to anyone. In the meantime, she couldn't promise anything. "I *need* to take care of him."

"Of course you do." He understood about family. "Christina told me about Toby. She said you wanted me to try to heal him. If he asks me, I'll do my best."

"Thank you, Silas." She put her arms around him, hugging him close. The desperation she felt about Toby eased just a little as his strong hands on her waist pulled her tight.

"But you have to understand that my type of healing doesn't necessarily mean a cure, Jordan."

She took a step back and scowled up at him. "For heaven's sake, I'm a doctor. Of course I know there aren't any guarantees. All we can do is hope." And fight. She'd fight for her brother's life with everything she had.

"Native healing goes further than hope. Sometimes, if the person's spirit has decided to leave, healing means helping the transition to the spirit world. You'd have to set him free, Jordan, so he could follow the path his spirit has chosen. You'd have to trust, not just him, but me."

He was asking her to let go of the outcome. How could she do a thing like that? She stared up at him, and in those clear, green eyes she saw her own reflection.

In an instant, it came to her that she was asking Silas to do the same.

She wanted him to love her, without boundaries, without timetables, without promises. She was asking him for unconditional love. Frightening as it was, she had to offer him the same in return.

She swallowed hard. Her hands were trembling. "I'll try, Silas. I promise you I'll do my very best."

"Good," he said. "I have this feeling that we'll make good medicine together."

And then he kissed her.

CHAPTER TWENTY-FIVE

NINE MONTHS HAD PASSED since that afternoon in Pacific Spirit Park.

Jordan smiled down at the baby girl cuddled close to her heart. Long, poker-straight tufts of coal-black hair stood defiantly on end, framing a small, indignant face. Hands the size of tiny acorns nestled under the baby's double chin, and her perfectly shaped bow lips made petulant sucking motions in preparation for the next meal, never more than an hour away.

"Welcome, baby girl," Jordan whispered softly— *really* softly. She'd rather not wake little Onida Rose Crow. Her niece was eight weeks old today, and Onida knew what she wanted and when she wanted it. She was a tyrant with the appetite of a glutton and a voice about five times larger than her diminutive body.

On this sunny May morning, Onida Rose was being welcomed by a circle of her family and friends. Her mother and father sat together on the other side of the ring of chairs. Patwin was holding Mary's hand, and the exhausted and slightly befuddled expression on his handsome face made Jordan want to laugh out loud.

Your daddy can't figure out what's hit him, she thought, looking back at Onida.

Patwin had been there when Onida made her dramatic entrance into the world. Mary's had been one of the shortest labors Jordan had ever attended. Fortunately, the family had been in the middle of dinner with Rose Marie and Peter at the time. Unfortunately, there hadn't been time to get Mary to a bedroom, much less the medical center.

Jordan and Christina had delivered Onida on Rose Marie's living room carpet, which would never be the same again. Patwin had fainted during the proceedings not once, but twice.

Christina had snapped photos of him out cold, lying on the carpet a few feet away from his newborn daughter. She'd pasted the pictures into the baby book she was putting together for her niece, and she was threatening to blow them up and post them on the bulletin board at the clinic.

In spite of her teasing, Jordan knew how proud Christina was of her baby brother. The entire family was proud of him.

Patwin had found work he was passionate about and was doing his best to support Mary and his baby. He'd volunteered as a coach for the boy's basketball team, and been so good at it he was hired as head coach. As well, he'd begun talking to the kids at the youth center about the dangers of drugs, and was now being asked to come to other communities as a spokesperson for the anti-drug campaigns in schools.

Jordan held the baby to her heart and rocked gently back and forth.

"Ahhhhh nook, ahhhhhh nook." She made the deep humming sound of welcome Silas and Christina had taught her. She took her time, as did everyone in the circle. When she sensed her blessing was complete, she gingerly passed Onida to Silas, sitting to her right. He said a prayer, everyone sang a song, and the blessing ended, thankfully before Onida woke up. Silas handed her off to her mother.

The circle broke up and everyone headed outside. Silas walked beside Jordan, his fingers interlaced with hers. His thumb traced the pattern on the wide wedding band he'd had made for her when they were married on her birthday in April. It was etched with the native symbol for eternity.

"The boat will be here any minute," he said.

Jordan nodded. "Let's walk down to the dock and see how Toby and Wanda liked being media mavens."

After spending a lot of time with the Ahousaht elders, Toby had become fascinated with their stories of building wooden boats in the traditional way, without chemicals or power tools. Toby drew up plans, and just before Christmas he and Patwin had started work under a makeshift tent, with an ever-growing number of grandfathers supervising. The project soon became everyone's baby, and most of the village ignored the rain to watch the boat take shape.

Michael's mother, Wanda Nitsch, had always dreamed of being a filmmaker. She used the video camera her husband gave her for Christmas to document the building of the boat. She'd then incorporated audiotapes of the grandmothers reading Sandrine's stories with the visual images of the boatbuilding and sent the completed documentary off to a contest in Vancouver.

Wanda won first prize—which meant the film was being aired on several major networks, and she and Toby were being overwhelmed with interview requests.

"Looks like half the village had the same idea," Jordan said as they neared the dock. Christina was already there, and she waved to them.

"Eli told me Toby was buying Christina an engagement ring in Vancouver," Silas said.

"How the heck did Eli know that? Toby hasn't even asked Christina yet."

She still occasionally forgot that there were no secrets in Ahousaht. Well, maybe just one. But it wasn't something that could be hidden very long. All the same, she and Silas were enjoying it while it lasted.

"Oh, Eli said it was easy. He saw Toby sizing one of the rings from Christina's jewel box."

"That kid is diabolical." And Eli was also beside himself with joy because Toby was going to be his dad and teach him how to build boats and take him sailing and buy him a new bike. Jordan knew the litany by heart, as did the rest of Ahousaht.

"There's the taxi now."

Charlie steered the boat in with more of a flourish than usual. Wanda was the first to scramble to the dock. She lifted Michael into her arms, and her family and friends cheered as she did a little victory dance for them.

Toby was next, and he also got a round of applause and some shrill congratulatory whistles as he stepped down to the dock. Christina gave him a great smacking kiss. The two of them, arm in arm, came walking over to where Jordan and Silas were standing.

Jordan tried not to assess her brother's health, but it was a hard habit to break. She noticed that his limp was still there, but it was slight. He'd gained weight these past few months, the skeletal look was going, and working outdoors had turned his face and arms almost the same copper color as Christina's.

"Hey, Mr. and Mrs. Keefer, it's good to be home again." Toby gave Jordan a quick, hard hug and tapped an affectionate fist against Silas's shoulder.

A special bond existed between her husband and her brother, the camaraderie of two warriors who'd gone into battle side by side and come out victorious. Jordan didn't know all the details of the healing process Silas and Toby had agreed on together. She did know that her brother's blood tests showed an ever-decreasing amount of neurotoxins, and that each passing month he looked healthier, more vibrant and more like his old self. It was a miracle, and Jordan didn't question it. She'd come to believe, as her husband often said, that healing was a mystery and a grace. She was profoundly, humbly grateful that both had touched her brother.

"I bought some fancy wine in Vancouver," Toby said. "Let's go to my place and see if Christina can guess where it's from." He led the way to the apartment at the back of the medical center. He'd taken it over the previous autumn when Jordan had moved into the cabin with Silas.

"I even bought some wineglasses," he went on when they were all seated around the old wooden table. He uncorked the wine, hiding the label and poured a small amount for Christina. She rolled it around in her mouth.

"That's easy," she said. "It's Domaine Chandon, high-end champagne, but they're not allowed to call it that, because it's not grown in the Champagne area of France."

Everyone cheered and clapped. Toby handed glasses around and poured.

"None for me," Jordan said when her turn came. The others looked at her, and she started to giggle as she watched Christina put two and two together.

"They're having a baby!" Christina squealed to a perplexed Toby. She got up and jumped up and down, squealing, "They're having a baby, they're having a baby!"

"This calls for a toast," Toby declared. He held his glass high.

"To the future," he said. "Good health and happiness."

"To babies," Christina said. "And to Jordan, who had the good sense to marry my brother."

Silas had his arm around Jordan's shoulders. He sipped his wine and turned to her, and her breath caught as she looked into his eyes. Their beautiful clear green depths shimmered with unshed tears.

"To my wife," he said softly. "To our children, our grandchildren and the unborn generations ahead. May each of them find the other half of themselves." And he chanted the only native words Jordan understood.

"Hiy! Hiy! Hiy."

With deep gratitude.

If you enjoyed what you just read,
then we've got an offer you can't resist!

Take 2 bestselling love stories FREE!
Plus get a FREE surprise gift!

e**HARLEQUIN**.com

The Ultimate Destination for Women's Fiction

Becoming an eHarlequin.com member is easy, fun and **FREE!** Join today to enjoy great benefits:

- **Super savings** on all our books, including members-only discounts and offers!

- Enjoy **exclusive online reads**—FREE!

- Info, tips and **expert advice** on writing your own romance novel.

- FREE romance **newsletters,** customized by you!

- Find out the latest on your **favorite authors.**

- Enter to win exciting **contests and promotions!**

- Chat with other members in our **community message boards!**

— To become a member, —
— visit www.eHarlequin.com today!

INTMEMB04R

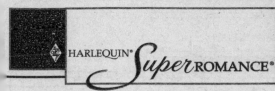

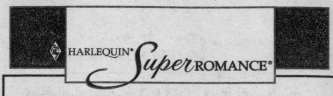

HARLEQUIN® *Super*ROMANCE®

It's worth holding out for a hero....

Three brothers with different mothers. Brought together by their father's last act. The town of Heyday, Virginia, will never be the same—neither will they.

Tyler Balfour is The Stranger. It seems as if his mother was the only woman in Heyday that Anderson McClintock didn't marry—even when she'd been pregnant with Tyler. So he's as surprised as anyone when he discovers that Anderson has left him a third of everything he owned, which was pretty much all of Heyday. Tyler could be enjoying his legacy if not for the fact that more than half of Heyday despises him because they think he's responsible for ruining their town!

Look for **The Stranger,** the last book in a compelling new trilogy from Harlequin Superromance and Rita® Award finalist **Kathleen O'Brien**, in April 2005.

"If you're looking for a fabulous read, reach for a Kathleen O'Brien book. You can't go wrong."
—Catherine Anderson,
New York Times bestselling author